BRAXTON'S CENTURY
VOLUME 1

JR STRAYVE JR

Cover designed by Teresa Espaniola

This book is a work of fiction. Names, characters, places, and incidents either are products of the author's imagination or are used fictitiously. Any resemblance to actual persons, living or dead, events, or locales is entirely coincidental.

J.R. STRAYVE, JR.
Visit my website at www.jrstrayvejr.com

Printed in the United States of America

First Printing: January 2021

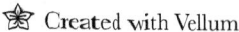 Created with Vellum

It is an honor and a pleasure to dedicate Braxton's Century volume 1 to my dear friend and content editor, Trisha Gooch. This is not the first book I've published but is the first book I wrote. With that came all the inexperience that accompanies a first-time author. Her patience, compassion, and oh so painful 'tough-love' made this book possible. Without her prodding, encouraging, and scolding it may never have been published.

Thank you, Trisha.

1

CUPULA INFERNO

Everyone at the Aurelio Palace in Southwestern England—staff, family, guests—was in an uproar. Ten-year-old Prince Braxton, third son of the Prince and Princess of Wales, had quite amazingly concocted a successful scheme to generate light and stench. The latter permeating most of the huge and commodious palace. An inferno with the characteristics of what turned out to be a manure bonfire was ablaze indoors!

The young prince thought it would be fun to have the senses of all palace occupants awakened by the stimuli of the glowing flames and acrid smell. He had thought little about the outcome of his actions, as he was not accustomed to facing consequences. He was equipped with charm, intelligence, and pleasant looks. All that was needed in a young princeling.

At this moment he cowered behind a life-size statue of an obscure ancestor perched upon a pedestal towering over him. The young prince's face and clothing were covered in sweat, grime, and the stench of manure and pieces of straw. Peering wide-eyed at the blaze on the rotunda's marble floor; shaking, he mumbled to himself, "What have I done?"

Weeks earlier, Prince Braxton had been in the palace's carriage house, watching from a distance as young stable boys played near a pile of what appeared to be manure, laced with copious amounts of straw. The boys were kicking a ball amongst themselves shouting, laughing, and making great sport. Braxton wanted to join in but knew he would not be welcome. Servants traditionally avoided him. He yearned to have friends his own age. Having a friend, any friend would do.

Following one particularly enthusiastic kick, an ill-placed lantern was toppled by the errant ball. Braxton gasped and strained over the windowsill to get a better look.

As the lantern tipped over, flames from its candle set the straw ablaze. Josh, one of the older boys, darted over to the tool shed and grabbed a shovel. He ran to a pile of earth and clay, repeatedly filling his shovel and extinguishing the fire with six or seven loads. Watching Josh extinguish the fire impressed young Braxton. He wondered, who is this boy?

As Josh finished his task, he looked up to the carriage house secondstory balcony and saw a drop-jawed Braxton peering down at him. He felt his heart skip a beat. He thought the olive-skinned, blond, blue-eyed prince was beautiful. Josh, the thirteen-year-old son of the head coachman, respectfully tipped his hat toward Prince Braxton. The prince, resigned to his friendless state, watched Josh walk away and join his friends in their games.

———

On the occasion of his prank, however, Prince Braxton did not anticipate family or guests would be returning to their bedrooms just before the maids were to light the morning fires. Had one absented themselves during the night and not returned to one's bedchamber before the fires were lit, reputations could be sullied.

This early morning, Braxton's oldest brother, Prince Dominic, was leaving Lady Allison's chamber. As he passed through the northeast second story promenade, he was surprised by a 25-foot flame soaring in the middle of the intersection of the northeast and east promenades. The intersection was roofed by a marble and crystal dome, rising a towering 45 feet.

Anxiously whispering to himself, "What in heaven's name is that?"

He ran toward the fire, gagging and stumbling, convulsing as the smell of manure and smoke permeated his lungs. Dominic nearing the flame, noticed his younger brother, Prince John, leaving a bedchamber not his own, but that of Lord Ramsey.

Dominic shouted, "John! Help! Fire!" He then collapsed onto the floor.

"Fire" echoed throughout both promenades and into every chamber as disoriented, partially dressed occupants streamed into the walkways. Gasps stifled screams as the noxious odor and smoke poured through the passageways. Young Princess Diedre, only four-teen years of age, had been awakened some minutes earlier by the smell of smoke. She had worked her way down from the third-floor bedroom she shared with 12-year-old sister, Princess Carmen.

On the landing between the third and second floors, Princess Diedre reached for the fire gong, and though she weighed little over five stone, struck it with all her might. The sound of the gong was not loud enough to awaken everyone, but it caught the attention of Sally the maid as she descended from the fourth-floor female servants' quarters.

Sally ran to the princess and wrapped her arms around the young royal. Adding her hands and strength to that of Princess Diedre's, they pounded the gong propelling a thunderous sound throughout the palace. Realizing the situation at hand, people in the far reaches of the palace instinctively located a gong near them and commenced hammering away, echoing the warning from Princess Diedre and Sally. All inside and outside the palace were alerted to the fire having broken out.

The underside of the cupula absorbed the intense heat spiraling up from the fire below. The lead caulking, holding the crystal panes within the iron lattice work framing the dome, softened. High above the rotunda floor, the glass shifted.

———

Mercedes, the Princess of Wales, awakened by the sound of the gongs, screamed at the soundly sleeping Prince Richard.

"Richard, get up, get up! Fire, Richard! The children!" She wailed, yanking him from his slumber.

Richard stumbled out of bed oblivious to everything she had said except, "fire" and "children!"

His slow reaction and even slower movement panicked Mercedes.

She picked up a pitcher of water and tossed it in his face.

The shock extinguished Richard's confusion, and he shouted, "Yes! Yes! Where, where is the fire?"

Mercedes grabbed hold of Richard and the two raced toward the third floor to gather their children.

Smoke billowed as the palace fire continued to burn. Braxton untied a course rag fastened to a wooden bucket's handle and held it against his nose and mouth to shield him from the putrid fumes. The massive stone statue continued to conceal him as the frightened prince watched the unfolding chaos.

Braxton jumped backward, startled by crystal panes crashing to the floor, set free by the softening lead. At first the glass sprinkled, then rained not unlike a hailstorm. Lethal panes dove downward, smashing, and propelling shards across the expansive polished marble floor.

Prince Braxton knew without a doubt he was in danger of being impaled by the shards. Suddenly a fragment cut into his lower right leg. He grabbed his injured shin and leaped to the concealed opening behind the statue leading to a dark passage inside the palace walls. As the panel closed behind him, he took the soiled rag he had held covering his face and secured it to his leg, knotting it in the light of a single candle.

Prince John, frightened not only by the confusion of the fire and smoke, was equally panicked about what his brother might have seen. John grabbed his unconscious 18-year-old sibling Dominic, dragging him down the marble and gilded promenade toward his own chambers, far from the confusion. He placed his brother on the bed and made certain Dominic was still breathing.

He opened the windows allowing fresh air in to displace the smoke wafting into the room. Closing his bedroom door as he exited, Prince John quickly returned to the scene of the fire knocking on doors to make sure that the occupants had vacated all rooms along the promenade.

Inside the passageways, barely lit by the candle, its flame shielded by the boy's hand, Prince Braxton ran as fast as his short legs allowed.

He hopped up a spiral utility staircase to the third-floor nursery. Throwing off his clothes, he donned a full-length nightshirt and jumped into bed, sweating, and shaking with fright. His lower leg throbbed, but fear masked the pain. Small amounts of blood stained his nightclothes and bed sheets. He whimpered, exhaustion taming his anxiety. The frightened boy curled into a ball. The blackened candle and candlestick that had witnessed the bedlam in the rotunda below rested on the floor next to the now fading prince.

Servants and stable hands sought to organize a bucket line to douse the fire but encountered massive confusion. Where were the buckets? All had vanished from their places. The stable boy's father quickly solved the problem.

"Go to every stall in the stables and rip the buckets off the walls and bring them to the line!" bellowed Josh's father.

Josh ran from the stables to the palace. He entered through the main hall and shot up the ornate staircase. Hoping not to be punished for failing to use the servant's entrance and stairs, he ran down the southeast promenade following the sound of crystal crashing onto the marble floors. Buckets began to appear on the scene filled with water—a disaster in the making! The stench hit him head-on. He knew exactly what it was. The first bucket of water thrown onto the fire served not to diminish but to spread flames across the marble floor.

All drew back from the heat and flames as several thrown water buckets enlarged the raging fire. Flaming manure and straw burned hot now covering twice the marble floor area. Crashing crystal panes inflamed the panic.

Josh knew the answer to the dilemma was smothering the fire with clay and dirt. But how could they get clay and dirt up to the palace's second floor?

Six French doors leading onto the second story outdoor garden flanking the rotunda were flung open by palace guests and servants fleeing to safety. The fire, fueled by gusts of air created by the now open doors, swelled like a sleeping giant stretching its limbs in every direction. Transformed into flying knives, crystal shards fell to the marble floor. The only protection lie within the outer colonnade encircling the rotunda.

Josh raced to the pile of empty buckets abandoned by the frightened crowd having seen the fire grow when showered with water. The well-intentioned, now confused, and paralyzed, had dropped their buckets and fled out into the garden.

The alert lad took three buckets in each hand and ran through one of the open French doors leading directly to the garden's raised planters. Planters filled with multitudes of blooming flowers and topiary. As if possessed by a demon, he commanded the bucket as both a shovel and receptacle, plunging it deep into the soft earth. He then handed off the full bucket to a liveried footman gawking at his performance.

Josh shouted, "Take it and throw the dirt on the fire!"

As if following an order from the Prince of Wales himself, the footman leaped toward the open French doors to execute the order. Josh repeated his actions until there were forty or more servants, nobility, and others following his lead, each taking buckets filled with planter soil to smother the fire. Prince John took notice of Josh performing the herculean effort, and with frantic and focused actions, directing the compliant adults.

Reaching the top of the stairs leading to the third floor, the Prince of Wales directed his wife toward Braxton's rooms as he ran toward the princesses' bedchamber.

Mercedes flung open the door to Braxton's suite, the waning

single candle illuminating the young prince. His face was filthy. She could tell immediately it was soot that ran across her son's face. The noxious smell! She jumped toward him, swallowing his small body in her outstretched arms. The smoke and acrid odor of the charred manure had not yet reached his chamber, yet the smell was thick on his body, hair, and clothing. Princess Mercedes felt her son's body shaking against hers.

Meanwhile, Prince Richard stumbled upon Princess Diedre and Sally, collapsed against the gong they had tirelessly rung.

The princess was still panting from her efforts on the gong, yet stammered excitedly, "Papa! Papa! We rang the gong together; we were the first ones to ring the gong!" Then pointed to Sally and said, "This girl helped me the whole time! She is very strong too!"

The prince wrapped his arms around Diedre, lifting her tightly against his body.

He kissed her forehead then turned to Sally saying, "Thank you so much for what you have done. Help me find Princess Carmen!"

The Prince ran down the hall carrying Diedre and searching for Carmen, with Sally following closely behind. Unbeknownst to family members sheltered on the third floor, the

fire below in the rotunda was extinguished. Now wide open to the elements, the dome buffeted by a mild breeze like the flue of a chimney quickly drew what remained of the smoke out of the palace.

Prince John directed the guests to the palace library, instructing the head butler to arrange refreshments. It was unlikely they would return to their rooms as the fumes had made most of the palace bedrooms uninhabitable. As a precaution, the prince ordered blankets and champagne to help settle everyone's nerves.

John, accompanied by a footman, went to check on Dominic, whom he had deposited in his own bed over an hour earlier.

Perusing her youngest son's bedchamber while holding his shuddering body, Mercedes knew Braxton must have had a hand in the blaze. But she wondered, How? Why? Fright spread throughout her body. She feared for the young prince.

"Oh, my son, how can I protect you from the shame of this incident?" Her mind reeled as she tightened her embrace on her shivering child.

Richard was relieved to find Princess Carmen tucked in bed soundly sleeping. Moments later he noticed Sally had found a rocking chair and had fallen fast asleep. The prince knew he must ask Mercedes to inform Mrs. Crompton, the housekeeper, of the maid's heroics.

Suddenly startled, the prince gasped, "Oh my God, Mercedes! Braxton!" He turned, left the room, and raced down the hall toward Braxton's bedchamber.

Prince Richard stopped outside Braxton's room. He could hear his wife and son speaking softly.

Mercedes had turned to Braxton still in her arms, and whispered, "Il mio figlio prezioso, cosa hai fatto? E cosa posso fare per proteggerti? My precious son, what have you done? What can I do to protect you?"

Braxton had gotten himself into this jam out of boredom and his mischievous nature. Creativity and an imagination had fueled this prank. His endless energy and frustration with being left on his own had led to this debacle.

With eyes still closed, the prince slowly turned his angelic face toward her and dolefully looked up at her whispering, "Angelo mia madre, mi dispiace, per favore amati. So che sarai sempre e per sempre per me. Anche io per te." "My mother angel, I am so sorry, please love me. I know that you will always and forever be there for me and me too for you."

Prince Richard, standing outside the door, did not speak his wife's native Italian well, but he sensed a tone of secrecy, pain, and fear in their voices.

He gave his wife a moment more alone with Braxton. Then entered the room and knelt beside Mercedes holding the now sleeping prince.

The household had calmed down as the sun made its appearance above the horizon. Most of the guests and servants were inclined to rest. The previous night's events had for the foreseeable future had altered everyone's plans.

For the Prince of Wales and his family, it was time to vacate the palace. Finding out the cause of the fire and identifying the perpetrators would come soon enough.

2

ON TO THE CAPITAL OF THE WORLD!

The Prince and Princess of Wales had two choices: they could go to their castle in Scotland or make a day's journey to their expansive home in London. The prince was reticent to be too far away from Aurelio Palace until plans for its restoration were completed. His primary concern was funding the restoration. He was wealthy, but his assets were not liquid. The most significant part of his wealth was the immense Chiacontella dowry from his wife. They would go to London.

———

Twelve hours following the fire, all guests had departed. Family and servants were preparing to depart Aurelio Palace. The magnificent structure, constructed of a variety of Italian marble, South American gold and silver was, at this moment, uninhabitable. The palace, a wedding gift from the bride's parents, had been refurbished in 1840, the year Prince Richard and the Countess Mercedes de Chiacontella were married.

Twenty hours after guests had departed Aurelio Palace, the

family was preparing to board the carriages for a trip that would span a full day. The air was crisp as they said their farewells to persons staying behind to care for the palace during the refurbishment.

An air of excitement permeated the family anticipating their arrival in London, knowing they would more than likely be there for the duration of the social season. They imagined experiencing all that London had to offer. The youngest family members and household staff had no real idea of where they were going. They did not care; they were leaving the countryside for the most exciting city in the world!

Prince Richard and Princess Mercedes stepped into their magnificent royal carriage drawn by six stunning and sturdy horses. A postillion rode forward, two coachmen sat in the driver's box, and two footmen in the rear. Mercedes sat with her gloved hands folded on the ermine cover placed across her lap and legs to protect her from the morning chill.

"Richard, I feel as if our lives are about to change, to change forever. I don't know why, I just do." The concern on her face, a face that was normally buoyant and full of life, caught her husband's attention.

Sitting close beside her, Richard whispered, "Life, as you know, is a journey. How it is weathered is up to the traveler. Fortunately, we have each other." He caressed his wife's face, kissing her.

The two young princesses and their maids were ensconced in the second grand, but less spectacular, carriage. They were followed by a similar carriage carrying the three princes. The equipage following the family consisted of three ordinary carriages, each containing eight passengers, including tutors and senior servants. Four large covered wagons carried a total of twenty servants, footmen, and baggage. The Prince of Wales' mounted Royal Guard of twenty made up the front and rear of the caravan.

Important artwork and artifacts, along with silver and valuable pieces, were all safely relegated to secure storage rooms in the basements of the Aurelio Palace. The most important pieces traveled to

London in the baggage wagons. Prince Richard left twelve soldiers behind to ensure that the household remained secure.

The Prince and Princess of Wales shared little conversation. Exhausted, as the events of the previous two days whirled about their heads. They pondered what life would be like when they opened the house in London. The day prior, Princess Mercedes had dispatched ten palace retainers to London to open the grand home and prepare for their arrival as best they could on such short notice.

In the third carriage, Braxton, uncharacteristically silent, sat facing the back of the carriage toward his brothers. He was not yet excited about the trip, as he had spent most of the previous day recuperating. It was not until the aforementioned evening when the palace was quiet that he set about putting his things in order. He was overwhelmed with the thought of being caught. If those conducting the refurbishment found the fifteen foul smelling buckets he had used to haul the incendiary fuel from the stables hidden in the passageways, he would be exposed.

Braxton snuck out of bed the night before and had located the buckets he had left in the secret passage after constructing his towering inferno. He spent more than an hour carrying them back to the stable, accomplishing the task unnoticed. He had retraced his steps through the underground passage that led to the outbuildings housing grain stores and tack.

This passage had been constructed one-hundred-and-fifty-years earlier as an escape route from the palace. The concealed network was dark, dank, and full of rats and spiders, but that did not hinder the young prince. The system of hidden tunnels was his secret passage, as were all passages that ran throughout the palace. Braxton made the best of the arduous task, moving bucket after bucket, slowly regaining his confidence. He positioned the buckets under the stable floor and after five trips back and forth to the palace, was ready to return his borrowed instruments to their rightful place.

Braxton turned a bucket upside down and stood on it. Reaching up, he raised the trap door, disturbing multitudes of rodents and bats nestled safely in their darkened sanctuary. The sound of sharp claws scurrying blended with the clicks, squeals, and flutter of bats fighting to flee, was scary. More deafening was the silence above when he quietly raised the trap door. Debris from the floor above fell on his head and face, and down inside the back of his shirt.

Racks that held the mass of tack and harnesses used for all manner of things related to the palace stable concealed the trap door leading from below the stable floor. He feverishly set about placing the numerous buckets, one by one, on the floor above. He climbed up and into the stable, closing the veiled trap door beneath him. Braxton then crossed his way over to the large double doors at the rear of the building. Ever so slowly, and being careful not to make a sound, he unlatched the doors opening out into total darkness.

He jumped at the thud of the door hitting the side of the building escaping his grasp and then froze in place. The cold air gripped his face rushing through the open door. A crisp breeze caused his eyes to tear and nose to moisten. He did not notice a figure looking down from a second-story window in the building across the yard. Sensing no one nearby, the stealthy prince made several trips into the yard, placing the buckets near a pile of fresh hay situated just outside the wooden double doors.

Unknown to Braxton, Josh watched from his bedroom window in the building across the yard.

Braxton's task now complete, he returned to the tack room and secured the double doors. He then darted toward the racks, descending into the passageway below. He reached up, closed the trap door, and scurried back to the palace.

The young prince entered his bedroom through the concealed panel, undressed, and jumped into bed. He sighed and turned about his covers once or twice. Convinced he had not been discovered; he dove into a deep slumber.

In the dark of night, he had not seen his mother sitting in the armchair across the room. Observing his actions, knowing this was not the time to confront him, she sat loving her son and, once again, feared for him. What was to be done? How could she tame or harness this whirling dervish?

Mercedes continued to sit in silence, ruminating on how to take charge of this high energy, genius son of hers. No doubt, the nanny had to go. She was not up to the task.

The princess began to reminisce. She was comfortable sitting in her son's room. She felt safer for them both, keeping a watchful eye on him, protecting him.

She chuckled, recalling the time her precocious son had concocted the idea to place a 'Black Plague' sign on his bedroom door, demanding that no one enter. While the nanny set off to sound the alarm and evacuate the palace, he sat comfortably on the floor of his room next to the fire consuming an entire tray of sweets intended for that night's dinner guests. Braxton had absconded with the plate from the pantry earlier that evening, distracting the kitchen staff by letting four live chickens loose to run wild in the kitchen creating a furor.

She whispered to the darkened room, "Dearest Braxton, what is to be done?"

"Braxton," said Dominic, "why are you so quiet? Aren't you excited?"

Braxton looked up at the second in line to the throne and turned his attention to the carriage floor and said, "I don't know."

Dominic teased, "Well, if I had any idea you were going to sit and sulk, I would have insisted you ride with the girls and not with us." John came to Braxton's defense, as he always did, nudging Dominic and saying, "Leave him alone, Dom. You can be such an unsavory fellow. Can you not see the fire has upset us all?"

Braxton leaped off his seat and propelled himself toward both his brothers. He hugged them effusively, then curled up on the seat between them like a puppy, resting against John's leg, positioning himself for a safe and secure nap.

"Braxton, I have a question for you," Dominic said patting his brother's head.

The young boy did not move or respond.

"Do not bother to pretend you are sleeping. Where were you during all the commotion the other night?"

"Other night?" murmured the young prince.

"Yes, the other night." Dominic, with a smirk on his face, tapped John on the shoulder. "I know where you were, John. We shall address that later."

John, caught totally off guard, shifted his weight causing Braxton to lose his balance. Scrambling to catch himself, Braxton managed a slouched sitting position between his brothers.

"Why are you harassing us, Dom?" asked John.

"I'm not harassing you. I am curious. When I ran down the promenade toward the Rotunda, you and Ramsey were… well, never mind…"

"Yes, never mind! There was too much smoke for you to have seen anything," blurted John.

"Suit yourself, I know what I saw. You had better be careful."

Braxton decided this was a good time to get out of the line of fire and moved across the carriage to where he had been sitting earlier.

———

Josh sat in one of the baggage wagons pondering the two times he had seen Prince Braxton up close. The first was as he put out the fire in the courtyard and felt Prince Braxton's gaze. The second was witnessing Braxton piling the missing buckets next to the hay in the yard. It was too obvious to be true. Had that fire in the palace been the work of a prince of England? The more he thought about it, the more excited and nervous he became. London might be fun after all. He could only imagine what Braxton would come up with in the city!

Prince Richard sat unsettled. The fire had ignited in him not only the realization of his own mortality, but the safety and vulnerabilities of his family. He closed his eyes and wondered, what is to become of my family? They could have perished in the fire. My life would have ceased to have meaning. And Mercedes, what if I had lost you? Tears formed beneath his closed eyes.

The prince reached over and took Mercedes' hand in his and settled back into the carriage's luxurious upholstery. The sound of the rolling wheels on the gravels and clopping hooves soothed his nerves. A wistful smile appeared on his face as he thought back almost twentyfive years, back to his youth.

In 1839 the Prince of Wales had been on his grand tour, which aristocrats traditionally embraced as signifying their advent into maturity. As the second in line to the throne of the world's most powerful nation, his tour was unlike any other nobleman. He was tasked with visiting most of the significant royal courts in Europe, and many minor royals and nobles as well. He was related to most of them and the kingdom was, by necessity, allied with many of them. So, his tour would not be as enjoyable as other young aristocrat's excursions. He had responsibilities and duties to fulfill as crown prince.

Rome was the final stop on his tour. It provided the lifechanging occasion to meet Cosimo, Count de Chiacontella. Despite being supremely handsome, smart, athletic, and charming, the count possessed a comfortable humility attracting everyone to him. He was known to be very wealthy but did not flaunt the family fortune as much as did his father, the Duke de Chiacontella.

———

The Prince of Wales and the Duke de Chiacontella's introduction happened at a state banquet hosted by the pope. Festivities were held at the magnificent Apostolic Palace in the Vatican. Never, other than in Versailles and perhaps in Vienna, had Prince Richard seen such opulence. The vast luxurious beauty of the rooms communicated the heights of secular achievements of man, while enhancing the feeling of an intimate proximity to God.

Richard stood enraptured by his surroundings. He turned slowly, enveloped by the bright luminescent paintings bringing the soaring walls to life, depicting the Aramaic biblical stories of old. He was overcome with the drama and emotions so vividly illustrated. The crown prince felt light-headed, gripped by the majesty and divinity of the saints and ancient heroes the paintings thrust upon his senses.

Regaining his equilibrium, he gazed into the heaven that was Michelangelo's ceiling. Richard's body shivered as he contemplated the glory of God and the Holy Trinity. If only all mankind could grasp what was revealed to him—a world that could experience the glory and divinity represented here would surely be a better place. Richard stood stunned, overwhelmed, and humbled. His transformation from an indulged prince into a man of compassion, humility, and understanding took hold. Prince Richard, at that moment, embraced a will to love his fellow man. Opposing his previous belief that they should meet his expectations.

———

Count Cosimo de Chiacontella was acutely aware of his surroundings. Educated well beyond his peers, he had little use for the trappings associated with his birth. He projected confidence augmented by serenity. He did not have the swagger of a young aristocrat. He was comfortable with everything about his life and the responsibilities commensurate with his position, leaving it up to others to get to know him—if they cared to do so.

His Royal Highness Richard, the Prince of Wales, wanted to know who this exceptionally handsome, self-possessed courtier was. Etiquette required an introduction.

Cosimo's sycophantic father possessed little of his son's charm, being instead self-absorbed and arrogant. In a small way it worked to Richard's advantage. The Duke de Chiacontella was obsessed with making this introduction. During the requisite tour of the Sistine Chapel,

His Holiness, the Pope, and the Duke made polite conversation with His Royal Highness. Richard would one day be the king of the most influential nation on earth. The two older men wanted to

bring England's heir into their fold. The young prince surmised
their intentions and believed he could serve his king and government by getting to know the two men better.

"Cosimo, come here," the duke bellowed across the room to his
son, calling him away from a bevy of young, and not so young, aristocratic ladies.

"Your Royal Highness, may I introduce my son, Cosimo, Count
de Chiacontella?" Turning from Richard to his son, the duke said,

"Cosimo, let me present his Royal Highness, the Prince of
Wales."

Cosimo bowed and Richard extended his hand, which the count
took into his, feigning the perfunctory act of kissing a ring.

"Count, it is a pleasure to make your acquaintance."

"The honor is mine, Sir," Cosimo said, looking intently into
Richard's eyes. Richard exchanged the look. The prince and count
felt a comfortable chemistry, of which both his Holiness and the
duke made note.

Cosimo had, of course, previously taken notice of the young
prince. His first impression was that Richard was performing his
duties and did not appear to be impressed with the exalted company
as much as he was with the glorious architecture and surroundings.
The chapel and its essence of spirituality inspired Cosimo. He
sensed that Richard felt it as well.

Protocol required that Prince Richard be seated at the head
table with the older princes of the church and nobility. The evening
came to a close. Richard, the guest of honor, was about to leave the
assembly when Cosimo drew Prince Richard to the side.

"Your Royal Highness, may I be so forward as to invite you to
join me for a ride tomorrow morning in the seven hills overlooking
this ancient city?"

"Thank you Count, for the invitation. I have never ridden in
those legendary hills and shall jump at the opportunity."

The following morning was bright and brisk. The pair met,
accompanied by their respective equerries. Anticipating the freedom
of a good jaunt, each contemplated excusing their respective
escorts. Venturing out beyond the confines of the Apostolic Palace

and Rome appealed to them both. This positive energy encouraged and lifted the men's spirits, promising an excellent ride and a pleasant morning.

"My dear Count, with your permission, I have asked my men to allow us space to run the horses and enjoy the countryside."

Cosimo responded enthusiastically, instructing his attendants to do the same.

The men set off on their excursion. Out beyond the city and heading up into the hills surrounding ancient Rome, they picked up the pace. A free-flowing conversation ensued. They discussed the city, its beauty, and its history. They talked of politics, alliances, and conflicts faced when dealing with many of the challenges occupying Europe and beyond. Lost in conversation, they continued riding at a comfortable pace into the early afternoon.

One of the prince's aides rode up alongside the pair. "Your Royal Highness, would it be possible to water and rest the horses?" The soldier's request brought to their attention the time of day, the hours that had passed, and the fact that not only the horses, but the men following some distance behind, required rest, water, and sustenance.

Amused at their lack of attention to this reality, Richard cheerfully remarked, "Certainly, pardon us. We shall rest at the next village. Agreed Count?"

As the aristocrat's horses were attended to and all were taking nourishment, Prince Richard and the count decided to stroll about. Richard turned the conversation toward a more personal bent. He inquired of the young count as to where he had acquired his obvious serenity and self-assurance. Cosimo dumbfounded, coughed, never having had anticipated the future king would deign to converse in a manner so personal.

Observing the count's surprise, Richard asked Cosimo for a favor.

"Count, I hope that I don't presume too much by asking this question." He stopped for a moment and picked blossoms off a tree and lifted them to his nostrils, gently inhaling the fragrance. "I am, in all honesty, consumed with the responsibilities I one day will assume as king. I am, frankly, not prepared to carry the burden. I am, however, resolved to find the strength, knowledge, and the will to rise to the lifelong tasks that lay ahead."

Cosimo took the blossoms from Richard's hand. He smiled and buried his nose in them. "Lovely."

Richard marveled at the spontaneity. They resumed their walk.

Cosimo addressed the prince, "I think I have some idea of what you are experiencing, though not on the same scale. While I only concern myself with a duchy and banking, I will not be on the world stage such as will be you."

Richard smiled appreciatively and continued, "I would like to be friends. Friends speak frankly and more openly when there is less formality. So, may I suggest that when we are in private, we use our given names? I feel that this would abet frank, open, and enlightening conversation. Would you grant me that honor, Cosimo?"

Again, Cosimo caught off guard, did not give any indication that it was anything but an ordinary request. "Well, of course, Richard." He offered his hand.

Richard took Cosimo's hand and said, "Thank you." They walked along in silence.

Cosimo saw Richard shudder

"What is it your... Richard?"

"Nothing. I was just thinking."

"About what?"

"I can't and shouldn't say."

Cosimo turned to Richard, "You know, I too, sometimes have thoughts that I cannot, or rather feel I should not, share. You can trust me."

Richard, looking into Cosimo's eyes, believed he could trust this man.

Cosimo returned the gaze. For a moment, they both experienced a feeling of warmth bordering on sensuality.

Facing the Prince, Cosimo placed a hand on each of Richard's shoulders and in a matter-of-fact tone uttered, "Richard, I would like to extend an invitation to our home, Villa Incantarre. You must meet my twin sister, Mercedes."

Richard, returning from his reverie of days long ago to the present day, reached over and took Mercedes' hand in his. Mercedes awakened from her own thoughts and turned to smile at her husband.

———

The carriage journey to London continued with Braxton curled up on the seat opposite his brothers. Dominic leaned over to check on him.

"He is sleeping," said Dominic. "Exhausted. I am sure it has something to do with the fire."

Though the youngster appeared to be sleeping, was only dozing. The sly young royal remained still. Peering beneath one eyelid he noticed his brother John remove a flask from his coat, a flask always on hand.

The young men tapped into a second flask. Their conversation moved from the trials of packing for their migration to London to the events of the night of the inexplicable fire.

"John, how did I end up in my rooms?"

"I deposited you there when you collapsed in the promenade."

"Yes, I remember calling out to you. Thank you, John."

"I awoke mid-morning as the guests were leaving the palace. I was terribly confused and left my bed to see what had transpired. I walked down to the rotunda and was surprised to see that the fire and its evidence were in large part gone. Gone as if nothing had happened. The place had an odd odor, and I noticed discoloration throughout the rotunda and the nearby promenades." Dominic thrust his head back and took a sip, not losing one tiny drop, and continued. "Oh, and yes, it appeared the glass from the dome had wreaked havoc. What on earth happened?"

Taking the flask from his brother's hand and drinking deeply, John said, "Well, brother, I carried you back to your rooms after you collapsed from inhaling the smoke." He took another swig, wetting his lips and quenching something deep in his belly.

"John, the last thing I remember was calling out to you as you and Ramsey embraced."

John stiffened; his face flushed in disbelief. "Dominic! That is not fair… and it's libelous."

Dominic sat back and casually replied, "Well dear brother, I saw what I saw. What I have suspected for a while."

Dominic then folded his arms and said, "You and Ramsey are in a dangerous spot. What exactly are the two of you thinking? If you get caught, it will be ruinous. You need to get over this childish, insidious play." He commandeered the flask from his brother, slowly putting it to his mouth. Wiping away the residue, continued, "My lips are sealed. However, if your secret is revealed, I fear the consequences. It is my sincerest wish that you and Ramsey take hold of yourselves. The family does not need a scandal. And you might not survive the disgrace."

Braxton heard every word. This was not the first time he had thought about what he too had seen. Not certain why but hearing it from someone else soured his stomach.

The ten-year-old had not only suspected John's dalliance, but he also knew it had happened because he had seen it. Upon first observing their unexpected behavior, Braxton was curious as to why his brother John and Lord Ramsey would be physically intertwined. After observing them on more than one occasion from a concealed panel where he peered into John's room, Braxton simply thought their actions odd and boring. He somehow knew it was best not to reveal what he had observed, and not to share with his brothers what he knew. Feigning sleep, no more, he fell into a deep slumber.

———

"Richard, we need to discuss Braxton."

Princess Mercedes believed the carriage ride from the Aurelio Palace to London provided her an opportunity to have her husband's full attention. It provided the perfect milieu to discuss pressing family matters. Foremost in her mind was what to do with Braxton. It was apparent that he had outgrown his nurse and needed to be challenged intellectually and physically. His aptitude and energy far surpassed anything she had seen in her other children. This activeness of mind and body, coupled with his precocious nature, troubled her. It could be an indication that one disaster might follow another in the young prince's life.

"Yes, we do need to discuss him," Richard said reluctantly, stretching his neck.

"The fire," exclaimed Mercedes.

"Yes, the fire." Richard turned, offering his full attention.

"I hate to admit it, but I think he was very involved." Mercedes took a deep breath. "Because, when I found him that night, he was hot, sweaty, and covered in dirt and smelled of manure." She paused and brought a lace handkerchief to her face, wiping a tear. "If I did not know better, I would think he had played in the ashes, but I do know better. He may have planned the whole thing." She buried her head in her hands. The jostling carriage and hooves hitting the pavement muted her sobs.

Richard wrapped an arm around her shoulder and pulled her close. "My dear, I think, I mean, wasn't it apparent that night when you found him in his room? What is it that upsets you now?"

"There is more. I've discovered more since that night," she sniffed. "Richard, he is far more advanced for his age than we thought. When we renovated the palace over twenty years ago, I mentioned the long-abandoned service corridors. Do you remember?"

"Yes, dear, I do, though I don't think I ever ventured into them."

"When I was a little girl, Cosimo and I explored and played in them for hours on end. I know the service passages and escape tunnels intimately. Cosimo and I would spy on the family and guests."

"Escape tunnel?"

"Yes, we found that by accident. It's filthy and disgusting, terminating in the stable complex."

"I guess that has something to do with Braxton's pyrotechnics?"

"Yes, it certainly must."

Richard sitting up abruptly, encouraged Mercedes to do the

same. "You are correct. We must do something to control Braxton's wayward energies. You have a solution, don't you?"

Mercedes tilted her head toward Richard then looked toward her lap. "You know I do."

Prince Richard agreed with her assessment of Braxton's needs.

"Well, my dear, what do you think should be done?"

"I know that he is still very young, but we put in place changes. I am making inquiries for engaging a tutor. I also think he could use some companionship his own age." She paused momentarily, looking, and continued, "I have no idea who we could get to spend time with him.

But I am up to the task to finding someone. What are your thoughts?"

"Whatever you decide, I will support you. But please remember, we are not at Villa Incantarre. Things are more reserved here in England than in Italy, particularly as it relates to the Duchy de Chiacontella." He paused, his soft eyes feigning hardening. "Don't go and engage some mystic from the East!"

Mercedes gave him a playful jab and whispered into his ear, "No promises, dear."

Princess Mercedes had other concerns regarding her children. She was not comfortable and feared for their futures in the dynamic and changing world, feeling her daughters most vulnerable. Mercedes tested her husband's patience. "Richard, I would also like to address a couple of issues regarding the older children."

Smiling at her in his uniquely playful way, "Mercedes are you taking advantage of the fact that I am held captive in this carriage and cannot run away?"

"Yes," replied his wife.

"Well, as I have no choice, go on!" He settled back, knowing the conversation to follow would take some time.

Mercedes explained to her husband it was important the princesses become more aware of the greater world. It was vital they became able to relate to those outside their gilded circle of sycophants and royalists. The devoted mother was looking desperately for a way to familiarize her daughters with the lives and reality of the vagaries and dangers of the world outside their limited experiences. She was afraid for their survival and happiness if they did not become capable of adapting to the changing world. She felt strongly understanding others in the real world would better prepare them for the future and whatever their lives might bring.

"Richard, it has not been that long ago. 1848. Europe was ablaze with anarchy and revolution. But for the grace of God, your father could have lost his crown. The mercurial French forced their king, Louis Phillipe to flee the Tuileries Palace disguised in the middle of the night, huddled in a cab! It was sheer luck the Austrian emperor kept his crown.

Tens of thousands died across Europe."

Richard listened patiently. He had no choice and was confident his wife would do what was best for the family. When she finally finished speaking, he took her face into his hands, stroked her hair to one side, and lovingly kissed her. The sensation of her warm lips on his caused him to embrace her in a kiss more prolonged than expected.

They were both delighted there was still enough time left in the ride to London to take pleasure from each other's company.

———

Prince Dominic was the eldest son and second in line to the throne. He had a foreboding that things would not go well for him should he become king, but was not sure why. He felt somewhere deep inside, in all likelihood, if he were crowned king, his reign would be inconsequential and perhaps brief. Dominic's primary concern was that if he did not produce an heir, his brother John, next in line, could present a problem having unthinkable ramifications. Though amicable and compliant, his brother appeared to have no ambition and no avarice. Everyone enjoyed having John around as they would a loyal dog or dedicated servant. He was great company and a safe friend, but his relationship with Lord Ramsey...

Gerald, Viscount Ramsey, descended from a long line of nobles. He was handsome, intelligent, and well educated. He was not socially ambitious. He was already at the top of the social ladder. He did not need to be center stage as he was on stage by right of birth and innate talent. However, he lusted to be relevant and needed to be needed—to be part of the scene. John provided that for him. John needed Lord Ramsey and John's needs made Ramsey relevant. The match was good for them, but not for the crown.

3

THE WORLD OF LONDON

Very late in the afternoon, the royal entourage arrived on the outskirts of London. As they neared the metropolis, roads grew crowded and noisy. Ruts increasingly jostled the caravan the closer it came to the well-worn streets skirting the city.

As they approached the metropolis populated by over three million people, the pace slowed, the air thickened and grew unpleasant.

The carriages and wagons made consistent progress as the troop of royal cavalry, flying the Prince of Wales' regal standard, cleared the way. Onlookers moved aside for this remarkable procession of elegant closed liveried carriages bearing the royal coat of arms, escorted by brilliantly uniformed cavalry in polished boots and glistening armaments.

"Braxton! Get your head back in the carriage!" Exclaimed Dominic, pulling at Braxton's coat, trying to rein him in. Braxton resisted and unknowingly tripped the handle securing the carriage's door. The scrappy youngster was flung out of the vehicle, landing in the mud and debris of the London streets.

Tumbling face first into the brackish filth, he lay momentarily still. Lifting himself up he saw Dominic leap out of the still-moving caravan of carriages and heard him hollering, "Braxton! Braxton!"

Dazed, the young prince watched Dominic charging toward him as the carriages and wagons moved on. It seemed as if he was in a dream. A dream interrupted by laughter coming from the people in the street reveling in his misery. The tedium of their hard lives interrupted, they guffawed, jeering at the aristocrat wallowing in mud and grime.

Within moments of Dominic's lifting him up out of the mire, Richard and Mercedes appeared, accompanied by guards and retainers. Spotting the crown prince and princess, the crowd hushed, showing respect, some hats in hand. Others tried to bow or curtsey, something few had ever attempted.

Josh, carrying a horse blanket, hopped out of one of the wagons. He pushed his way through the crowd, squirming past guards and finding himself beside Braxton.

Braxton, covered in foul-smelling refuse, stood alone. No one spoke.

Josh stepped forward handing the coarse woolen blanket to Braxton saying, "You sure stink. No one will want to ride with you." Braxton looked sheepishly at Josh, accepting the blanket, and wrapping it around his shoulders.

Directing his attention to his parents, he said, "I am sorry, I didn't mean to…"

Mercedes interrupted, "I am grateful you are not injured."

His head held down, he muttered, "Yes, Mama."

Josh tugged at the blanket, saying "Come ride with us. We're used to the smell."

Braxton looked at Josh and stuttered loudly, "Real… really?" He looked toward his father. Richard shrugged and turned to Mercedes.

She offered, "Well, I am not certain that is a good idea."

Dominic grimaced and said, "Why not, Mother? It serves him right. Smell him! John and I do not care to have that in our carriage."

The crowd erupted into laughter in search of a break in the tension.

Richard said, "Mercedes, all appears to be well. Besides, it will do him some good."

Everyone, including Braxton, looked to Princess Mercedes.

Taking in Braxton's pleading eyes, she smiled, and desiring to please her son gave a slight nod.

"I shall have clothing sent to the stables when we arrive. No one cares for that aroma to permeate the house," Mercedes said, then blew Braxton a kiss.

The crowd roared in approval.

Braxton jumped up and clapped his hands twice, exclaiming, "Thank you, Mama. Thank you, Papa."

Josh took hold of Braxton pulling him through the crowd making way for the odiferous young prince. Arriving at the back of the baggage train, the occupants made room for Braxton. Those in the wagon did not know whether to defer to their young master or make fun. Sniggering could be heard sparking Josh to come to everyone's rescue.

"This is the prince. He has a foul air about him. Be done with it."

Braxton, not entirely oblivious to his dirty state, looked around and hoped these people could be friends. He grinned and said, "I am Braxton. Call me Braxton. I am sorry I stink."

"That'ud make you a stinkin' royal, wun't it?" came from deep within the wagon. Dead silence permeated the vehicle as it rocked and creaked rolling along the uneven road.

A moment later Braxton replied, "Exactly!"

Laughter and jibes rippled through the travelers.

Josh teased the mud sodden prince, "When was the last time you had a mud bath?"

Scowling, he answered, "First time, hope it is my last."

Josh leaned over toward Braxton and whispered, "I saw you put'n the buckets in the yard."

Braxton hunched forward wrapping his arms around himself. He replied quietly, "You saw no such thing."

"Yep, sure did, but I'm not squealin', it's our secret," Josh said, slapping the prince on his back. He then wiped his soiled hand on the edge of the blanket that had fallen off Braxton's shoulders, exclaiming, "Eww!"

The prince snorted and asked, "What is your name?"

"Josh."

"I am Braxton."

Josh shook his head side to side and chuckled, "Yeah, I figured."

———

Braxton's head spun taking in the city as the wagon proceeded through the city. He had never experienced such activity and noise before, nor had he seen so many people! Entering this new world engulfed his senses.

Twilight approached. The entourage drew nearer the alabaster marbled Arch Gate, serving as the main entrance to Renaissance House.

The Prince and Princess of Wales' London residence was centered on a 110-acre park surrounded by a thick stone wall standing more than twice the height of a guard on horseback.

There were three additional entrances to the estate. These lesser gates were not nearly as grand as the main gate. Use of the Arch Gate was limited to family and official guests. The Equus Gate was for all things related to maintaining the grounds, stables, horses, and all other manner of feathered and furry creatures living on the property. The other two entrances were utilized by servants and tradesmen.

Rules of etiquette were strict in London; today only the family carriages entered through the Arch Gate. The remaining transport and conveyances peeled off to their respective entrances. As the family passed through the imposing Arch Gate, the estate manager and his staff lined the drive standing erect, hats in hand, heads bowed.

The drive curved along a small lake, framing the imposing manse sitting atop a large, elongated knoll overlooking the well-manicured park.

Renaissance House's staff of eighty had formed up to welcome the family. They stood shoulder to shoulder, the butler, and head housekeeper nearest the royal carriage, it having come to a halt in front of the chateau.

The London residence had been constructed in the architectural style of the Loire Valley chateaux. It was commodious, sprawling, and reached to the sky. If it were not for the park that surrounded it, the chateau would have dominated the horizon for miles around, demonstrating once again the Chiacontella talent for concealing wealth and grandeur. The well-laid out park shielded the magnificent edifice from the outside world with tall centuries-old oaks standing proudly behind the 30-foot-high granite wall bordering the park. The primary structure stood on two acres surrounded by ten acres of Baroque and Neoclassical gardens and niches extending intermittently throughout the park.

As the family disembarked and walked past the assembled household staff, through the vestibule, and into the main hall of Renaissance House, they entered a gloriously appointed and soaring room. The grandeur overwhelmed them all. Even though Richard and Mercedes had lived in, and frequented the chateau, the eminent looming reality Richard would one day ascend the throne engulfed them. The couple realized they were destined one day to leave their country lives behind and step into an unknown future.

————

Braxton found himself placed in a large tub in the carriage house. Two women had stripped him of his clothing and had placed him in the hot water. Lye soap and firm hands removed all traces of dirt and odor. While scrubbing him, one of the hefty females marveled out loud, "You know, Master Braxton, if you was to be the heir, yu'd never be lef' wi't us. Yu'd a be put in yus own carriage, smells and all. Now, if you be the spare prince, yu'd still not be put in our wagon. But you be the spare's spare! He He!"

Tired and agitated, he did not bother to ask what she was talking about. "May I get out now? All this rubbing is removing every inch of my skin!"

The other girl remarked, "Get yourself on out and we'll get your royalty dressed. Someone'll be heading this way for ya soon." Braxton jumped out, toweled off and dressed in clothes a footman had delivered during his bath.

Nanny arrived to retrieve the freshly scrubbed and newly outfitted Braxton from the stables. The two exiting the washroom, Nanny prompted, "Do you not think it polite to thank these people, Your Royal

Highness?"

Braxton's bright countenance gave way to gloom. He stuck his hands in his pockets and looked at the floor and thought to himself, I do not want to go; I want to stay here. I want to stay with Josh, my new friend.

He looked up, turned, and nodded at the women standing by the wash tub and exited the room.

Leaving the stable complex, he walked up to the stable master and said, "Thank you, Sir. Thank you for your kindness."

"You are welcome, Your Royal Highness. You are welcome here anytime."

Surprise and glee covered Braxton's face. "Do you mean I may come back?"

"Yep," Josh piped in with a matching grin on his face.

Braxton returned the smile.

"Come, Your Highness," said Nanny as she took his hand pulling him away.

Braxton waved one hand back at Josh as Nanny drug him toward the main house.

Nanny took Braxton to the top floor of the Campanile Tower. A wing of the house noticeably removed from the family's other quarters. It had traditionally housed the nursery suite composed of a salon, classroom, two bedrooms, and the nanny's room. The ceilings stood fourteen feet high. French doors opened onto a full balcony traversing the length of Braxton's bedroom, the salon, and the classroom —which offered views of the park–the gardens, and most importantly, the stables.

———

Upon entering their private palatial rooms, Richard turned to Mercedes, lovingly placing his arms around her, and planting a light kiss on her forehead. He then rested his head on her shoulder for a moment. Raising his head and looking squarely into her eyes, whispering to her in a calm yet serious tone, "My darling, I love you and, above all, trust you with all my heart." He paused for a moment and continued, "I have a deep and somewhat uncomfortable feeling that we are about to embark on a magnificent and challenging journey. I want and need you to participate in every part of my life. And if I can provide that same support for you, please only ask."

Mercedes lower lids shimmered as tears filled the shallow wells.

She blinked a single wet drop out of each eye and looked up at Richard, saying, "Amore mio, tu sai che il tuo amore e la tua fiducia sono ben posti in me. Certo, sarò lì per te. E sì, ti sto chiedendo di fare lo stesso per me. My love, you know that your love and trust is well-placed in me. Of course, I will be there for you. And yes, I am asking you to do the same for me."

The prince's private secretary interrupted them, entering through the door left open by the couple. Bowing, he said, "Excuse me, Your Royal Highnesses, I was informed you requested my presence." Richard responded, "Yes, please have my son Prince Braxton brought to my study."

The secretary replied, "Yes, Your Royal Highness." He bowed and left the room.

Richard took Mercedes hands in his. "Dear, I must have a talk with Braxton. You are right. He is totally out of control. Something must be done."

Mercedes pulled Richard close, their faces inches apart. Pleading with her eyes, she said, "Richard, please do not be unkind. He is yet a boy."

Resting their foreheads together, Richard said. "Don't worry my dear, I will be firm, but gentle."

Richard removed himself to his study, closing the door behind him.

He strode to the desk and sat in a plush leather chair having legs and armrests made of gilded ebony. The chair sat alongside the empire desk, complete with hand-carved legs and gold leaf-encrusted details along the edges of the tabletop.

Consumed with his thoughts of Braxton, Richard, who usually took time to admire such beauty, wasted not one moment, carefully rehearsing what he was to say to his third son.

He stared out the huge ornate window. Its frame gilded in a delicate, intricate web of silver and gold sitting atop shimmering lacquered ebony framing enormous panes of glass. Richard looked past the exquisite craftmanship, seeing nothing but Braxton looming large in his mind's eye. The ramifications of what he must convey to his son swirled about his head.

4

MANY SEASONS ROLLED INTO ONE

Three sharp raps sounded on the study's mahogany door. The private secretary entered and announced, "His Royal Highness, Prince Braxton."

Having been announced, Braxton slowly entered the room and bowed, saying, "Father, you asked to see me?" He remained by the door and near the secretary as if the secretary might provide some sort of protection or sanctuary.

"Come here, Braxton."

Braxton stepped slightly back.

"Braxton!"

The young prince's eyes widened, his posture ramrod straight.

"Yes Papa?"

"Come here and sit down."

Braxton looked up at the secretary as if there remained some hope he would be saved from certain death at the hands of his father. The secretary let a slight grin escape and motioned with his head toward Prince Richard, then left the room closing the door behind him.

Braxton proceeded as if in a funeral march and a dirge playing in the background. Richard watched his ten-year-old son approach him as if he were the guillotine itself.

The young prince took a seat in front of his father who sat behind what appeared to Braxton was the largest piece of furniture he had ever seen.

Richard steepled his fingers under his chin. "Braxton, do you know why I want to speak to you?"

"No, Papa."

"Would you care to venture a guess?"

Braxton cocked his head and said, "You want some of my soldiers to put on your desk?"

"What are you talking about?"

Braxton shifted in the chair, then leaned forward, an impish look on his face, pointed at the desk's surface and said, "I was thinking this would be a good place to have battles with soldiers, and I do not think you have toy soldiers. So, Father you may borrow some of mine." Braxton's charms were hard at work.

Richard was aware of his son's talents. He sat up and placed his hands on the edge of the desk.

"That is very kind of you Braxton. If the situation were different, I would take your kind offer into consideration." He paused. "Now listen to me very carefully. You placed the family, our guests, and servants in great danger creating that inferno."

Braxton felt a chill course through his body. His head sprang up engaging his father's stare, his own eyes bulging. They sat in silence as Braxton's face turned a shade of light blue.

"Breathe, Braxton. Open your mouth and breathe." The stifled prince's face turned bluer.

Richard raised both his hands and slammed them palms first onto the desk and shouted, "Breathe!"

Braxton startled by his father's loud voice and hands striking the desk, gulped in air, hyperventilating. The frightened breathing turned to coughing, soon giving way to tears.

Richard instinctively sprang out of his chair and swept the hysterical Braxton into his arms. He held him and rocked him saying, "It is all right Braxton, calm down. I did not intend to frighten you. Please get ahold of yourself."

The boy continued inhaling through coarse breaths.

Richard carried his son to a nearby pull and rang for a servant as Mercedes entered the room. Seeing Braxton in such a state, she immediately asked, "Richard, what happened?" She ran over to Braxton and coddled the boy's face in her hands. "Braxton, what is wrong, why are you crying?"

He continued to blubber.

"He shall be alright. He just-just needs to calm down, calm down. When the servant arrives, ask for water."

———

Braxton's breathing returned to normal as he drank water offered by a servant, his parents alongside him.

Mercedes, patting Braxton's arm said, "Now that you are feeling better, I will leave you two to continue your discussion."

Braxton reached for her hand, in effect begging her not to go. She looked down with a smile, patting him on his head, saying, "You will be fine." She rose, gently squeezed Richard's hand, and exited the room.

Richard remained next to Braxton. "You were quite the sight to behold wallowing in the mud and manure this afternoon. How did it feel?"

The question took Braxton aback.

"Squishy and smelly, I guess."

"That is not what I meant. Did it feel embarrassing and humiliating?"

Braxton placed the glass on the table. He played with his fingers for a moment. "I guess it hurt a little, but not much. I got to ride in the wagon with Josh!"

Richard ran his fingers through his hair. "My God, Braxton. Did it ever occur to you that you could have been hurt or even run over and killed falling out onto that road? Did it ever occur to you how devastated your mother, brothers, sisters, and I would have been if you had been injured or died?"

Braxton lowered his head, looking at his shoes, slowly shaking his head back and forth. Quietly he said, "No Papa, I am sorry."

"Yes, yes, you have said that many times recently."

"Now Braxton, the fire in the rotunda. What was that all about? How did that come about?"

Braxton took another sip of water and stood up. Using his hands, he exclaimed hastily, "I was so frightened! The fire was monstrously large! I do not know how it happened! It was so much larger than the one in the stable yard. It became out of control so fast. All I wanted was to have some fun and stink everyone out. I didn't want to burn anything!"

Richard went over to where Braxton was standing and knelt in front of him, holding his son's hands, looking up into his face, "What stable fire, boy?"

Having his father's full attention, center-stage, he launched into his story, "Well, a couple of days before, I was…" Unleashing his innate sense for theatre, Braxton went on to tell his father everything that had transpired, from spotting the lantern tip over to returning the buckets to the stable yard.

Fascinated by his son's dramatic delivery, Richard remained on his knees, admittedly transfixed by the storyteller and his tale. There was only one thing he could think of to say to his extraordinary son.

"Braxton, you are a prince of England. You have responsibilities. I expect you to remember that. People could have died. Never do anything like that again."

Braxton hung his head and wiping his nose across the back of his hand said, "Yes, Papa. I'm sorry Papa." He then moved to his still kneeling father and wrapped his arms around him.

———

Richard left the next morning for an extended trip on crown business. Mercedes had a plan, many ideas coursing through her mind.

Richard was hardly out the door before Mercedes set about implementing those ideas.

Mercedes mused to herself, provided he was absent long enough; Richard would hardly recognize the members of his family upon his return.

Princess Mercedes had the opportunity she had always wanted– free rein to prepare her brood for the ever-changing world she felt looming. First on her mind was, of course, Braxton. He had the most potential and was still at an age where he was impressionable and moldable.

Following the sorting out the foreign intelligentsia residing in the capital, Mercedes arranged a soiree including the most excellently educated in London, Oxford, and Cambridge. Following the successful soiree, she then took steps to schedule five more gatherings. She organized a series of lectures delivered by some of the most learned men in England. Each of the talks would highlight educating the leaders of tomorrow. Her Royal Highness had her invitations distributed by liveried footmen. Each recipient was to be presented the invitation, whenever possible, in public. Public invitations extended by royalty, even foreign royalty, assured acceptance, and attendance.

Her actions stunned London society and academia. How could the princess, a foreigner at that, deign to postulate how to educate the English aristocracy? The concept of universal education was as alien to society in Britain as were the princess and her Chiacontella background.

With the king and his court in Scotland, and Prince Richard traveling, Mercedes was free to do what she wished. The third in the series of five lectures was completed before Mercedes experienced disapproval from the crown.

In a letter received from Richard, he wrote Mercedes, it pains me to have to bring this to your attention, but father is a bit concerned about the lectures you have hosted and subscribed. The prime minister and several lords are not entirely comfortable with the notice that is being given in the newspapers. I know you mean well, please take care to not let this matriculate into a spat vis-à-vis constitutional matter.

Mercedes replied. Thank you, darling for relaying his majesty's and the government's concerns. Fear not. The lectures are confined to education and the value they bring to the empire's youth. Certainly, no offense can be taken with my efforts to enhance the quality of education. The future of his majesty's and the government's empire weighs in the balance.

The first well attended lecture was followed by widespread controversial conversations permeating society and academia. A thought-provoking discussion on the philosophy of educating the masses, proved to be a somewhat controversial concept. Philosophical discussions centered on education being accessible to all classes. While many agreed that all classes should have access to education, there was great division as to how to make it available to the masses. Braxton, from his vantage point in the gallery, kept track of the words and new ideas flying about. He did not comprehend why very few seemed to want to act and move toward educating the masses. What was to be accomplished with these well-meaning lectures? Inwardly, even at his young age, he felt a gnawing futility.

The second and third fully attended lectures centered on science and mathematics. The fourth and fifth gatherings were configured to spark in-depth conversations about national and international politics. Because of the success of her previous gatherings, attendance was expected to exceed Renaissance House capacity. These final lectures were moved to the recently opened St. James Hall.

Mercedes' efforts successfully accomplished two things: She had planted a seed in the minds of others that changes must be made in the nation's education of its youth. Secondly, she had learned enough to put in motion a plan to upgrade the education of her own children.

The older princes might not agree to participate to the degree their mother wished, which would surely be a disappointment. However, the remaining three children would have an opportunity to partake. While the princesses were not totally comfortable with the upcoming changes, the changes thrilled Braxton. He had convinced his mother to allow him to sit in the gallery during the lectures attended by his older brothers. Inspired by the presentations, he formulated a plan for his education, all his own.

———

Mercedes was not often in Braxton's suite, as the nursery was somewhat removed from the center of the chateau. Typically, Braxton was brought to her mid-morning as she breakfasted or dressed for morning activities.

One afternoon, as Braxton was attending to his studies, his mother entered his room unannounced. Her person was such that she lit up his room as she did most rooms she entered. The spaces illuminated by her natural beauty, charm, and compassion.

Braxton had been fixated on his geography lesson. Sensing her presence, he looked up from his studies. She seemed to float across the room. He jumped up and ran to her arms. To him, she was the fairy princess of his childhood stories—Cinderella, Rapunzel, and Snow White all in one.

Still holding him, she kindly dismissed the nanny and placed her youngest son on the sofa next to her.

"Well, Braxton, how are your studies progressing?"

"Very well, Mama. I am studying maps of many countries that I will one day visit!"

"Excellent, my dear. What countries would you like to see?"

"Well, of course, I would love to visit your country, Italy."

Patting him on the head, she smiled and said, "I certainly hope so. It would be lovely to show you Italy myself."

"Mama, perhaps you could take me there today!"

Laughing she said, "Yes, today would be wonderful, but perhaps we should wait for Papa."

"There is another country, Russia," the young prince said.

"That is interesting Braxton. Why Russia?"

Braxton went on to say how he had heard wonderful stories about the snow, the Russians defeating Napoleon, tales of wolves, and roaring rivers alongside soaring mountains. His favorite stories were of Cossacks, and Peter the Great and his armies.

Russia too had been on Mercedes' mind. She had recently engaged a Russian-born tutor, Count Konstantin Volkov. The educator was from an old noble family that had served the Russian princes for centuries. Konstantin, like Braxton—was not the firstborn son, and unlike his soonto-be new charge, his family had lost much of their wealth. Konstantin was educated in St. Petersburg, Rome, and Paris. He was 21 years old. The young scholar was mesmerized by learning and demonstrated a penchant for teaching. He loved research, and where others saw black and white, he looked for grey. Konstantin was Mercedes' attempt to educate, stimulate, and challenge Braxton, hopefully distracting him from his preoccupation with childish and hazardous activities.

Mercedes was a linguist, but Braxton's abilities indicated he would one day exceed even her talents in this arena. She spoke Italian, French, Spanish, English, Latin, and Greek. Her fluency in Russian was limited at best. Because of that, she engaged Konstantin to teach the increasingly important language to all her children, not just Braxton.

Russia was a vast empire with the potential to dominate Europe and challenge England's predominance as the world's greatest power. She felt strongly that her family must be well prepared to deal with their royal Russian as family or foe.

A tall, angular, well-dressed young noble entered the room.

"Braxton, let me present your new tutor, Count Konstantin Volkov."

The young prince's jaw dropped.

Konstantin could have been a Cossack, as far as Braxton was concerned. The Russian strolled briskly forward and executed a crisp bow to his new pupil.

Braxton nodded and said, "Count Volkov, I am pleased to make your acquaintance and look forward to your tutelage. I hope you will be comfortable here and that I am worthy of your attention."

Konstantin smiled and said, "Your Royal Highness, I have every confidence you will."

———

Braxton's course of study was rigorous. He and the count spoke Russian frequently as the prince moved toward mastering the language.

They rarely spoke English as the young prince spoke Italian and some German, which often had to suffice when Russian was too difficult. The count focused on classical history, literature, grammar, math, geography, and some science. Forty-five-minute study periods were interrupted by meals, trips to museums and exercise. This routine occupied him twelve hours each day. He reluctantly agreed to an hour rest in the early afternoons. The schedule was followed six days out of seven. Braxton could not have been happier or more engaged, and Mercedes more pleased with his progress.

Konstantin grew weary from these long, arduous days, in part because Braxton rarely accepted knowledge without having to question it. Konstantin adored Braxton but preparing long lessons and then implementing them with his capable student consumed sixteen hours each day. Thus, causing the dedicated tutor to live in a state of physical and mental exhaustion.

Nine months into their academic journey, Konstantin met with Mercedes to explain his dilemma. He recommended Mercedes engage a tutor to instruct Braxton and the other children in Britain's constitutional law. This would give him a small reprieve and, as members of the royal family, it was imperative they know their prerogatives and limitations as royals. Konstantin felt this new tutor could also instruct Braxton in English grammar and literature. He further suggested the tutor could provide companionship. It was also time for Braxton to begin an equitation program. Familiarity and mastery of horses, hunting, and polo were vital to the young prince's place in society.

Braxton once again enthusiastically welcomed these changes. Now, the only thing missing in his life were childhood friends. A concern his parents and brother John embraced.

Princess Mercedes had a visitor. The Grand Duchess Princess Ekaterina had great energy, compassion, and wisdom. As the daughter of the current and aging Czar, she had a gravitas that few possessed. Her contagious smile and exuberance warmed many hearts. Ekaterina, a contemporary of Mercedes' mother had become Mercedes' lifelong friend, having spent many summers at the Villa Incantarre. Mercedes had learned over the years that traditional familial situations had been difficult for this naturally effervescent woman. The loving support offered by Mercedes and her mother was a godsend to the grand duchess. They provided love, stability, and the Chiacontella "magic" that saw her through the darkness and strife that enveloped her family and country in darker times.

Braxton, interrupting his mother and the grand duchess in the Japanese conservatory, immediately felt for reasons unknown that he had met his guardian angel.

"Young Braxton! Come here!" Chortled Ekaterina. Braxton quizzically obeyed his new friend, running up to her, bowing respectfully, and introducing himself as "Braxton, your obedient servant." This charmed Ekaterina to no end. She turned to his mother, took her hand, and asked her for a proper introduction.

Mercedes acknowledged the cue, "Your Imperial Highness, Grand Duchess Princess Ekaterina, may I present my precious son, Prince Braxton?

Once again, the young royal bowed respectfully, took Ekaterina's hand, and placed the traditional kiss on her ring. The grand duchess was enthralled, and precocious young Braxton thoroughly charmed.

To Ekaterina, Braxton seemed the reincarnation of her twin son, Peter, whom she had lost to the war, along with Peter's father.

Ekaterina mourned not the loss of her husband, Prince Gregor. Gregor had made no secret of the fact he had loved the elevated imperial position his marriage to Ekaterina brought him more than he loved her. His many affairs attested to that. She most resented him for the actions he had taken prior to and throughout the war, years earlier when in China; those actions leading to Peter's death. Maxim, Peter's twin, was now not available for her, as he was enslaved to a horrible existence. Ordered by the Czar to serve as a companion to the czarevich, who at 16 had already shown signs of madness.

Ekaterina had fled to Italy and then England to escape haunting memories and her pain.

And now before her was young Braxton. He was the incarnation of what she once dreamed, hoped, and imagined her husband and sons might have become. Her sons and her husband were dreams unfulfilled and Braxton was an amazing amalgam of so much she had dreamed for them all.

Braxton was the fresh and new, the phoenix, the embodiment of the magic of the Chiacontella ménage and her beloved Peter. Ekaterina committed to perpetuating her chimera and phantasma through the young prince.

The grand duchess complimented Mercedes on the perfection of her child. Braxton felt secure and empowered by her, just like he was when with his mother. The feeling of empowerment Ekaterina inspired in Braxton would grow into a prodigious power beyond even the duchess's comprehension.

5

THE STABLE BOY & THE GRAND DUCHESS

The following day, having exhausted his tutor, Braxton slipped away and found himself in the stables. Roughhousing with some of the lads, he deliberately tripped the slightly older, and larger, Josh.

Josh instinctively turned around and smacked young Braxton's jaw hard. The prince yelped stumbling across the straw-strewn stable floor, coming to a stop smashing into a thick wooden post before falling limp and unconscious to the ground. Instantly every boy in the area froze, looking over at Braxton's seemingly lifeless body and then at Josh. Their eyes appeared ready to pop out of their respective heads. As the shock passed, everyone except Josh quickly fled the scene.

The stable boy could not believe what he had done. He did not take a moment to think before scooping up the listless prince and carrying him to the chateau bursting through the first open door he could find; hollering loudly for a doctor.

Alarm sounded throughout the vast manse. It seemed that the entire household materialized in less than a minute, creating a crowd of over eighty staff and family members. The head house-keeper quickly gathered towels and ordered two maids to bring water, bandages, and blankets. The butler ordered Josh to follow him, still carrying the limp prince, to Braxton's rooms. Josh had begun to tire following the run across the grounds from the stables. Drenched in perspiration, his legs and arms burning from the exhaustive exertion, he struggled to keep up with the older servant. All the while, the nervous butler screaming, "Hurry! Do not drop him! Hurry up. Follow me."

The stable boy placed the unresponsive body on the prince's bed. Princess Mercedes and the grand duchess flew into the room, simultaneously asking, "What has happened? What happened?"

Josh answered back in an exhausted but agitated voice, "I hit him. I am so sorry, Ma'am. I just hit him!"

The two women bent over Braxton not looking at Josh. Mercedes cried hysterically, "Why in God's name did you hit him?"

Josh indignantly replied, "He hit me first!"

"What?" shouted Mercedes looking up at the stable boy.

The grand duchess instructed Josh to sit in a chair on the other side of the room. He did as commanded.

Braxton moaned and moved his head ever so slightly, causing the room filled with family and servants to forget Josh for the moment. The exception was Sally the maid. She brought him a glass of water and a towel to wipe off dirt and perspiration.

The two women carefully inspected every inch of Prince Braxton, lifting the hair from his neck, turning his face with great care, and examining his limbs and torso. They surmised he was not injured but filthy. Oh, and yes, he was going to have a nasty bruise or two.

A short time later a doctor arrived. Braxton awoke confused about all the fuss. The last thing he remembered was tripping his friend in fun and being on the receiving end of Josh's big hand.

"How did I get here?" inquired Braxton.

"That young man carried you here," answered his mother gesturing toward Josh.

Braxton looked across the room at a shaken and timid Josh, "Oh, hello, Josh. So sorry I tripped you. I hope I did not hurt you. From the looks of things, it appears you got the better of me!"

Everyone in the room stared in awkward silence, first at Braxton, then at Josh and back to Braxton, and again to Josh. A quiet giggle permeated the room; it was Ekaterina. Mercedes looked at her friend and also laughed, which ignited a twitter from the servants who quickly left the room in an attempt to contain themselves. Mercedes and Ekaterina laughed aloud, and Braxton followed suit

Poor Josh, unsure what to do and still very uncomfortable in these royal chambers, just sat there. Moments earlier, while the women inspected every inch of Prince Braxton, the stable boy imagined himself in front of a firing squad, sentenced to death for assaulting the prince. In this uncomfortable moment, he was hopeful he might get by with a severe beating from his father. Mercedes saw this as an opportunity to help Braxton learn a life lesson or two. She approached Josh sitting paralyzed in his chair.

From across the room, Josh heard Braxton say, "This would be an excellent opportunity for you to stand up and bow."

Josh looked over to Braxton, then up at the princess who stood six feet away gently smiling down at him. Josh slowly rose respectfully. That is all he remembered before things went black.

Later he found himself unsure of why he was now lying face up in a prone position on a sofa looking up at Braxton, placing a damp cloth on his forehead and peering down at him. Shock and exhaustion had taken its toll as Josh had fainted while rising from the chair. Fortunately, the prince had recovered enough from his unexpected tumble to attend to the person who both disabled and assisted him.

Mercedes pulled up a chair next to Josh and asked, "What is your name young man?"

Josh attempted to rise off the couch.

"No, stay where you are, rest," Mercedes insisted. Josh, wide-eyed, looking up at the princess, answered, "Josh." "Your Royal Highness," Braxton interrupted.

Mercedes glared at Braxton and said, "Never mind that, now."

She continued, "Josh, please tell me what happened."

Josh replayed the incident exactly as it had occurred.

Mercedes said, "Thank you, Josh."

"Yes, Ma'am."

Mercedes turned toward Braxton and said, "I think you owe this young man an apology."

Josh sprang up to a sitting position and exclaimed, "Please Ma'am the prince doesn't hav' ta apologize."

"Indeed, he does."

Looking down at the floor, the prince rubbed his hands together and said nothing.

Ekaterina interjected in Russian, "Braxton, we are waiting."

"He hit me too," Braxton returned in Russian.

Mercedes, annoyed that the two had spoken in a tongue that she, and she assumed Josh, did not speak, stood and said sternly, "Braxton, you initiated the confrontation. He was defending himself. It is time for you to take responsibility for your actions."

Braxton inhaling, shoulders back and stomping his foot said, "I am sorry for tripping you."

"That was more of a tantrum than an apology," Ekaterina said again in Russian.

Braxton folded his arm and then pointing at Josh and asked in Russian, "What about him?"

Mercedes, having figured out what Braxton must have said replied, "Does he owe you an apology? You tripped him, unprovoked. The decision is up to him."

All eyes focused on Josh.

Rubbing his head, Braxton blurted out, "I'm sorry. I'm sorry."

Mercedes rose out of the chair and with Ekaterina stood by the door leading into the room. "Very well, the two of you will spend the next twenty-four hours in these rooms."

Braxton and Josh exchanged looks of incredulity.

Mercedes went onto explain that meals would be brought to them. They were not to leave the suite of rooms and could only venture out into rooms contained within the suite. She insisted that this was an opportunity for them to sort out their problems. Apologies would normally suffice, but in this instance her punishment would require such close proximity that their actions would attest to the sincerity of a resolution to whatever problem had initiated the melee.

Braxton was delighted to have Josh's company as he never had a young companion to play with when at home. The young prince considered this punishment a fantastic lark.

Josh felt entirely different, frightened, as this place was unlike anything he had ever seen. The stable boy recalled two years prior, the night he extinguished the fire in the Aurelio Palace rotunda. The young waif did not know how to breathe in this extraordinary chateau, much less inhabit it. He felt nauseated, lay back down on the couch, and fell back to sleep.

When he awoke, he found Braxton freshly scrubbed and dressed, striking in appearance. Josh recalled the first time he had seen the young prince. He had looked up from the stable courtyard and witnessed Braxton on the second-story balcony looking down at him.

That was years ago, but he felt that same sensation now.

"You are awake! Time for a bath." Braxton said, gesturing to a huge tub of what appeared to be warm, clean water sitting in the middle of the room. "Take your clothes off and get in! I just had a bath. It is your turn. This room is smelling like you! I have opened the windows, but it is not eliminating the stench. Get going!"

Josh sat up stunned. He had never had a clean tub in which to bathe. His father always had the first bath, followed by his older brothers, so by the time it was Josh's turn, the water was filthy. That was why he always snuck down to the river, upstream from where the livestock spent their days, and washed up. He very much wanted to get into the tub of clean water. Yet he was too embarrassed to take his clothes off in front of Braxton and certainly did not plan on stripping off in front of the three house-maids standing close by. The women, their arms folded, stared at the stable boy daring him to disobey the prince. Josh remained glued to the sofa. The maids lurched forward, grabbed hold of him, stripped him naked and placed him in the magnificently warm water.

Josh did not stir, worried he might die of shock or pleasure.

Either way, he was convinced that before he could leave this place, he would die.

As was their routine with Braxton, the maids washed Josh top to bottom. The paralyzed stable boy hardly moved throughout the process. So many unfamiliar sensations ran through him. No one had ever bathed him like this before, not even his own mother. The young man hated it, yet he loved it. As Josh enjoyed the experience, the maids lifted him out of the tub, dried then dressed him in fresh clothes Prince John had outgrown years earlier. The clothing fit the stable boy quite nicely.

Braxton filled the time by entertaining himself with hand-painted toy soldiers on a mock battlefield that sat atop a table at the other end of the room. Occasionally he looked up to see Josh and laughed.

A fire was lit to warm the room as the open windows had invited a chill. Braxton summoned Josh to the table to see the mock battlefield. The stable boy stood in awe of the beautiful craftsmanship and detailed toy army pieces. The soldier's uniforms were painted red to represent the British infantry. The cavalry horses had riders atop them. There were tiny cannons, rifles, mortars, and all such military equipment, as well as tents, baggage trains, and camp followers. The scene was complete with a village, castle, river, and lakes. There were hills and valleys and a battlefield with the British on one end and a French army in blue on the other.

"Since you are my guest, you may be the British. I will be the 'Frogs'."

The invitation sounded interesting, but Josh had no idea how to take part.

"Your Royal Highness," said Josh, "I have never played this game."

"Never you mind. I will let you win." Braxton then set about explaining the rudiments of battle as he understood them. His father had been his first teacher, and tutors had augmented his understanding. However, Braxton learned most of what he knew from reading books and his endless curiosity, which led him to pick the brains of military men who frequented their home. Over time he had cornered several officers and invited them to come to his suite, see his soldiers, and assist him in fighting various battles. Braxton's charm and enthusiasm endeared him to even the most high-ranking officers who often joined him in his spirited play until rescued by his parents. Braxton was eager to instruct Josh. What fun!

Hours passed on the battlefield. The sun had set long ago, servants having rebuilt the fires three times, and closing the windows long before the boy's games came to an end. Mercedes left word, other than meals, Braxton and Josh were not to be interrupted. She and the grand duchess, having spied on them twice, decided the boys could be left unsupervised and to their own devices.

Finally, the boys grew tired and, without saying a word, Braxton extinguished the remaining candles that had not already burned out. He and Josh disrobed, climbed into Braxton's bed, and fell fast asleep. For the young prince and his friend, it had been a day to remember!

The following morning Josh stirred and opened his eyes. He gazed at the carved ceiling, fourteen feet above. Crystals dangling suspended in the gas chandelier refracted colors on all four walls.

Josh said under his breath, "That roof is so high."

He rolled to his side lifting himself onto an elbow. The room was full of morning light, revealing a sumptuous breakfast on a small table covered in white linen set with silver and china. Two chairs faced one another across the table.

Braxton was dressed and sitting at his writing desk updating his journal, completing entries that he had failed to make the night before.

The young prince had started this journal upon the family's arrival at Renaissance House two years prior. A family guest had shared this French saying with him once, "Be faithful to your journal and your journal will be faithful to you." Braxton knew that older members of his family kept journals and determined it was time he kept one as well. Committing in that instant to chronicle his hitherto brief but burgeoning life's experiences.

A devotee of intrigue and espionage, Braxton obsessed on how he might record entries in his journal without risking his many imagined secrets being revealed. He must come up with a secret cypher.

At first, he wrote every word backwards, which seemed to work well until one day, unexpectedly, he saw his reversed words inverted back to him. The many precious words he had so carefully inscribed in his journal were reflected at him in perfect form from the mirror next to his dressing table. After knocking a glass of water over on his desk, he hastily placed the journal in front of the mirror and was aghast at what was revealed in the reflective glass. This could be his undoing!

The voracious reader knew of ciphers, codes, and spies from books about soldiers and battles. When trying to solve the problem of keeping his secrets, he took time to scour the cavernous library at Renaissance House. Finding nothing that elaborated on creating codes, he invented his own, comprising transposing numbers to letters and letters to numbers. Braxton thought this code to be inventive, but not unbreakable. He felt secure enough to use it until something else came along, still convinced a spy would surely try to gain access to his journals!

———

On a chair next to the bed, Josh found fresh clothing and shoes laid out for him. Again, they were the finest clothes he remembered having seen. He marveled at the soft cotton undergarments, wool stockings, fine wool trousers, pressed white collared shirt, and smart jacket. He dressed slowly, marveling all the while at the finery. Inspecting himself in the mirror, Josh realized he was hungry.

The stable boy, feeling so proud in his elegant attire, walked to the table, and gawked at the many covered dishes. Slowly removing the covers one by one just enough to peek at the contents, he discovered eggs, ham, sausage, potatoes, scones, and pastries. There was enough food here to feed a dozen people. Never had he seen such a feast! Braxton joined him. They sat at the prepared table, each devouring large portions.

Witnessing Josh's table manners, Braxton was grateful he had listened to Nanny and given in to her demands he handle his cutlery properly. She had faithfully schooled him in how to dine as a gentleman: never leaning over his plate or shoveling the food into his mouth like a hungry lion tearing into its prey. Braxton determined it was best to have a footman spend some time with Josh later that day, as his table manners were difficult to endure.

Braxton thought how best to share other toys, books, and paraphernalia with the stable boy and yet not overwhelm him.

Suddenly, Josh wondered if his father knew where he was, expressing his concern to Braxton. The prince said his mother had instructed a footman to go to the stables and tell his parents she had requested Josh remain at the house. Josh was still trying to adjust to living in the royal household and could not fathom what the reaction would be when he returned to his world.

The boys became increasingly familiar with each other, making the most of their twenty-four hours together. Braxton kept track of time and inwardly grew anxious that the hour would soon arrive when Josh would have to return to his life in the stables.

At the appointed time, no one had come to retrieve Josh.

Soon enough, a footman entered the nursery carrying a silver tray. "Your Royal Highness, Her Royal Highness, Princess Mercedes sends this with her compliments."

"Thank you, Smythe," Braxton said retrieving a small envelope from the tray.

"Will there be anything else, Sir?"

"No thank you, that will be all." The footman left the room.

Josh asked, "Why does your mother not just come and see you or holler for you to go to her."

Braxton chuckled and replied, "I have rarely heard her raise her voice, certainly, never have I heard her yell. Bad manners and all that. Her rooms are distant, anyway. Her voice would not travel this far."

"She could come here."

"It is not done that way. I see her at appointed times or request an audience. I do not send notes, I have a servant relay my request.

It is not like that so much in the country. Things are less formal. When in London we have dignitaries, foreign ambassadors, and those with whom the family does not associate with regularly in the country. It can be tedious. Children are not welcome. I am forever in trouble for acting as if we are in the country."

Josh scratched his head and asked, "But why a letter? She could tell the man to tell you."

"That would never do, other than summoning me. If she or anyone else in the family has a message, rarely is in conveyed by word of mouth. Perhaps through a senior servant, but not often. You must have noticed that my family's personal life is kept very quiet. Gossip so often causes great confusion and can be harmful."

"It sounds like a lot of fuss about nothing," Josh sighed.

"It can be. Shall we see what all this fuss is about?"

"Yes!"

Braxton and Josh sat down, side by side, and stared at the envelope fastened with his mother's seal.

"What do you think is inside?" asked Josh.

"A letter," Braxton said.

Josh gently jostled Braxton and laughed. Braxton returned the favor and laughed as well.

"Open it, please!"

"I think not," Braxton teased. "Let us burn it!"

Josh grabbed the envelope and said, "You better not! I want to know what it says!"

"Well, open it then!" teased Braxton.

Josh looked down at the luxurious cream-colored embossed envelope affixed with a beautiful crimson wax seal covering a blue ribbon. Not wanting to crack it, he gently tugged at the seal while lifting the hardened wax from the envelope. He tore just a bit of the paper off with the seal as the envelope opened revealing matching stationery folded in half. Josh looked up at Braxton. Braxton looked back, smiled slightly, and nodded his approval.

Josh grinned, then deftly removed the stationery, handing it toward Braxton who, holding up his hand, refusing the letter, asking,

"Would you please read it?"

Josh slightly bounced his knees, and said, "I am a good reader, but not as good as you."

Braxton responded gently, "So, read."

"I am going to read a letter written by Her Royal Highness Mercedes, Princess of Wales." His hands shook as he unfolded the stationery. He held it upside down. Braxton reached over and turned the letter upright. Both boys giggled.

Josh read the letter to his friend and host.

Braxton and Joshua,

I want you both to know how very proud I am of you. During your time together you have shown yourselves to behave as responsible and caring young men. Thank you both for honoring each other's families in this manner. I hope that you will remain friends.

Braxton, it would be very hospitable for you to show your guest around Renaissance House.

Gentlemen, please visit me in the Japanese salon for tea. In the meantime, Joshua, I would appreciate you visiting your parents prior to teatime. Please ask them if they would allow you to spend another night as our guest. But do this only if it suits you.

Warmest regards,

Mercedes, Princess of Wales

The boys stared at each other in disbelief.

"Well, what did you expect, young prince?" said Josh sarcastically. "I am the perfect guest!"

With that, they rolled on the floor, laughing and wrestling until their sides ached.

Watching from the next room, Mercedes and Ekaterina smiled then disappeared unseen by the boys.

The rest of the day went as expected. Braxton enjoyed showing his friend parts of the chateau the stable boy had never seen before and would never have experienced if it were not for this most unusual situation. Josh was grateful for the tour. As they explored, he thought about how nice it was to see the way royalty lives, knowing full well that he would soon return to much humbler surroundings. Perhaps his thoughts were harsh, but true, none-theless. Remembering his station, Josh kept his thoughts to himself and made the most of the hospitality that felt quite genuine.

Following the princess's instructions, Josh found his parents, and relayed the contents of her letter to them. Though happy for him, they were concerned. They worried that having tasted the nectar of privilege afforded to those of birth-rank, it might be difficult for their son when he was required to return to porridge. Would he be forever resentful? They were frank in their discussion with Josh and emphasized how fortunate it was that he had been met with kind-ness and generosity. Josh's parents stressed that working-class and noble lives did not mix, and he would have to face that reality soon enough. Josh acknowledged what his parents told him. He could see their concern for the predicament in which he had found himself. Even at his young age, Josh was determined not to play the pawn.

When he returned to the chateau, Josh found Braxton in the kitchen enjoying a taste of sweet treats the pastry chef had just concocted in the huge kitchen. There were four fireplaces large enough for two pairs of grown men to walk into them. Only one was lit this evening. The other fireplaces were used when preparing for large meals and festive occasions. There were at least three scullery maids, plus undercooks, cooks, a sous chef, a pastry chef, and a head chef.

In aristocratic circles, one's status was elevated or diminished based on the competency and flair of culinary delights served to their guests.

Braxton and his friend took full advantage of being allowed below stairs, though Josh was unaware of the rules of etiquette in the castle. Children of the aristocracy, not adults, were permitted in the servants' domain. Braxton made the most of this custom knowing that it would be short-lived as he grew to reach majority. He felt that life was more exciting downstairs than it was in the more formal environment upstairs. Besides, the servants did not mind him underfoot if it did not interfere with the endless and tireless duties they were required to perform each day. This did not escape Braxton's notice.

"Your Royal Highness, your mother is expecting us in the Japanese salon," volunteered Josh.

"Yes, you are right. We better get up there. She gets annoyed when kept waiting."

Wiping cream from his face with a towel handed to him by the pastry chef, Braxton led Josh by the hand and up the stairs they ran. Reaching the main floor, they hurtled down the hallway past various state rooms. Approaching the salon, they narrowly missed careening into Prince John.

"Slow down, Braxton!" John said in an irritated voice. "Furthermore, who is this you have with you?" Pausing, he looked quizzically at Josh. "I know who you are. You are the lad that showed us how to extinguish the fire at Aurelio Palace. You are a hero! You saved the palace from ruin. Follow me!"

Prince John motioned Josh into the room where his mother and the woman he fondly called Auntie Ekaterina sat comfortably on a divan. In front of them lay a gleaming tea service surrounded by treats and pastries much like those pilfered by Braxton only moments before.

"Mother! This is the young man I told you about the day after the fire. He is the one who had the brains to use dirt to extinguish it! How on earth did you ever locate him here in London?"

Braxton wished he could crawl under a rock. This was not his finest memory.

Mercedes and Ekaterina alternately wove the story of how Braxton ended up being knocked sideways by Josh, delivering every detail in an amusing and lighthearted way.

John congratulated himself for uncovering the identity of the hero.

Everyone engaged in conversation with Braxton and Josh until John noticed it was time to dress for an unspecified social engagement set for later that evening somewhere in London. The two women though curious felt not obliged to inquire into Prince John's plans. Young maturing male's activities were best left alone and unrevealed.

Following John's goodbyes, the ladies and the two younger boys found themselves staring across the table at one another. The women had things to discuss, and the boys were obsessed on the treats beckoning them. Ekaterina seized the opportunity to ask Josh what his favorite item was amongst the treats. He responded by explaining that he had never tasted any of them.

"Well, I think we can remedy that." She motioned Josh to her side. "Now take a plate, put one of each on your plate, and enjoy them." Josh quickly reached for a pastry.

Braxton, not waiting for an invitation, followed Josh's lead. Mercedes then suggested that the boys take their plates and napkins and sit at a more sensible table to enjoy their feast. She felt a glow of warmth watching the boys chatter excitedly about the confections.

As they inhaled the sweet delights, Mercedes spoke. "Boys, the grand duchess and I have been thinking about how we might be able to arrange a way to allow the two of you to spend more time together. As of this moment, we are not sure exactly how to accomplish this. We thought if you are interested, we might be able to come up with an arrangement that would work for both of you and the respective households."

Braxton and Josh looked at each other quizzically not sure what on earth she meant.

Ekaterina, reading their minds, contemplated clarifying what she and Mercedes had in mind.

Suddenly, Braxton leaning forward and rushing his words exclaimed, "That is a capital idea! What say you Josh?" Josh turned his head downward and scratched behind his ear.

Mercedes turned to her young guest and asked what he thought. Josh shared with them he truly appreciated their kindness and hospitality and recognized it had been an experience of a lifetime and would always be a treasured memory. He went on to say he felt their worlds were so different and could not see how they could be combined. His primary concern was his future. How could he meet his responsibilities at the stable? He loved working in the livery and would be in danger of compromising his future if he lost the position.

The three sat in silence contemplating what Josh had shared. They knew he felt vulnerable and did not want him to think that he was being used. They hoped to protect his interests as well as those of Braxton. Mercedes broke the silence, "When I was a young girl in Chiacontella, my life was much less formal than here in England. I must confess I initially had great difficulty acclimating to the English court and customs. Josh, I can only imagine that it might be even more difficult for you."

Following a suitable pause wishing not to interrupt the princess,

Ekaterina entered the conversation, looking at Josh, "I think I can solve this problem if you will make a commitment, young man." This caught everyone's ear, causing them to sit up straighter and listen carefully. "I was very lonely growing up in my family's Winter Palace in St. Petersburg. I had my much younger brother and younger sister, but I never had a friend of my own."

Mercedes took her friend's hand and gently squeezed it, knowing the more recent pain that she had left out of this tale.

"I propose that you come to live here. You stay in Braxton's rooms. You will have tutors of your own and will participate in activities with Braxton as you wish. You will be clothed and treated as a gentleman. You will have a small allowance. In fact, we will not consider you a servant as you will enjoy the status as my ward. Whether you become regarded as family, only time will tell. I will happily bear all the expenses. Should you maintain yourself in a respectable manner, I will ensure that you receive a practical education suitable for any gentleman to sustain himself." Pausing and placing her folded hands on her lap she continued, "Think of it as a reward for extinguishing the fire at the Aurelio Palace."

Braxton's and Josh's mouths dropped wide open turning their gaze from the grand duchess and toward each other, to Mercedes and back to the grand duchess.

Speaking to Mercedes she continued, "Well, my dear, what do think of my proposal?"

Mercedes, flustered, amused, and intrigued replied, "Well, I think there will be many necessary details to consider and arrangements to be made. At first glance, I feel it is worth trying. What do you think, Josh? And you, Braxton?"

It did not take long for the four to assemble a plan. Braxton now had a friend and companion. Josh's life would be forever altered.

6

LOCOMOTION & MASTER HIGASHINO

"Hello Grandpapa," Braxton, shouted unannounced, entering the Renaissance House state dining room. His appearance and informal greeting to the king silenced the room.

The king pushed back from the table and bellowed, "Hello grandson, what brings you to dinner?"

"Why you, of course! And Grandmama, of course! Are you enjoying your dinner?"

"Well, honestly, it was rather dull until you arrived. Come!"

Skipping through the dining room toward the king, he chirped, "I shall, Grandpapa, as things seemed rather boring from the other side of the dining room door."

The king guffawed and laughter rippled through the fifty dinner guests assembled in their finery.

With that interchange, Braxton's reputation began to grow as a fun-loving, charming, and confident young prince.

With the advent of the steam engine, the world became captivated by locomotion and its tangible impact on London. Viscount

Ramsey's family had financial interests in growing railroad concerns.

During a picnic in the Renaissance House park with the Prince and Princess of Wales, Prince John, Viscount Ramsey and a business associate of his family, Major Stuart, the adults were bearing up under incessant interrogation by Braxton regarding a railroad currently under construction near London.

Braxton had made a habit of devouring the daily papers concerning the miracle of the railway and was intent on learning more.

The impatient young prince's tone took on an agitated ring. He felt he could not get information fast enough to satisfy his teeming curiosity. This behavior intrigued Major Stuart, as the nine-year-old's questions were typically those that might be asked by someone much older.

John and Ramsey tiring of the subject at hand and annoyed at Braxton's parade of questions broke off into their own conversation. Richard shifted in his chair.

"Braxton, come and sit over here by me," Mercedes said patting the seat of the chair next to her.

"But Mama, we are discussing trains, the railroad."

His father interjected, "What your mother is trying to say is that you need not dominate conversation. Let others partake in the discussion."

"They are Papa, they are answering my questions. And very well, I might add."

Braxton's remark brought laughter to the guests, all resigned to the young prince having charmed his way back into the center ring.

The major threw out crumbs of information regarding track gauges. Braxton commented on the disparity between track gauges in England and America. The major, laughing off Braxton's comment said that it was unlikely that those trains would ever meet, so the difference in size was of no concern.

Braxton retorted, "Yes sir, you are correct. But wouldn't it make more sense to have the same gauge in the colonies and here so that

England could manufacture and export its train carriages to America without having to retool?"

The entire party and its chatter abruptly silenced. All heads, including John's and Ramsey's turned toward Braxton. He smirked, knowing he had captured everyone's attention. He dared not lose it.

"Sir," he said now standing and addressing the group while looking at Major Stuart, "I think that if America and Europe would standardize railway manufacture the entire world could be criss-crossed by railways that fit together nicely."

"Your Royal Highness," Major Stuart said, if you think we could persuade your parents to agree, perhaps you could join me for a visit in our London offices and then venture out to see some rail construction lines outside London."

The invitation bowled Braxton over with excitement. His parents, having heard every word, anticipated an onslaught of pleading ad infinitum to accept the invitation. They knew their acquiescence was a fait accompli.

Thinking strategically, Braxton compelled Prince John and Ramsey to join him and the major for the outing. Later that afternoon, John in tow, the two of them convinced his father and Dominic to come along as well.

With his father present, Braxton counted on no stone being left unturned. Braxton would then be in the position to learn and absorb more information than would have been offered had Prince Richard not accompanied them.

———

Braxton excused himself from the picnic and made his way for the chateau's main library in search of the afternoon papers and the latest news on racing and the railroads. As he entered the Japanese Salon, his attention was drawn to an artist focusing on his work. The beautiful logographic kanji, the derivative of ancient Japanese symbols, caught his notice. There seemed to be an endless parade of kanji and kana characters on the panels that were themselves pictures. Always curious, Braxton stopped in the center of the room, transfixed, his arms dangling at his side.

Seiko Higashino was not a particularly diminutive man, unlike most of his Japanese countrymen. He stood five foot ten inches tall and weighed almost 160 pounds. His frame though light, appeared strong and sinewy. His complexion was pearl-like, almost translucent. Raven black hair tied in a small bun at the back of his head framed his face. Eyes like pools of ebony reflected a calm but commanding soul.

The artist was restoring centuries-old panels that made up the walls of the Japanese Salon, the same part of the house where Braxton and Josh had met with his mother and the grand duchess. Seiko Higashino was alone in the room attending to his work when Braxton wandered in through the open French doors leading from the terrace.

Higashino would not have normally stopped his work to notice anyone, as it would corrupt the meditative state he had entered focusing on his task at hand. But in this instance, he sensed Braxton's fascination. As if the prince was a sponge, fixated and absorbing the logographs.

Braxton did not notice Master Higashino observing him as he immersed himself in the strange symbols whose meanings he did not comprehend. The longer he studied the poetic and beautiful puzzle patterns, the more the symbols began to emerge and demand he decipher them.

After a moment, the artist went back to his work; Braxton continued to stare, pondering the art. As his eyes followed the patterns across the panels Braxton noticed the pieces interrupted by other sections containing kano, a Japanese artform originating in the Fifteenth and Sixteenth Centuries. He would grow to love this school of art. Once again, his eyes were drawn back to the kanji and kana characters, only to be distracted by taking note of Higashino painting the characters using a brush of a strange design.

In a respectful quiet tone, the prince said, "Excuse me, Sir. I apologize for the interruption. However, please allow me to say how much I admire what you are creating here."

Master Seiko Higashino turned and looked at Braxton. The prince made a short bow, turned, and exited the room thinking to himself, why have I never considered those forms? I have been in that room a hundred times.

7

OFF TO THE RACES

Braxton was determined to gain access to the horse races. Josh was his entrée. Josh knew the lay of the land and was considered by the stable and track workers to be one of them. But things were somewhat different now. Josh's recent change of status from stable boy to Braxton's companion presented new challenges. As a stable hand, he had always had free and easy access to the racetracks, stables, and paddocks. That had changed. Now dressed and perceived a young gentleman, he had joined the ranks of those kept at a distance by the stable hands and trainers and was viewed with some suspicion.

The transformation had cost Josh his anonymity. The evolution was difficult and lonely. Braxton and his tutors worked diligently, facilitating Josh's goal of transforming into the ephemeral gentleman he could never have envisioned.

As the two were still minors, their presence was tolerated, much as they were in the kitchens of the Renaissance House and other stately homes of the day. Setting about their plan to learn as much as they could, they maximized their time behind the scenes. They were on a mission.

Braxton had a keen sense few people possessed for sizing up

horses and riders. Josh was fair enough at it but marveled at how Braxton could dissect the personality of both the rider and mount by mere observation. Even more extraordinary was the way he could pair them, finding the perfect complement of one to the other. The boys kept Braxton's skill a treasured secret.

Braxton selected horse and rider combinations at trials and offtrack meets. His choices often outperformed the most sophisticated handicappers. The youngsters poured over race programs and fliers, reviewing bloodlines, and having countless conversation with owners, trainers, and jockeys. Since no one thought much of the two boys perceived innocent interest in racing, information flowed easily and often carelessly.

Braxton's family position gave him carte blanche entrée to all unofficial events. He amused and confounded those whom he questioned and engaged in conversation.

One day, accompanying John and Ramsey to a garden party, Braxton and Josh made a proposal.

The prince and viscount were seated in an open pavilion drinking from a glass punch bowl. Braxton and Josh approached them.

"Brother, it seems as if you two are a bit bored. As are we. Shall we go see the ponies?" Braxton said keeping one hand in his pocket.

Ramsey leaned back in his chair, one hand holding a glass and the other placed behind his head. "Really, Braxton? You know you're not old enough."

John laughed and asked, "Why would we want to take you to the races?"

The former stable boy's impudence was revealed when he retorted, "Because you are not having much fun and we can help you make some money."

John quipped sitting up straight in his chair. "I'll be damned, Josh, if you are not entirely too forward."

"Well, he is right-on and the two of you know it," Braxton said defending Josh.

Ramsey put one hand on John's shoulder and addressed Braxton and Josh, "What is the plan, boys?"

"We have some rather confidential information. We need to get to the paddocks to verify it. If you two can let us off and meet us in the paddock later, we'll share what we know."

John said, "We have little to bet, seeing as how no allowances are to be had for a fortnight."

"What're you two going to use for money?" Ramsey asked.

Josh and Braxton shared playful grins and chuckled, turning to face the other two.

"That is our point, gentlemen," Josh said shoulders back and chin high.

Braxton interjected, "We will tell you which horses to bet on. You will finance the bets. All four of us share in the winnings."

"How do we know you will provide us winners?" John asked.

"You don't, but we've done damn well guessing winners at trials!" Braxton shot back with hard deliberate eyes.

"For God's sake, Brax, don't take it so personally. Besides, if we get caught, we will hear about it from you know who," John said.

"Father's reactions have never bothered you two before. Besides, it is better than hanging around here. If you keep dipping into the punchbowl, you will end up losing what money you do have. Now, I have called for the carriage. Time to go," Braxton said, a smug grin radiating upon his face.

Bundling the boys into the closed carriage, they made their way to the track. The carriage dropped Braxton and Josh at the trainer's entrance. The older boys agreed to meet them just inside the paddock prior to the first event. The young boys made their way to the stables.

Finding a program, the boys located a discreet area and sat to study the entrants. Concentrating on the first half dozen races, they discussed each horse and rider. Reaching a consensus, they placed each pair in order of worse to best. Next, the boys analyzed each mount as it was paired with its jockey. To confirm their choices and get a better feel, they visited each horse in its stall and watched warm-up runs whenever possible. The boys listened carefully to the racing chatter surrounding them. While making their way through the paddock, they overheard a jockey volunteering to tip a run toward a long shot in the third event.

John and Ramsey met them at the paddock as planned, a little worse for drink. Josh discreetly handed Ramsey the picks for races one through six, omitting the third race. When asked about the missing bet, they vaguely referred to it as "suspicious." Josh and Braxton disappeared into the stables to seek more information on the remaining races.

———

"I am going to watch the race," Braxton said to Josh sitting on a bale of hay.

"Me too."

"We cannot both go. Actually, neither of us are allowed in the stands."

"Why you?"

"Ah c'mon, Josh. You can sneak into the next race. If we go together, we will surely be noticed."

"Yeah, maybe you're right. Go ahead. Meet me back here, right?"

"Right. Keep an eye on things and a listening ear while I am gone."

The young prince maneuvered himself onto a perch on an elevated platform covered in festive bunting just at eye level and close to the finish line. He partially concealed his position with the help of copious bunting and the crowd of people in their finery bustling about. The band was playing popular musical production tunes interspersed with patriotic marches. Waiters worked in between the boisterous aristocrats, serving beverages and cigars. No one appeared to take notice of him.

He knew his pick must win. If John and Ramsey did not make money, they could not be recruited to participate in his future plans.

Braxton had his brother bet on a horse called Silver Candy. This mount was a three-year-old with little history and an undistinguished pedigree. But there was something there not apparent to even wellschooled track aficionados. Braxton had studied his bloodlines, which standing alone were unremarkable, but collectively offered promise. As luck would have it, the jockey in the bulletin had been substituted with a favorite of Braxton's called "Fat Bob." There was nothing fat about Bob other than his pie-shaped face and oversized hands. Fat Bob could get more out of a horse than any jockey in the circuit. Braxton was counting on it.

An exquisitely dressed, statuesque octogenarian, Grand Duchess Ekaterina, and her lady-in-waiting, swept up the platform stairs to stand alongside Braxton. The startled prince jerked his head back slapping his hands against his cheeks.

"Well, Braxton, how would you suggest I place my bet?" He tensed up certain he would wet himself.

The rise in his vocal pitch blurted out mischievously, "Carefully?"

"Carefully on which horse?" She asked, wiggling her eyebrows, suppressing a grin.

"Silver Candy," Braxton said, his face turning impish.

"Stay right where you are."

Ekaterina then turned to one of her ladies-in-waiting and instructed the baroness to take the twenty-pound note which Ekaterina proffered and place two bets to win, at ten pounds each, on 'Silver Candy.' The grand duchess looked down at a dumbstruck Braxton, took him by the hand, and escorted him to the Royal Enclosure.

As he entered the box with the grand duchess, he turned and bowed to her, excusing himself and walked toward his parents. All in the enclosure focused on the underage Braxton. Conversation ceased. His mother feigned no surprise, offering him her hand which he took and bent over kissing it. He bowed to his father. Prince Richard grinned wryly and said under his breath, "You know what to do next?"

"Yes, Papa."

He bowed once again to his parents. Realizing he was the center of attention, he embraced it. Standing erect and smiling a Cheshire Cat-like grin as confidently as a 12-year-old-going-on-30 could, he took wide steps and with a steady gait, approached their majesties.

Spying Braxton, his grandmother placed one hand on the king's arm. The king and queen stood staring at the willful prince. How were they to handle this blatant breach of court etiquette, presenting oneself underage and uninvited?

Ekaterina approached the king and queen and curtsied. "Your Majesties, what do you think of my handsome young escort?"

The question allowed his grandparents to recover and search for a gracious way out of this predicament, the entire court anticipating something gloriously explosive.

The king, with a slightly reddened face, cleared his throat. "Braxton, what are you up to this time?" He then looked down his nose at the grand duchess.

She returned his look with a cherubic smile and a curtsy. "Your Majesty, how could you not approve of such a magnificent choice of an escort?"

The king's mouth opened as he roared with laughter, "By Zeus Ekaterina, you've done it again! You have created a silk purse out of a sow's ear. Jolly good!" He continued to laugh slapping Braxton on the shoulder. The king's laughter, followed by a pregnant pause, caused all within eyeshot to break out into applause and laughter.

Always on the lookout for ways to ingratiate himself, the young prince performed a sweeping bow, kissed his grandmother's hand, turned, and bowed to onlookers. His theatrics were returned with amused laughter from courtiers and those outside the enclosure. The king offered Braxton his footstool for a seat. The prince assumed his position just in front and between the amused monarchs.

The starter pistol's resounding bang announced the start of the first race. All jumped to their feet. Braxton stood on the stool between his grandparents. His quiet stance morphed into an animated bouncing from foot to foot. The king and queen suspected he had a vested interest beyond his enthusiasm for horses. Glancing over at Mercedes and Richard, Ekaterina sent them a look confirming that something was astir. Not bothering to pay attention to the race, the Princess made her way to the grand duchess. As the race progressed, Ekaterina in hushed tones informed Mercedes of the wager Braxton had advised her to place. The princess brought her hands to her mouth in surprise at the revelation, a gesture the queen did not miss. However, her majesty had not heard the conversation. She waved her daughter-in-law to her side. It took only three furlongs for the queen to hear the story from Mercedes. She too, cupped hands to her mouth in surprise. The three women pondered what might follow. The king remained oblivious to this feminine distress. He was too involved balancing Braxton as Silver Candy having started out toward the rear, slowly moved ahead in the pack. His majesty did not have an entry in the first run and was only mildly interested in a small wager he had on Cinnamon Tobacco. Cinnamon Tobacco had started behind the pack as well. His jockey was encouraging it as best he could, and in fact got more leg out of the horse as the race proceeded.

Fat Bob on Silver Candy battled the dirt flying up from the horses in front of him. They persevered and gained ground. Rounding the first turn Silver Candy was quickly coming up on Cinnamon Tobacco. The jockeys urged their mounts forward. The field tightened as the leaders drew closer together.

Hurtling down the backstretch, Silver Candy extended his forelegs further than he had ever done. He appeared to be lifting off the track, almost floating above it. His nostrils flared rhythmically and sweat from his neck pelted Fat Bob's face. The jockey no longer had to push. The horse was possessed with urgency and increasing speed.

Silver Candy passed more horses widening the gap, hooves pounding the earth. The racehorse hugged the rail with a burst of power and thunderous hooves hammering, pushing mounts out of his way. His throaty blasts emanated, accented by air blowing forcefully out flaring nostrils routing the competition, screaming imminent victory.

Confusion swept the field as the two poorly ranked horses Silver Candy and Cinnamon Tobacco broke to the front of the pack. Silver Candy pounded forward and into the mix. The others faded and Braxton's pick flew past the leaders, completing the race eight lengths ahead of the second-place finisher, Cinnamon Tobacco.

The king almost toppled over attempting to keep a very spirited and ebullient Braxton from falling off the stool. "Please Braxton, calm down a bit, I am entirely unable to keep you upright," the king laughed, holding on to the young prince. His grandfather, though exhausted, had rarely experienced such an exhilarating race.

Ekaterina, vested in the race and despite the excitement, maintained her composure throughout. She was so amused with Braxton's theatrics she had forgotten all about her 14:1 winning ticket and was reminded of her good fortune when the baroness returned presenting her with her and Braxton's winnings.

Ekaterina, bowing to the king and queen, handed Braxton his share. She smiled, curtsied, and returned to her seat. Everyone occupying the Royal Enclosure and surroundings were dumbstruck, even more so when the grand duchess indicated their shared winnings were made possible by the young prince.

Braxton, winnings in hand, turned to his grandparents, bowed, and walked over to his father, beaming. The youngster kept one pound and gave the remainder to his father for safekeeping. He then turned to his parents and the grand duchess, bowed, and ran off in search of Josh. As things settled down in the Royal Enclosure, Mercedes and Ekaterina took a turn. They needed air.

Richard could not stop thinking, what is Braxton up to? He felt a family meeting was in order. He worried his son's activities at the races could damage their name, as they had experienced a great deal of pressure from continuing negative press about the monarchy.

The crown's popularity had fallen precipitously over the last twenty years, because of rebellion in Ireland and the lingering labor disputes throughout the kingdom. The upheaval of the 1848 uprising had opened wounds that still festered. The crown had worked tirelessly to regain their subjects' trust and good will by making countless public appearances and subscribing to many charitable foundations.

Unbeknownst to the family, the king's and Braxton's race day jocularity had been captured by photographers and the press. This was a horse race that would be pictured and reported on in every corner of the empire.

The second, fourth, and sixth races went well for the young prince. It was not until the eighth race that Mercedes and Ekaterina caught up with Josh and Braxton, witnessing the youngsters exchanging information with John and Ramsey. Summoning the two older boys, the ladies made short work of getting the entire story out of them.

Interrogation over, John and Ramsey quickly said what they had to say, bowed, and departed to place their bets. Not wanting to waste what they had just heard; the ladies instructed their attendants to place wagers for them as well. Thanks to Braxton's tips, the family experienced a profitable day at the track.

That evening, Braxton collected his winnings from John and retrieved the funds he had entrusted to his father. Josh collected from John as well. Braxton kept the amount he had won to himself. It was a substantial win. Braxton had won £250 sterling, a more than respectable purse.

———

Various headlines touted the royal family's day at the races:

KING HOLDS ON GYRATING GRANDSON'S DURING RACE

PRINCE BRAXTON, 4th IN SUCCESSION WINS 14:1 BET!

HIS MAJESTY REINS IN PRINCE LONG SHOT SILVER CANDY CLENCHES 1ST PLACE!

The following day's papers were full of photographs of Braxton being steadied by a beaming king and grandfather. The informality of the event both shocked and pleased most readers. There were, of course, those who felt it inappropriate or vulgar. But even the most cynical could not deny that the handsome young Prince Braxton brought warmth, happiness, hope and a sense of family to the empire.

Their majesties were surprised and intent on capitalizing on the perception created by the positive press. More family outings were planned.

Braxton and Josh no longer had any semblance of anonymity and could no longer move about unnoticed in the paddock. It would be much more difficult to ferret out the inside information on the horses.

Braxton had to devise another means by which to advance his scheme.

8

RETURN TO THE AURELIO PALACE

The following day Prince Richard and Princess Mercedes were lunching with their five children at a large round satinwood table. Dominic sat to his mother's right, followed by Braxton to his right, then John to Braxton's right. Diedre was nestled next to John, with Carmen between him and their father. The table set with floral patterned china, crystal, and a low centerpiece of multicolored roses, the source of a light spring fragrance. The casual meal found them chattering and teasing Braxton about the previous day's events. "Braxton, what are you going to do with all that money you won?"

Diedre asked. "I heard it was a tidy sum."

"Yes, little brother, surely you'll want to have a wonderful party and invite all of us!" exclaimed Carmen.

Though taunted, Braxton did not squirm, but sat up, puffing out his chest. "None of your business."

"Yes, it is! We are family and we want to know everything," chided

Dominic and continued teasing, "Besides, we're very proud of you so be nice to us."

John sat silent, focused on his soup. He felt particularly protective of his favorite brother. He lifted his head and placed his spoon on the plate beneath the soup bowl. Resting his hands on the table, and speaking to no one in particular, "You should be kinder to Braxton. Yesterday was a big day and he should be...just stop teasing him." John pursed his lips, inhaled, and continued, "As we all know, Braxton has many gifts. Picking winners is one of them." John lifted his glass in a toast, "To our brother Braxton."

Everyone raised their glasses.

"And our son," said Prince Richard as he and Mercedes joined in the salute.

Braxton's face reddened, erupting into a shy smile. "Thank you."

Placing her glass on the table, Diedre said looking directly at her brother John, "I suppose now you can pay a few of your debts with your track winnings, John."

"Whoops," Braxton said.

"That was a bit severe, Sis," said Dominic.

"Well, I would like to see the 10 pounds he owes me. And Carmen,

I am certain, would like to be repaid the…"

"Enough!" Richard said, laying his napkin on the table. The whole table jumped at the sound of his stern voice. "This is not proper lunch conversation. Please keep such matters private between yourselves."

Richard lifted his wine glass toward John, "Son, you will make good your debts immediately."

"Yes, of course, father."

Mercedes attempted to soften the mood. "Now Richard, let us get on with the good news we want to share with the family."

Richard sat back pulling on his ear. "Kindly give me your attention." He looked around the table, making brief eye contact with each of his children. His gaze settled on Braxton. He grinned at the young prince and then directed his attention to Mercedes.

Richard continued in an enthusiastic and upbeat voice, "Children, the Aurelio Palace restoration and repairs are coming to an end. Two years and thousands of pounds Sterling into it, our home awaits our return."

Blank looks and tight lips adorned the sibling's faces. No one responded.

Richard cocked his head, puzzled. "Haven't any of you interest in returning to the country?"

Mercedes shifted in her chair next to Richard and commented, "We thought you missed our home?"

The young princesses each took one of the other's hand in theirs and sat expressionless. John exhaled and folded his arms.

Dominic surprised himself and everyone else at the table clucking his tongue against the roof of his mouth. Catching himself, he stopped, then mumbled, "Sorry."

Braxton leaned forward in his chair and said, "I want to return, but

I'll miss London and the racing." He paused for a moment, then said, "Could we possibly return our departure to the end of the racing season? Papa? Mama? Please." Braxton pleaded, folding his hands in mock prayer.

Dominic twisted his lips into a pursed grin looking at Braxton and joined in, "Yes, father. There remains only six, maybe eight weeks in the Season. I know John and I would be insufferably miserable in the country having missed the remaining festivities."

All sat quietly, some focused on Richard and others looking down at their plates or staring at nothing.

Placing his elbows on the table and steepling his fingers, Richard said, "Hmmm. Well, I suppose that would be all right. I just thought you all missed Aurelio. That you would want to return as soon as possible."

Prince Richard sat back, gripping the arms of his chair contemplating the plate on the table in front of him. He looked over at Mercedes, noting her soft eye contact, and said, "Very well, we shall stay until the end of the Season. Everyone happy?"

"Yes! Thank you, Papa!" echoed throughout the room.

———

Braxton remained at the table fidgeting with his napkin. His brothers and sisters had left the room stealing glances his way.

"Braxton, is there something else? Are you not pleased with the arrangement?" Mercedes asked.

"Why yes, Mama." He sat looking at his parents.

His father opened his mouth, placing the tip of his tongue on the bottom of his lower front teeth. He then inhaled, "Okay, what's on your mind, son?"

Braxton exaggerated his return to an erect sitting position and tightened his lips together and said, "I must go to the bank. The Chiacontella Bank. Mama's bank."

Mercedes wiped her mouth with the tip of her napkin and questioned, "Braxton, what on earth for?"

"To, um… to open an account with my winnings. Uncle Cosimo said to always choose a sound bank. It is sound, isn't it, Mother?"

"I certainly hope so, dear. That is where your father and I maintain our funds." She adjusted her skirts appearing to wait for either Richard or Braxton to say something.

"So, I asked Auntie Ekaterina to take me."

Richard, adjusting his cravat, asked, "I see, son. Why the grand duchess and not your mother or me?"

"Well, I have heard you and Grandpapa and Grandmama say one should not be involved in commerce, you know, the crown and all. So, I thought since I am the spare's spare…you know… Dominic is the heir, then John, and then me. John's the spare, and I am his spare…"

Both his parents exchanged quizzical glances. Braxton smiled at them. He lifted his chin and said in a strong voice, "Therefore, those rules shouldn't apply to me." Braxton sat back; confident he had made his point.

"Would you please leave us?" Mercedes said addressing the two footmen. The footmen ceased clearing the table, bowed and left the room, closing the doors behind them.

Braxton looked down at his plate and fiddled with the silverware. A gentle breeze wafted in from the gardens through the open French doors.

"I see," said his father, "That you continue to be occupied with the fact that you're not likely to be king one day."

"Excuse me father, it is not that I won't be king that concerns me. I do not wish to be king."

Mercedes leaned forward and said, "Braxton, why would you say such a thing? Surely it is an honor, a divine gift!"

Braxton inhaled and placed his elbows on the table, his chin resting on his folded hands. "Mama, I care to do something else with my life. Something exciting, like travel! Being king is too confining.

Grandfather does not rule; he reigns. The prime minister rules."

"Where did you learn this?" Richard asked, speaking to Braxton, and glaring at Mercedes. "Is this part of that modern education you have been advocating? Is It?"

Mercedes coughed into her napkin, straightened her posture, and said facing Richard, "In part it is, Richard." She then directed her comments to Braxton and said, "And I am proud of you, son."

She returned her attention to her husband and said in a confident tone, "Braxton has been attending to his studies of the constitution. I so hope the other children have a similar grasp of the subject."

Richard's face assumed a pinkish color, his teeth clenched.

The three remain silent for a moment.

Braxton began again, "I feel our lives are planned out for us and we cannot do as we please. Why should I not be allowed to go into business? Father will be king, then Dominic. If not Dominic, then John. I am content to be me. I will have opportunities none of them shall have." He relaxed sitting back in his chair.

Richard drummed his fingers on the table, staring at his son, saying nothing.

Mercedes removed her handkerchief from her sleeve and held it in her hands. "Excuse me, but I see some merit to what you have said, Braxton. I like to think we are modern, and open to change."

Richard asked, "The two of you do realize, of course, the difficulties engaging in commerce could cause the crown and the government?"

Both Mercedes and Braxton gave a slight nod.

"It is unlikely, and improbable, you are going into business. All the same, should it happen, it will take time and artful planning to convince the powers that be. Thank God we have time, you are still young yet, Braxton."

The young prince sat twisting his napkin as his father continued, "Would it be too much of an inconvenience for your mother and I to accompany you and your auntie to your uncle's bank?"

Mercedes and Braxton directed a double-take at Richard.

"I agree with your mother. We are modern, and we want to be supportive of every member of our family."

Mercedes reached over and placed her hand on Richard's arm and whispered into his ear, "Thank you, I love you, Richard."

Braxton's excitement was undeniable. "Yes, that would be marvelous. May we go now?"

————

Braxton committed to making the best of his remaining months in London. He visited the track at every opportunity. Josh and Braxton recruited John and Ramsey to take them to the racecourse. When John and Ramsey were not available, Ekaterina and Mercedes often played the willing accomplices. By the middle of May, Braxton had accumulated over two thousand pounds through well-placed wagers. Feeding tips to others also earned him a percentage of their winnings.

Braxton and John sat in an open Landau returning from the track.

Both dressed in the latest spring fashion, sporting colorful waist-coats and neutral bowlers.

"You know, Braxton. If word gets out to father or the king that you are passing on tips and making money off our friends, it could be a great scandal. That would be the end of your adventures at the track," John said.

"I have thought about that. Making money off others has been highly profitable, but you are correct."

He turned and faced his brother, a small smile on his face, "I have another scheme in mind."

"Of course, you do, Braxton. What is it and may I have a piece of it?"

Braxton looked directly at his brother and said, "I am going to purchase several horses before we leave London. Then it will be obvious to all that I am engaged in the sport and there will be less to talk about. I shall continue to do as I please." He then looked away and out at the passing crowds and said, "It remains to be seen how that will involve you."

"Do you really think you can pull that off?"

"You shall see soon enough," Braxton said, observing the bustling streets and tipping his hat to those who recognized him from his numerous newspaper photographs.

————

Ekaterina, Mercedes, and Braxton sat in an open Landau traveling back from an afternoon concert, discussing the program when Braxton changed the subject. "You must keep my confidence if I am to share something with you." He sat, staring across at the two grand ladies seated opposite him.

Mercedes asked, amused. "Why whatever could you be talking about?"

"Do I have your confidence, Mother, Auntie?"

"Who have you murdered?" Ekaterina asked first in a severe tone, then betrayed her jest crinkling her eyes.

"Oh, the horror!" laughed Mercedes.

Braxton remained silent, not amused.

"For heaven's sake, Braxton. What are you talking about?" Mercedes implored.

"Confidence, confidentiality, do I have it?"

"Yes, of course you do. You should not have to ask," Mercedes insisted.

"Obviously, you have our confidence. Now out with it," Ekaterina demanded.

"I'm going into the horse racing business."

Mercedes fanned herself, and in an exasperated tone said, "You know the king would not approve and your father will not allow it."

Braxton folded his arms. "I hope you are wrong. Regardless, I have two secret weapons."

Mercedes asked, "Pray tell young man, what are these secret weapons, as you call them?"

Ekaterina tapped Mercedes on her arm. "Us. We are the secret weapons. Though I have never thought of myself as a weapon, I have yielded a few, metaphorically, as you well know, dear."

"I see," said Mercedes, whipping the fan. "What is your scheme and what do you expect of us poor defenseless, ignorant, but useful creatures?"

He leaned forward, swearing them to secrecy before sharing his plan with them. As always, the two women ended up supporting his plan, thankful that Braxton would finally have an outlet for his pent-up energy.

———

The young prince had spent a significant amount of time studying every horse that ran that year. By the end of his studies, he knew more about them than most of their owners. Like a chess player, he was planning moves three and four years out. The prince kept an eye on auctions for prematurely discarded mares and stallions he thought were likely to produce good racing stock. If paired well, after acquiring these undervalued horses for a fraction of their true worth, he could make a fortune.

The money he won from wagers supported his purchases, but he needed additional funds to pay for their maintenance for up to three years. Based on his meticulous notes and calculations, Braxton required another one thousand pounds to support at least three stallions and three breeding mares.

Braxton set to work, like a spymaster, positioning Josh, his brother John, and Lord Ramsey to ascertain which horses their owners were planning on selling. He also encouraged Mercedes and

Ekaterina to discover what some of the more successful owners intended to do with their racing stock at the end of the Season. He paid several of his acquaintances at the track to inform him of who planned to sell, who wanted to buy, and what they were interested in purchasing.

Meanwhile, Braxton and Josh charted combinations of sires and dams that appeared favorable, prioritizing his picks. However, this intense research limited the time he could spend wagering at the races.

"I'm short several thousand pounds," said Braxton, placing his arms behind his back, gripping one wrist with the other hand, pacing fiercely.

"Just go pick it up at the track. At most, it will take you a day or two...if you are careful," Josh said looking up from the pile of papers on his worktable in Braxton's rooms.

"The problem is, I have not been to the track in weeks and have not kept abreast of track activity."

"Neither of us have," Josh remarked and continued, "That comes from weeks of looking into the past, studying and researching the bloodlines."

The prince fumed as he said, "My entire plan will be ruined if I go into it without the funds to see it through. According to Uncle Cosimo, undercapitalization destroys most new business ventures. I will not be a..." Stopping in mid-sentence, Braxton hit his forehead with the heal of his hand. "I've got it!"

"What? A self-inflicted headache," laughed Josh.

"No! I know how we can get the money!"

"Borrow it?"

"No, no, no. Make it. Make it by winning a big race and winning big."

Josh asked with a bit of sarcasm in his voice, "Your highness, just how are you going to do that?"

Braxton knew there were three large purses to be won at the Royal Ascot in July. He set his sights on winning one of them. He planned and strategize acquisitions. The determined young prince would have to make early purchases prior to the auctions toward the end of the season. He had his eye on four horses he felt were under-valued and under ridden. He had heard Silver Candy was injured and finished running for the season. However, he had four half-siblings with similar bloodlines. The prince set out to learn more about them.

Braxton instructed Josh to locate the four horses. Next, he dispatched his brother John and Lord Ramsey to make inquiries about purchasing them. They too, sent surrogates in their stead so as not to ignite undue interest.

Finally, after Josh had reported back as to the location of the horses, Braxton set out to see them for himself. He borrowed clothing from one of the stable boys whom he enlisted to join him on the day trip to inspect the horses firsthand.

Braxton observed the horses from a distance. He liked what he saw and returned home directing proxies to place offers for three of the four animals. Following considerable negotiations, three of the horses were purchased for £2,100.

After tallying his purchases and expenses, Braxton had only £300 remaining. He had yet to pay the entry fees and come up with the money to house his herd and acquire jockeys to ride them. If Braxton did not win big at the Royal Ascot, his venture would fail.

For the time being, he stabled his horses at Renaissance House. The chateau's park had a track for running and exercising the horses, but it had been generations since the Chiacontellas had actively raced in London. Braxton invested minimally in updating the track to make it safe for his prized animals. Josh took over the maintenance and management of the three horses. Wanting to stamp a mark on his enterprise, Braxton renamed his horses Extra-ordinaire, Valorious, and Fabuloso.

Fat Bob and three trainers were hired to prepare the horses for race day, using a training schedule that Josh and Braxton had designed with the help of Fat Bob. When Braxton became danger-ously low on funds, he returned to the track and won just enough money to keep the enterprise afloat.

Josh asked Fat Bob to recommend jockeys for Fabuloso, and Valorious, as Bob had insisted on riding Extraordinaire himself.

The day of the Royal Ascot Queen Anne Stakes would soon arrive. The event boasted a purse of £85,000, four times the largest purse ever paid. Braxton felt pleased to have three horses of the same caliber as Silver Candy in the race.

He also had the best jockeys money could buy. Not because he had the money to pay them their full fees. He promised them more, drawing up a contract offering to split ten percent of the purse with the jockeys if they won, placed, or showed. He now had world-class horses, the best riders, and the power of greed working for him.

The race crew named the three horses and their riders, 'The Unbeatables.' Word spread that the king's grandson owned a team of horses, all three of which would participate in a single high-stakes race. Everyone at the track wondered how such a young and inexperienced owner could have assembled what might prove to be an excellent racing team.

Richard and Mercedes, meanwhile, were proud of their son but had grown concerned his passion for horseracing could negatively affect the family's public image.

Ekaterina did not concern herself with her public image and planned on betting large sums on The Unbeatables as a mark of support for Braxton. The old dowager spent part of each day encouraging him and monitoring his welfare. As Mercedes did not want to be perceived as an overbearing mother, she relied on Ekaterina's discretion and frequent reports on her son's unimaginable venture. The king and Prince Richard visited Renaissance House track at least three times a week. The entire household was caught up in the looming race.

All of London was mesmerized by the young prince's venture and the upcoming extraordinary event. Newspapers and periodicals were full of news and updates on 'Prince Braxton's Race.' How was it possible a thirteen-year-old put together this exceptional team? Word quickly spread his winnings at the track had financed the entire operation. Though people were doubtful, and some scoffed at the idea a young boy could participate let alone win such an event, most wanted to believe the impossible was possible.

Paris, Berlin, and Vienna had also heard of the evolving tantalizing story. Ekaterina made certain Moscow and St. Petersburg were provided regular updates on Braxton's progress and the impending competition. Wagers poured in from all over the continent, raising the purse to £153,000 sterling.

9

IN PURSUIT OF THE STAKES

The head of the London Metropolitan Police Service, also known as the Scotland Yard Commissioner, addressed Prince Richard.

"Your Royal Highness, I very much appreciate the position with which the family finds itself. All at the Yard are keenly aware of the exposure the family will have traveling to and from the Ascot Races. His majesty has made his concerns very clear to the prime minister and

Scotland Yard."

The prince paced, covering his mouth, rubbing his lips with his fingers. He took a chair opposite the commissioner. Folding his hands in his lap, he said, "As you know, Commissioner, London has a population of over three million. It appears that my son, Prince Braxton, has become popular with the people. That is certainly a positive development but could also be dangerous. Europeans and even the

Americans are caught up in all the hullabaloo concerning the Queen Anne Stakes. For heaven's sake, even the Grand Duchess Ekaterina has stoked interest in Moscow and St. Petersburg!" The prince shook his head.

The commissioner sat erect, his back not resting against the chair.

His hand lay on the head of an elegant silver and walnut walking stick. "Yes, that is true, Your Royal Highness. We have taken all that into consideration."

Rubbing the back of his neck the prince paused and looked the Scotland Yard man directly in the eye and said, "Please elaborate on the steps you have taken to ensure everyone's safety."

"Sir, we have the Metropolitan Police, detectives, and elements of the 60th Rifles. We also have the King's Life Guard assigned to securing the safety of the royal family. Men from the Wellington, Victoria, and the Royal Artillery Barracks will also make up the contingent."

"Will any be mounted?"

"Yes, Sir. The Wellington and Victoria Barracks, Sir." The commissioner leaned forward, "We will also have plainclothes detectives inside the racecourse." He sat back against the chair and continued, "Soldiers and police will line the route from Windsor Castle to the Ascot grandstand and royal enclosure entrance. Those not holding a ticket will not be allowed within 500 feet of the event, Sir."

"Are you certain all precautions have been taken?"

"Yes, Your Royal Highness."

Royal Ascot finally arrived. Win or lose, all eyes were on the young prince. A bright blue cloudless sky and mild breezes embraced the throng as the royal procession emerged from Windsor Castle. The king and queen led the procession in an ornate open Landau. It was followed by another Landau carrying the Prince and Princess of Wales, Princess Diedre and Princess Carmen. The ladies held colorful parasols against the brilliant sun.

Princes Dominic, John, Braxton, and Viscount Ramsey trailed behind in an open carriage. More carriages followed bearing courtiers and dignitaries.

The mounted King's Life Guard, resplendent in their brilliant red uniforms and shimmering helmets, rode at the front and rear and alongside the procession. The clatter of the horse's hooves on the cobblestones, fluttering banners and flags, and the cheers from the assembled crowd rounded out an idyllically picturesque day.

The horses drawing the open carriages moved at a quick trot, traversing through the village and toward the race grounds. Nearing the village of Ascot, more cheering, flags, banners, and music filled the air.

Prince John and Viscount Ramsey sat with their backs to the coachman. Dominic, as the heir, and Braxton, as the cause célèbre, sat facing forward. All four dressed in grey morning coats, dark trousers, and top hats.

"What do you think of the 'stovepipe?' It is your first time," John grinned and teased Braxton.

"It feels rather odd. I hope it remains on my head."

Ramsey teased, "Do not concern yourself, you will become accustomed to it. All you require is an adult-shaped head to hold it in place. That will happen soon enough."

Braxton sat continually adjusting his hat.

"It seems entirely unlikely; however, I certainly hope so."

While enjoying the attention, he remained fixated on the upcoming race.

Braxton internalized his celebrity status. From that day on, no matter how his horses performed, he hoped he would be respected for who he was, not who his family was. Through his efforts, he was his own person, intent on living his life on his terms and not the crown's.

The mood intensified a quarter of a mile from the entrance to the Ascot Parade Circle. Horses pulling the carriages tensed, interrupting their fluid movement forward. Mounted soldiers worked to quiet the anxious animals on which they rode. The royal family all took note, sitting more erect and scanning the crowds, the ladies clasping the hands of whoever was sitting beside them. Catching sight of Prince

Braxton, the enthusiastic crowd let out a huge roar of "Hurrah! Braxton! Braxton! Braxton!" The undulating crowds pushed steadily against a wavering police line.

Police fired shots into the air to ward off the crowd.

"Richard!" Mercedes screamed startled by the sound of the shots only yards behind them.

Richard rose out of his seat and looked back beyond the footmen posted at the rear of the carriage.

"Look Papa!" Carmen screamed, having risen from her seat. The horses lurched unsettling the carriage and tossing Carmen into her mother's lap.

The Landau carrying the three princes and Ramsey had come to a halt fenced in by a thick crowd cheering and waving wildly, still shouting

"Braxton! Braxton! Braxton!"

The mounted guardsmen were unable to get close to the horse drawn vehicle. Men in the crowd took hold of their mount's bridles, limiting the horse's movement. There was nothing the guards could do, outnumbered thousands to one.

Shouting and wrestling one another for position, the over-charged masses swarmed the carriage.

"We're cheering for you," one man shouted.

Another hollered, "We'll fix the race if ya wan' us ta!"

Another shouted, "We're betting on The Unbeatables!"

"Come with us, we'll take you to the track," Hollered one man now hanging onto the sleek Landau door.

The young prince leaned away from the man and up against John, clenching his hat in his hand.

"Braxton don't panic! They like you!" John said.

"They like me too much!" Braxton replied attempting to squeeze himself between John and the leather upholstery.

Three men dressed as laborers forced the door open and leapt into the Landau. They pushed Dominic and Ramsey up against the back of their seats.

One of the three turned to Viscount Ramsey, smiled, and joyfully shouted, "Pard'n me, me lord, but we be borrowin' the wee fellow for a bit!"

Ramsey's mouth fell open and his eyes blinking, stuttered, "You must not, that is the king's grandson!"

"We knows who 'e be. Never you mind, we be takin' good

care of

'im! 'E's the prince, the people's prince!'"

The men lifted Braxton off his seat and onto hands and arms pulsating and yearning to hold him high for all to see.

Oblivious to Mercedes helping Carmen from her lap, Richard said gesticulating, "The mobs surrounding the boys! My God! They have Braxton!"

Eight of the king's Mounted Guard surrounded the king and queen's carriage. The coachman unleashed his whip thrashing the six horses into a gallop. The postillion astride one horse repeatedly came close to losing his balance, fighting to keep the team together, avoiding falling to his death beneath the churning hooves.

The crowd, seeing Braxton carried aloft by the exuberant men, surged forward to join the parade, crashing through the police line.

The fervent mass of men, women, and children had brought the royal procession to a halt. The royal family stood in their carriages, drop-jawed, watching their youngest member being carried triumphantly down the street toward the racing compound. The passionate crowd chanting and claiming him the "People's Prince."

Braxton sensed he was not in any overt danger but feared he might be dropped and trampled. He kept his movements as still as possible, trying to aid the mass of hands holding him high. The men carrying the young boy tossed him about, fumbling and prodding, frightening, and confusing him.

Soon the bearers calmed down and smoothed out their carry.

Braxton regained some of his confidence, sat up as best he could and waved to his worshippers, his hat miraculously still in hand.

The prince's initial shock had turned to forbearance, then morphed into excitement when the men finally held him securely. That feeling changed into warmth and compassion noting the people taking pride in him, their prince.

Held by a large man on his shoulder and now vertical, Braxton feverishly waved his hat to the crowd. Arriving at the Ascot circle, the princely cargo was lowered to the ground. Bewildered, he attempted to straighten his clothing.

The Mounted Guard had untangled themselves from the crowd.

Hooves beat the pavement and blaring police whistles scattered the masses. The prince's bearers vanished into the throng. The police now formed a line separating the crowds from the Parade Circle and track entrance.

The people's prince stood alone, his clothes rumpled and cravat askew. Arms at his side, he observed those that had been charged with protecting him, heading toward him. They had failed him.

Although Braxton had reveled in the experience of being carried aloft by a cheering crowd, he realized he had no control over what might have happened to him. His thoughts returned to that terrible night of the fire at the Aurelio Palace, rekindling his fears.

The guard and police came to a halt thirty yards from the prince.

The parade circle was broad and empty. Where there should have been hundreds of people bustling about, men astride their mounts and people overflowing their carriages, there stood only Braxton.

Stomach churning, he waited stone-faced for his family to arrive. Placing his top hat on his head, no one within earshot, in a low monotone he said, "I promise. I promise I will never again allow myself or my family to be vulnerable again. So help me God."

The Scotland Yard chief detective having just heard about the manhandling of a member of the royal family sent detectives to protect the prince.

The family arrived in the Parade Circle. The clip-clop of the horse hooves echoed eerily. The band did not play, and the onlookers stood, staring, saying nothing. Flapping flags, bunting and banners were the only sounds as the carriages came to a halt opposite Braxton.

Mercedes was first to reach the ground. She rushed up to her son, coming to an abrupt halt two feet short. Her skin bunched around her eyes and pressed lips betraying anguish said, "Braxton, dear, it appears you are quite popular."

"Yes, Mama, it does indeed," the prince said, concentrating on remaining upright. Quietly he confided to his mother, "I am looking forward to finding a place to sit."

"Yes, I'm sure you are. Do the best you can. We will be inside soon."

Mercedes then reached over to straighten Braxton's cravat and smooth his coat.

Braxton responded to his mother's attention with a slight but grateful grin.

Richard approached mother and son, motioning the detectives away. "Son, how are you fairing? Prince Richard took hold of his wife's hand and placed it in his.

"Fine, Papa," Braxton said as he moved alongside his mother.

"Come Mercedes," Richard said in a firm but quiet tone.

From behind, John's voice carried forward, "Brax! You have all the fun. We get a heart attack and you a hero's welcome!"

Richard, Mercedes, and the unsteady prince paused and turned.

"John!" Mercedes said. She smiled a mother's smile at Dominic and John. "Really boys," she whispered.

In a higher-than-normal pitch, the spare's spare responded to his brother's jibe. "Yes, I suppose I was the first one here to welcome all of you."

As far as the crowds, the court and onlookers could tell, the royal family had managed well what could have been a disastrous situation. The royals had been schooled in keeping a stiff upper lip. They did indeed conceal their horror and fear for what could have transpired.

———

The Guard escorted the king and queen to the safety of the Royal Enclosure. "What the devil is going on?" the king demanded of an adjutant.

"Sire, it appears that the crowd absconded with Prince Braxton. They carried his royal highness on their shoulders along the route to the Parade Circle."

"Is he safe? Is he unhurt?"

"Yes, Sire. It appears he is safe and remains uninjured. Scotland Yard has assigned four of their men to him. He and the men are standing in the Circle."

"What? Why isn't he in here where it is safe? He can be such an aggravation." the king demanded.

"Sir, I believe he is waiting for the rest of the family."

"Good for him. Something I wish I had done had her majesty and I not been whisked away when shots were fired."

The king's secretary approached the king and said, "Your Majesty, the Yard commissioner is here and wishes to speak with you."

"Send him over," the king said, deepening his tone.

"Yes, your Majesty."

The commissioner entered and bowed. "Your Majesty."

The king held up his hand, "Don't say a word." The monarch pointed his right index finger within inches of the commissioner's face. He glared, then spat out, "You and your staff will report and wait for the prime minister and me at the palace! You are dismissed!"

———

Fans overwhelmed the stands and concourses in anticipation of the greatest equine match of the year. Every color and variation of the rainbow was presented by ladies parading about in colored cotton, embroidered tussore silks and summer woolens. Exotic hats, gloves, and parasols complemented their attire. Smiling and nodding, they were the centers of their own worlds.

Fashionable men exhibited monochrome semi-tailored jackets and stiff collars sporting wing tips. Curious cravats, some extravagant and some colorful, were all that was left to distinguish one gentleman from the other. Top hats crowned most every head.

The Royal Enclosure was positioned in the center and twenty feet above the track in the pre-eminent viewing stand. Bunting, banners, linens, and upholstery touting the king's racing colors adorned the enclosure.

———

"Papa," Braxton said taking his father's elbow in his hand, "Would you please accompany me to the stables?"

Mercedes looked quizzically at Braxton, then Richard. "Is everything all right Braxton? You are not injured?" Richard turned his attention to Braxton.

"No, Mama. I seek Papa's advice."

Richard looked at Mercedes, patting her hand. "We will return shortly."

Mercedes, dressed in a vibrant blue chiffon dress, skirts billowing in the summer breeze, appeared to have shrunk into the sea of azure fabric. Biting her lip, she said, "Be careful you two. We have had enough excitement today and there is surely more to come." She inhaled and sighed, "Go about your business, but hurry back."

Richard kissed her cheek and took hold of Braxton, placing an arm around his son's shoulders.

Father and son walked away, similarly dressed in top hats and morning coats. "Look," whispered Mercedes, speaking to no one in particular, "Braxton is almost as tall as his father. He is growing up." She smiled; her spirits somewhat lifted.

"Braxton, so what advice are you seeking?" Richard asked the prince as they exited the enclosure.

"None, actually," Braxton said sheepishly, lowering his head and looking back at his father.

"None? Then why... oh I see."

"I am just a bit nervous and did not want to suffer the crowds and their questions alone," Braxton whispered to his father.

"Certainly yes. I understand. Glad to be of service. Now shall we check on those animals of yours?"

Braxton's posture improved, his face upturned, smiling "Yes, Papa, let us do just that!"

Prince Richard felt odd, as if he were following in the wake of his 13-year-old son but did not mind. Braxton's command of himself and his own affairs filled his father's heart with pride.

Richard and Braxton took note of the other owner's race horses, then Fabuloso, Valorious, and Extraordinaire - The Unbeatables.

Josh and the racing teams bowed to Crown Prince Richard and Braxton. The staff and royals then engaged in restrained, but somewhat animated conversation, doing their best to contain their excitement.

At various times during the day, Braxton insisted his mother, his brothers, sisters, the grand duchess, and even the king walk with him to check on the horses. He was nervous, as was the rest of the family.

The royals discussed the position in which they found themselves. They speculated among themselves they might leave the race as a phenomenon of global proportions or as silly fools. They tried not to think about the latter and attempted to remember how they had been placed in this position. It was clear Braxton was an exceptionally clever boy. It was also obvious he was intent on charting his own destiny. Their hope was he did not intend to chart their destiny as well.

———

The Queen Anne Stakes was the last race of the day. Hours passed as Braxton busied himself inspecting his horses. He whispered into their ears, "I know you can do this. Win! Win together! You're a team; believe in each other."

Shortly before the Stakes race, the prince broke away from his family and trainers and gathered the jockeys and their mounts. The riders held their horse's reins as all stood in a circle. The animals were calm, as if it were any day, not the premier race day it was. They occasionally pawed the ground, snorted, and shook their heads. The jockeys stroked their mount's long snouts, rubbing behind their ears and patting their shoulders.

Braxton stood solemnly, swallowed, and said, "You have done it. All six of you. You have worked together, and victory is within your grasp. I am so proud of what you have accomplished these last weeks. Dedication and hard work will prove victorious today. I have every confidence you will win! Each and every one of you. Congratulations on your coming victory, for you have already won in spirit. A spirit that will be manifested when you bring home the Queen Anne Stakes Cup today!

10

THE QUEEN ANNE STAKES

Twelve horses entered the Queen Anne Stakes, all owned by aristo-crats. All well trained and ridden by competent jockeys.

The event was monitored via telegraph. Updates would be provided in intervals to all of Europe, St. Petersburg, Moscow, New York, Chicago, and San Francisco. Teletypes were situated to transmit the progress of the race from start to finish. Each change in position was dictated to a series of four telegraphers, each updating every change in position.

At the receiving end of the telegraph, men armed with mega-phones and strong voices shouted out each message as it was received. This benefited the large crowds assembled in each of the cities listening to the races progress. The time differences of up to nine hours in cities around the world did little to deter the international audiences' interest.

Braxton's entries were not favored in the program. They were long shots. Just for sport and for their people's prince, many small wagers, again, just for sport, were placed on The Unbeatables. The larger bets went to the odds-on favorites. Braxton did not bet that day, having kept

200 pounds in reserve to care for his animals regardless of the outcome.

———

The final race was upon them. The horses with the best recorded times in that year's races were given favorable positions, starting at the rail, and moving outward. The contenders, jockeys astride, were led one by one to the starting gates and locked in place. None of the three Unbeatables had run exceptionally well during the season, and as a result were given the 10th, 11th, and 12th positions. This placed them furthest from the rail and at a distinct disadvantage.

The Unbeatables' jockeys were dressed in matching colors. Each wore a purple jacket with scarlet sleeves and gold braiding. Fabuloso's jockey wore a black velvet cap trimmed in gold. Valorius's rider wore a scarlet cap trimmed in silver piping. A purple cap adorned the head of Fat Bob astride Extraordinaire. White silk trousers completed each rider's ensemble.

Jockeys struggled to contain their mounts. The cacophony emanating from the cheering stands fueled the already over-excited animals. Orderly progress to the starting line was impossible. To the untrained observers, the horses and riders appeared at odds with one another. One jockey was thrown from his horse but quickly sprang up off the ground and remounted. More than once, trainers leading horse and rider lost control of the leather, losing contact with their charges. The jockeys struggling with their mounts spread out behind the gates, widening the distance between them and the other horses.

The noise from within the stands subsided as concern for safety pervaded onlookers. Gradually the mayhem subdued, and the horses were locked into their respective gates one by one. The overzealous animals, thrashing, kicking, and snorting inside their respective gates, accented the solemnity now infusing the stands.

The starter's pistol rang out with a bang as the flag went down and the gates sprang open. The horses in the first three positions bolted out of their gates in full view of the grandstand and royal enclosure. Thundering hooves kicked up the dirt on the track as ear splitting cheers erupted. They were off!

Horses 4, 5, and 6 swiftly followed in file as the three front leaders ran neck and neck down the course and through the curve, entering the backstretch. The Unbeatables gathered steam as they moved forward, side-by-side. The intensity and power of their movement caught and transfixed the crowd's attention.

The Unbeatables' display of raw power thundering down the center of the track alarmed the seasoned racing crowd. Horse 3 tripped and rolled, crushing his jockey. Dirt and tack flew in every direction. A collective groan of horror erupted from the crowd.

The crowd saw the 5 horse leap over the horse laying on the track. Upon landing, 5 clipped 2, causing it to stumble, narrowing avoiding spilling them both.

The jockeys reined their horses around the fallen animal into the turn.

Horses 1 and 2 lost ground to 5. Jockeys on horses 6 and 7 wildly whipped their animals as The Unbeatables gained on them.

The Unbeatables moved toward the rail and alongside two other riders. Positioned twelve lengths behind the leaders, they were five abreast.

The leaders entered the last turn running side by side, clawing at the turf sending sod, soil and horse sweat into the air. The Unbeatables following suit, entering the turn, and leaving 6 & 7 behind, blanketing them in track debris.

Exiting out of the turn and barreling down the home stretch, the race fan's fevered pitch began to chill. Cheering turned to silence as shock consumed the crowd. They gaped in wonder at the display of raw speed and courage galloping toward them.

The Unbeatables surged! The crowd came to life with a ground-shaking roar. The Unbeatables were three lengths behind the leaders, horses 1 and 2. All eyes were on the finish line.

The Unbeatables closed in on the leaders. Fat Bob knew he need not urge his horse forward, Extraordinaire was consumed with winning.

Braxton's team burst forward, still lined up evenly and now only two long lengths behind the horses in first and second place. Easing off the inside track, they formed up abreast to sprint to the finish line. The Unbeatables exploded with shared energy and charged forward.

Extending their legs, they gained on the second-place runner and passed him fifty yards from the wire. They surged again, flying by the leader. Only the thundering hooves pounding the turf could be heard as fans, silenced by what they were witnessing, watched in paralyzed disbelief as the Unbeatables cross the finish line three abreast.

The crowd erupted, deliriously shouting, stomping, and grabbing whoever was next to them. Horns blew and the bands struck up a victory refrain. A glorious roar filled the heavens.

The Unbeatable's jockeys sat back on their saddles, waving to the fans as they fell into a trot, cooling their animals.

Braxton, like many in the crowd, had stood in stony silence the entire race, his countenance projecting confidence. Only one photographer had taken his eye off the race long enough to snap the young prince's photograph. This picture was soon emblazoned across the world's newspapers, memorializing Prince Braxton's victory forever.

As the news spread throughout the major cities around the world, reactions were similar. The next day papers carried stories, photographs, and illustrations, real and imagined, of the Queen Anne Stakes finish.

Overnight, His Royal Highness Prince Braxton became a worldwide household name. The nickname "Brax" caught on fast with fans around the world.

Photographs of the finish had to be analyzed. Who was the winner? Which horse had garnered second or third? Determining the final order was no simple task. It was widely believed the judges conducted a coin toss to determine the results of the race. Regardless,

The Unbeatables collected the entire purse of £153,000, making Braxton, in his own right, a very rich young royal.

"Braxton come with me. In fact, all of you come with me," ordered the king, addressing his family.

The royals headed to the paddock and their carriages as the crowd continued to holler and shout.

The king faced his family and bellowed, "Each of you will wave to the crowds as we circle the course. We do not need another incident like the one arriving at Ascott earlier. Something must be done to draw the people's attention and keep them in place while the horses are taken to safety."

The royal family climbed into their carriages. This time, Braxton was in their majesties' carriage, standing as his grandparents sat, waving to the throng. The king steadied Braxton, reaching up and taking hold of his free hand. The prince waved to the crowds. With victory behind him, he longed to be with his Unbeatables.

The victory lap proved to be a safety valve, allowing the crowd to blow off the steam of adulation for the young prince and his fairytale victory. It also served as another valuable lesson for Braxton – he had learned of the unpredictability and uncontrollable nature of crowds. This experience strengthened his resolve to always be in control of his life.

———

Braxton was grateful his father was alongside him as he accepted the trophy in the winner's circle. The color had drained from Prince Braxton's face and his legs felt as if they would fail him. He needed the support of his family to get through the celebration.

John and Ramsey approached Braxton.

John placing his arm around his brother's shoulders exclaimed, "Congratulations little brother!" He paused, patting Braxton's back, saying, "But I think you look a bit peeked."

Braxton folded an arm against his stomach. "I am not feeling so well."

Looking at Braxton, Ramsey said, "He is exhausted, John, perhaps a tad undone."

John whispered in his father's ear, "Papa, I think it is best we take him home. This has been a tremendous day, months in the making and he is still but a boy."

Ramsey said, "Come Braxton, we are taking you out of here!"

————

The next morning the family threw itself into preparations for their return to the Aurelio Palace. It had been over two years since the fire, and all were eager to see their newly renovated home. Braxton sent a footman to request a private audience with his parents.

He was immediately summoned to the Japanese Salon where the Prince and Princess of Wales were discussing the closing of Renaissance House and opening of the Aurelio Palace. The princess sat at a large oval inlaid mother-of-pearl black enameled table piled high with notebooks and papers. Prince Richard stood next to her in conversation with his aides and upper servants.

Braxton, announced, entered the room. The five foot eight-inch-tall 13-year-old wore long brown trousers, a vest under a dark frock coat and a white shirt tied at the collar with a slim black cravat. His blond hair was slicked down in the style of young gentlemen of the 1870s. Members of the household bowed or curtsied as he approached his parents. Whereupon he bowed to his parents.

"Papa. Mama. I know you are so very busy, but I have a matter of some importance and a request."

"What is it Braxton?" his father asked, handing papers to one of his aides.

Braxton spoke in a confident, mature, yet differential tone. "It is a matter of some delicacy. I was hoping we might speak in private."

He commanded the room's attention with his upright stance. The young prince's previous unremarkable bearing now exuded gravitas. He had caught everyone off-guard, as they first looked at Braxton, then his parents, and back to the maturing prince.

Mercedes displayed a subtle grin and an approving nod.

Prince Richard signaled, and the room emptied, leaving Braxton alone with his parents.

Richard's sincere smile framed his words, "Tell us, Braxton, what is it? Are you well? Yesterday was a frightening experience for you. It was also exhilarating, but a tiring day. We understand if you are not feeling yourself today."

"Thank you so much, Papa, Mama. You need not have worried. John and Ramsey took excellent care of me. I slept well and have had a restful, yet contemplative morning."

"Contemplative? That sounds interesting," his mother teased. "Whatever have you been thinking?"

His father chuckled and pulled up a chair alongside Mercedes. "Contemplative, eh? I am intrigued."

Braxton held a sealed envelope in his hand. He placed it on the lacquered table, positioning it in front of his parents.

"What is that?" Richard asked, neither he nor Mercedes reaching for the packet.

"Braxton, does that envelope have anything to do with your request?" His father asked, nose wrinkling.

"It does. It contains a draft. Payment." He paused, bracing himself for the words to come.

Both parents shifted in their respective chairs, gazing in serious focus at the mysterious packet.

"I owe you an apology and financial payment for the damage I unintentionally caused at Aurelio Palace. I started the fire. I am truly sorry. I was foolish. I was irresponsible and did not understand what I was doing." He paused for a moment and continued, "I do not wish to discuss it. Papa and I have had that conversation. I only ask that you accept my sincerest apology."

Seated, Richard and Mercedes stared as Braxton delivered his apology. When he had concluded, they rose and walked around the table to Braxton.

He stood eye level to his mother and only an inch or two shorter than his father. Both parents wrapped their arms around him. His mother pulled back and kissed him on the cheek. Mercedes said, blinking back tears, "We forgave you long ago."

Richard rested one hand on Braxton's shoulder and smiled. "We are deeply proud of you son."

The Prince and Princess of Wales returned to their gilded and yellow silk upholstered chairs. The doting parents watched their son pull up a matching chair and join them at the table.

Mercedes and Richard exchanged proud glances.

Braxton leaned back and placed his elbows on the arm of the chair, steepling his fingers. "I listened to the engineers and the accountants during the last couple of years as they were planning and implementing the refurbishment. I know that much has been done to enhance and redecorate the palace. Far more than required to repair the damage for which I am responsible.

"I am a wealthy man now." He paused. He folded his hands in his lap. "I can afford to compensate you for the expenditures which my irresponsible actions required.

"With your permission, I shall pay a visit to our family's bank to deposit my recently acquired winnings. As I am sure you are aware, I depleted my other monies, all but a couple hundred pounds, investing in the Unbeatables.

"When I return, I shall have covered the note compensating for the Aurelio Palace expenses, and will have tended to other business.

"What other business?" the princess asked, looking first at Braxton, then at Richard.

Braxton continued as if he had not heard the question. "Again, with your permission, I would like to handle my affairs from the Aurelio Palace. I would be honored to have both of you as counter signatories on my accounts. That should provide peace of mind as to my handling my finances.

Braxton pushed back in his chair and stood. "As you are both otherwise engaged today, would you allow Auntie Ekaterina to accompany me to the Chiacontella Bank?"

Mercedes raised her eyebrows. and Richard followed, letting out a deep-throated cough.

Richard looked at Mercedes and commented, "Well my dear, I don't see any problem with this. Braxton is acting with honor, integrity, and purpose."

Mercedes motioned Braxton over; he obliged her. "Braxton, there is one problem with your plan. I insist that your father and I join you and Ekaterina on this errand. It is important that everyone see you have our continued support. This will stand you in good stead as you continue your life's ambitious journey, though not yet of age. We want everyone to witness the confidence we have in you."

Braxton softened his demeanor, his shoulders loosened. He rose from his chair and walked around the table, bending over, and giving both his parents an affectionate hug followed by a grateful "Thank you!"

The grand duchess met Braxton and his parents in the port cochere, joining them in the carriage preparing to escort Braxton on his errand. Conversation centered on the move back to the country. Of particular interest to Braxton, they rattled on about his horses and plans.

The enthusiastic prince shared that he was formulating a plan for stabling, breeding, and training. He described his ideas for taking over an underutilized and somewhat neglected part of the vast Aurelio Palace stables.

Midway in the conversation Ekaterina observed, "Have you noticed Mercedes, Richard, that we have, shall I say, been hood-winked?" She was grinning with pursed lips and sparkling eyes looking directly at Braxton. "Perhaps that is too severe a term, but descriptive." She paused as all exchanged knowing glances.

"Yes, of course," Mercedes said chuckling. "But what is your point? It should be obvious our young man had this tête-à-tête planned all along."

Richard broke in, "I'm getting rather used to his methods. I also saw this coming." He tapped Braxton on the knee. "Go on young man, what is it you want?"

Braxton utilized the carriage ride to obtain his parent's permission to operate a section of the stables as his own. He subsequently agreed to the grand duchess's suggestion that he pay all expenses relating to stabling his horses.

"Josh, we have done it!" Braxton said slapping his friend on the shoulder. The two were amid supervising the preparation for moving the racing team to Aurelio Palace.

"We have done what? Or rather, you have finagled what?" Josh mused out loud.

"We not only have the stables at Aurelio, but the entire east end of the stable block, all of it!"

Josh placed himself in front of Braxton.

"All of it?" Josh asked in an incredulous tone.

"Yes, now we can house the horses below and the team in the garrets above!"

"And the training grounds, the palace track?" Josh asked in a high pitch.

"That as well!"

"Great news, Braxton! Great news! Pray tell, what is the catch?

"No catch."

"Braxton?"

"Well, uh, um, maybe a little one."

"How little?"

"I, uh we, pay for all upkeep, expenses, and some maintenance."

"That sounds fair, although the track and enclosures will not be inexpensive to maintain. No rent?"

"No rent."

Josh place himself in front of Braxton, his hands on his friend's shoulders. "Well done, Brax!"

"I thought so," Braxton grinned, congratulating himself.

Late one afternoon, a few weeks later, Mercedes entered Braxton's rooms, dressed all in black. She wore a long-sleeved full-length black dress and a small black cap atop her coifed golden hair.

The sound of her rustling skirts had not aroused his interest as he continued making entries in his ledger. The fragrance of lavender awakened his senses. He sniffed and wiped his nose with the back of his hand. He kept writing.

"Mama?" he queried, still focused on his papers. He placed his quill on the inkstand and turned toward his mother. The sight of her dressed in this unexpectedly severe manner caught him off-guard.

Earlier that morning he had seen her otherwise attired, in a gaily colored summer dress and matching parasol. Now in one hand she held a white handkerchief and in the other a black armband.

"Mama!" He stood, "What are you doing dressed in black? Has someone passed? Grandpapa? Grandmama?" "Please, come here," she whispered.

Braxton required a mere five steps to reach her. He took both her hands in his, looking first at her, then down at her hands. "Who?"

Their eyes met again; tears ran down Mercedes' face. Braxton placed his arms around her and pulled her gently against his shoulder. Braxton's jacket muffled her reply. "Ekaterina." His body and limbs contracted.

Mercedes placed her arms around the middle of his back. They stood holding one another, saying nothing.

"I am dreadfully sorry, Mama. So very sorry," Braxton mumbled in a hollow voice.

They released one another but continued to hold each other's hands.

"Braxton, she passed peacefully. She had dismissed her maid this morning and lay down on the divan in her rooms. I went looking for her, as she had not kept our date to go for a walk in the gardens. I knew when I saw her, she was no longer with us."

Mercedes took her handkerchief and wiped her eyes.

He released his hold on his mother's hands and stepped back. "Thank you, Mama. What do we do now? You know I will do whatever I can for you, for her, for all of us."

Holding up the armband, she said, "I suppose you need put this on. Let me do it for you."

Braxton held out his arm as his mother placed it around his upper arm.

"I can't believe she's gone," the prince said, choking, his eyes pooling.

Mother and son embraced once more.

———

Later that day, the Imperial Russian ambassador and entourage arrived at Renaissance House to receive the grand duchess's body. The family observed strict mourning. Preparations to depart London for Aurelio Palace came to a halt.

A week later, Braxton studying in his rooms, a footman appeared announcing he had been summoned to the chateau library.

The prince was announced entering the room, "His Royal Highness, Prince Braxton." The young man found his father and mother sitting with the Russian ambassador and several other serious-looking men. The ambassador and other men rose and bowed to the prince. Prince Braxton could not help but notice a large crate placed off to the side of the room. He bowed to his seated father and mother, then nodded to the ambassador who had taken his seat and was leaning forward in his chair, surrounded by several others unknown to Braxton.

All dressed in black.

The fifteen-foot-tall windows that allowed oceans of light into the room had thick moribund drapes drawn across them. The flickering light from gas-lit chandeliers and sconces was all that held the dreary room from falling into total darkness.

Speaking in Russian, "Your Excellency," Braxton addressed the ambassador.

The ambassador jumped to his feet as Prince Braxton addressed him.

The prince continued, "Please accept my condolences for the loss of Her Imperial Highness, The Grand Duchess Ekaterina. She was a dear, dear friend and I cannot adequately express the grief her passing has caused my family and me." He paused for a moment to collect his thoughts. He swallowed, and continued, "Again, my sincerest condolences to her father, His Imperial Majesty the Czar, and the Russian people." Braxton punctuated his precise Russian dialogue with a crisp bow.

Accepting the young prince's condolences, the ambassador bowed and in Russian, the czar's representative replied, "Thank you, Your Royal Highness. You honor her memory with your excellent command of the Russian language."

"It is she who honored me, regaling, and teaching me all things Russian. She cherished and so missed her fatherland." Braxton smiled, remembering out loud, "We spoke only Russian when together. She taught me a great deal. I am grateful. Grateful to have known her, Excellency."

Everyone's attention turned to Prince Richard as he walked across the center of the room and over to the crate.

Richard placed one hand on the tip of the crate and turned to his son, saying, "Braxton, the grand duchess has been very generous to you. She bequeathed you four important paintings. I know you remember the artwork she shared with you at the British Museum. Many of those paintings were on loan from the grand duchess."

"On loan, father? She never indicated such to me. They were hers?"

"Yes, son. We were not privy to that information either." He paused and looked over to Mercedes, and asked, "Mercedes?"

The princess wiped her eyes with a lace handkerchief. She stood and joined her son, taking one of his hands in hers and walked him over to Richard and the large wooden crate.

With tear filled eyes, she sniffled and said, "I had no idea so many important pieces belonged to her." Pointing to the crate, Mercedes said, "These now belong to you."

He could not believe what he had heard. Braxton raked one hand through his hair, his voice cracked, "Me? She has given these…to me?"

Braxton had always recognized and appreciated the grand duchess's attachment to, and knowledge of so many magnificent canvases. The Rubens, the Brueghel, the Botticelli, among so many other great works, would always be precious to him. He would be forever grateful for her gifts.

11

COSIMO

Cosimo de Chiacontella, now Duke de Chiacontella, arrived several months after Braxton and his family had returned to Aurelio Palace. Of the many family dwellings he had frequented, the prince and princess's country home were a favorite of Braxton's Uncle Cosimo. The duke had lived there for many months at a time as a young child.

Two decades had passed since Richard and Mercedes' betrothal. Cosimo took a moment to reminisce. Cosimo, then a youthful man in his early twenties, had been sitting in the loggia with his parents, the duke and duchess, on a lovely summer evening at the Villa Incantarre. They were discussing his sister Mercedes' dowry.

"Father, with the dowry now arranged, we need to make payment," Cosimo said, toasting his parents. The Sun had disappeared behind distant mountains. Within the loggia overlooking one of their many vineyards, candles flickered behind the multicolored Murano glass lanterns resting atop the balustrade. A multitude of flowering plants provided a carnival of fragrances carried on the back of a warm breeze flowing across the vines, rising up the hill, buffered by the Villa Incantarre.

"Yes, Cosimo. I know this," his father sighed and fidgeted. "I just do not understand how Consigliore Vanatti was unable to negotiate a more agreeable financial settlement."

"My dear, if you don't mind... it is a fair settlement," Cosimo's mother reassured her husband, patting his arm. "After all, she is marrying the future king of England."

"Vanatti and I have spent a great deal of time coming to this arrangement," Cosimo said.

"It is a great deal of money," huffed the duke.

Cosimo, clenching his jaw said, "Yes, father, it is. But I believe I have found a solution that will lessen the amount of gold needed to fulfill the contract... a great deal less, in fact."

"What is your plan, son?"

"A gift. A wedding gift of great value."

Cosimo stood from his chair and paced the length of the loggia. His movements, captured in the rising moonlight, cast shadows along the terrazzo floor. He stopped and rested his hands on the balustrade facing the vineyards, his back to his parents. "Aurelio Palace."

"Never!" Shouted the duke, veins rising across his forehead. "Aurelio is the crown of all our homes throughout Europe! Have you taken leave of your senses? As I recall, it is your favorite. I will not agree to this!"

"Calm down my dear, it is just a proposal," purred the duchess.

"I will calm down, but the answer is still no," her husband said, drinking the remaining half glass of wine. The overweight duke sat up in his chair and reached for what was an empty bottle. "Damn it! Thousands of vines and all we have is an empty bottle."

"I'll send for more," Cosimo said snapping his fingers and lifting his empty glass.

A servant immediately appeared carrying a carafe of Chianti.

"Give it here," Cosimo barked.

He filled his father's glass, then his mother's and finally his own, impatiently waiting for his father to speak.

"Why Aurelio? Why not just send the money?" the duke said, wiping his mouth with his hand after emptying his glass.

"Father, because we don't use the Aurelio Palace and its upkeep is a financial burden. Giving the house to Mercedes and Richard would decrease the amount of gold needed to fulfill the dowry."

"I thought we could afford this, Cosimo! I assumed being grandfather to the King of England was bound to be expensive. But I still do not understand why we should give up Aurelio," he said, petulantly.

The duchess rose from her seat and stood behind her husband, placing her hands on his shoulders, quietly saying, "We are giving the palace to our daughter, the future queen of England, and one day, her son, our grandson, will be king."

The duke sat up and murmured, "I will be father to a queen and grandfather to a king." He sat back in his chair.

Cosimo inwardly savored his victory. He had won. Richard would remain in his life.

The duchess continued, "It will provide status and prestige to our family. The Chiacontella will become one of the most influential families in Europe. But that in and of itself is not the reason we should do it. Please remember, we will still have Renaissance House and its vast park in the center of London."

The duke jerked his head around to address his wife. "What do you mean, that is not reason enough? You confuse me, woman."

Cosimo remained silent, still savoring the fruits of this conversation with his father.

The rehearsal time spent, with his mother, earlier that afternoon had prepared him to withstand his father's temperament and facilitate his persuading the duke to agree.

The duchess returned to her chair and took one of her husband's hands in hers. "The palace is old. It is in need of extensive and expensive repairs. The costs maintaining it are prohibitive, more than Villa Incantarre, and we are rarely there to enjoy it." She released her husband's hand and reached for her wine glass.

"Bravo, Mother," Cosimo said clapping his hands. "I could not have said it better myself." He lifted his glass in his mother's direction. The duke paused, then lifted his and toasted them both.

———

Cosimo's heart ached continuing to reminisce, thinking back months prior to the conversation with his parents about the dowry 20 years ago. Before Prince Richard had been introduced to his sister, Countess Mercedes.

Prince Richard and Count Cosimo had journeyed from Rome to the Villa Incantarre. They had become fast friends, learning about each other's countries, and enjoying one another's company. Neither had wanted their time together to end, conspiring to extend it by making excuses to stop for days at a time.

The two young noblemen prolonged what should have been a sixday journey into a three-week excursion, often lingering in small towns for days at a time. They sought the hospitality of rich merchants and nobles well known to the Chiacontella.

Soon, their close friendship assumed a different attraction. They both experienced a craving, a longing to be close, to touch one another. They fought to fend off the magnetic draw that continually pulled them closer, but the yearning tugged at their hearts. Was it a deep bond, a passionate friendship or more? One day, as they were dining, Richard could no longer keep his feelings in check and spoke haltingly to Cosimo.

"Cosimo, there is something I need to ask you," Richard said, taking shallow breaths.

Cosimo smiling, placed his hand on Richard's.

Richard gasped and jerked his hand away.

Cosimo left his hand on the table, his countenance tightening.

"What are you afraid of?"

"Nothing. I am sorry. You startled me," Richard replied, rolling his lips. Then gazing into Cosimo's eyes he set his hand back on the table next to Cosimo's. Looking down, Richard used his other hand to pick up the count's and place it on his own. "Now, there," Richard said staring into Cosimo's eyes.

"Come to my room after the banquet," Cosimo breathed.

Richard looked into his friend's eyes, and not hesitating replied, "Yes."

———

That night, after the dinner guests had departed their host's palazzo and the household had retired, Cosimo heard three light taps on his door. He opened it to find Richard holding a candlestick illuminating his sparkling eyes.

"God, I thought you weren't coming," Cosimo whispered breathlessly, pulling Richard into his room.

Richard closed the door behind him and placed the candlestick on a table. He took his hands and laying them on Cosimo's shoulders said, "How I have wanted you to want me."

They moved toward one another; their lips touched.

Cosimo wrapped his arms around Richard's back, pulling him close. Eager, yet unfamiliar with such passion, they shed their garments, the flickering candlelight revealing their strong, young silhouettes.

The men gently kissed one another like tender lovers. Then, as their passion surged, they unbridled the lust they finally acknowledged and joined their bodies in a writhing oneness.

———

The new lovers met the next night and evenings following. They stole time together bribing their servants and lying to their hosts. But most importantly, they found the time they needed to be together.

Cosimo and Richard would spend the early evenings separated from one another, each in the company of willing ladies. Yet both knew they yearned for one another. At the end of the evenings, their social obligations paid and their secret safe, they rushed to a prearranged rendezvous.

One night, Cosimo lay against Richard's back, his arms enfolding the English prince. "Tomorrow we arrive at the Villa Incantarre. Tonight, is the end, our last time together."

Richard sighed, "Yes, tis the end."

"Thank you. Thank you for…"

"Cosimo, thank you."

Richard turned over and held Cosimo's face in his hands. He

drew their mouths together, setting fire to what they knew would be their last night together.

———

The prince and count exchanged loving glances before proceeding through the gates leading to the Villa Incantarre.

Approaching the villa, Cosimo had regaled Richard with the 800 year-old history of the ducal seat. The Chiacontella duchy had come about as the direct result of an influential cardinal's request to a dying pope.

The cardinal wished to be exiled from Rome and had asked his withering friend, Christ's Vicar on Earth, to banish him so that he, the cardinal, could escape the politics and intrigue that would envelop the papal states upon Saint Peter's successor ascending to heaven.

The Pope's heir presumptive was a mean and cruel priest who held grudges. Only through his power and evil talents did this papal candidate make his election to the papacy all but certain. Those who were not under the virulent Prince of the Church's spell were fleeing. To stay in Rome meant misery, ruin, and perhaps death. There existed a list of enemies. Cardinal Chiacontella was on it

Cardinal Chiacontella knew exile would remove him as a threat to the pretender and his drive to secure the Holy See. With the dying pope's help, Chiacontella left Rome in disgrace. Following his departure from Rome, he was never spoken of again in public, at least in the Vatican proper.

The cardinal retired to his family's estate. Five years after his return he inherited the dukedom from a deceased cousin.

Years earlier, the cardinal-duke had been the minister of the papal finances. The cardinal had gained considerable experience in international finance. He knew all the important players.

The cardinal-duke established the first Chiacontella bank during the 9th century. As duke, he used surrogates to represent his interests. The duchy grew into a mid-level player in European finances long before the infamous Renaissance banking families emerged hundreds of years later.

As Richard and Cosimo approached the Villa Incantarre, Cosimo said, "Our dukedom has over 200,000 people. And it is protected. See those mountains in the distance?" Cosimo pointed toward the horizon. "They keep enemies and highwaymen at bay." Turning in his saddle and pointing in the opposite direction, he said, "Wide rivers and strong currents, plains strewn with volcanic crags, and marshes also serve to isolate Chiacontella. We are blessed with natural boundaries."

"Chiacontella is fortunate," Richard said. "Our island nation enjoys similar protection. We too, are blessed."

As they rode through the forest leading up to the villa, the men returned to more personal matters.

"I envy you, Richard."

"What do you mean? Why should you envy me? You will one day be duke, and all this will be yours. Not only this but a vast banking and trading empire."

Prince Richard continued, "You will rule, I will reign. You will have power and I'll be a puppet parroting whatever my government tells me to say."

"Richard, you will be king of the greatest empire the world has ever known!"

"I will reign from a gilded cage. These weeks with you will be the only real freedom I will ever see." Richard shifted forward in his saddle, snapped his reins, startling the horse from a slow walk into a cantor.

Cosimo sent his mount forward as he thrust his heels into the animal's sides.

"Slow down Richard, there is something else."

Richard responded by tugging lightly on the reins and assuming a firm seat. He brought his mount to a walk. The men, again, rode side-byside.

"My twin sister, Mercedes, Richard."

"Are you tossing me off to your sister?" Richard asked, staring ahead. He did not see the look of shock coursing across Cosimo's face.

"Tossing you off? How can you say that? That is not it at all! It is the only way I know of to keep you close. I do not want to lose you. We cannot, we must not and cannot be finished."

The two men rode on in silence, absorbed by their own desires but knowing their lives were not their own.

————

Three weeks prior to this day, Mercedes had received a letter from her twin brother. Cosimo had mentioned he was returning to the villa with a newfound friend. She had thought little of it. Cosimo was social, amiable, and always engaging interesting people to entertain the family.

At present, there were three or four of these acquaintances residing at the villa. They had long worn out their welcome and had exhausted what intellect they had to offer the family. Soon Mercedes' father would usher them out. She assumed this man would be the same. She would be amused for an undetermined amount of time, and eventually, not so amused.

Though the family was geographically isolated, they experienced the best that science, art, education, literature, and philosophy offered, vis-à-vis their long-term house guests. Their guests' knowledge was recorded and cataloged by scribes and preserved in the Chiacontella library.

The duchess had been informed a large procession approached with Cosimo at its head. The report intrigued Mercedes and her mother. Cosimo and Richard rode side-by-side as their entourage arrived at the villa.

————

"I hope you will find my sister pleasing."

Richard replied tersely, "She is your twin sister. No doubt I will find much to like. She is not you. That, I do not find attractive."

Cosimo ignored Richard's retort. "When I wrote my mother and sister, I didn't mention exactly who I was bringing. She has no idea who you are."

"That will be interesting, dear count. Perhaps your father has written. From the little I know of him he does not strike me as the type to keep a confidence."

"Really, Richard, that may be true, but it is very unkind of you to say such a thing. He is my father and soon he will be your host."

Cosimo took a breath and continued, "I asked him not to tell mother or my sister. I want it to be a surprise. They are certainly expecting some frumpy university don, or the like. Won't they be surprised!" Cosimo said slapping Richard on the shoulder. "Oh, and the not so discreet duke, my father, will not arrive for several days."

Cosimo, with his azure eyes and olive skin, gazed at his lover, enjoying the wisp of musky scent that was always present around Richard. His friend's light complexion, broad shoulders and long, wavy auburn hair ignited desire in the Italian's loins.

At that same moment, Mercedes sighted the strong Englishman from afar. Cosimo has brought me a present. She smiled. How thoughtful, she mused to herself.

The stranger's coat of arms, emblazoned on standards carried by attendants, looked familiar. The countess searched her memory and recognized the colors. She felt faint. She gasped with the realization that her brother's friend was the future king of England.

The duchess, sensing her daughter's sudden apprehension, supported her with an arm around her waist.

"Mother, you know who that is, do you not?"

"We would both be wearing dunce caps did we not."

The duchess clasped her hands and continued, "That brother of yours! Not warning us! I care not how old or how big he is I shall take a strap to him."

With an edge in her voice, Mercedes responded, "I will help you, mother."

The young woman held her breath, regaining her composure.

Struggling to maintain a civil tongue, she said "If our visitor was not so handsome, I would clobber Cosimo the moment he dismounted."

Mercedes took her mother's arm, and they descended the villa's steps to the plaza. The duchess smiled widely, waving to the new arrivals, not betraying her anger and frustration with her son.

Richard barely noticed the Chiacontella duchess, as his attention was drawn to the tall, athletic, golden-haired siren beside her. Mercedes was dressed in a long cotton gown of pastel colors. The matching ribbons intertwined in her hair rested on her shoulders, then cascaded down her back. She radiated youth, vitality, and a delicious warmth.

"Breathe, Richard," Cosimo cajoled.

"I cannot," Richard said under his breath.

Mercedes' grip on her mother's arm tightened.

"I can see why Cosimo kept him a secret," the duchess whispered to her daughter. "Are you still angry with Cosimo?" She chuckled.

In short breaths, Mercedes whispered, "If this man can string two words together, I shall make him mine." The two ladies swallowed their laughter.

"You do know what this is all about, don't you, Mercedes?"

"Yes, I believe I do."

The duchess said between her teeth smiling at the men, "And are you up to considering it?"

"As if I have a choice. When father and Cosimo team up, as I am certain they will, whatever does it matter how I feel?"

Both ladies recognized Cosimo intended his twin sister to become queen of England.

Such a marriage would destroy the duchy's anonymity. The power

and wealth, which flourished in isolation, would be threatened. Cosimo had recognized the threat but uncharacteristically disregarded his instincts and judgment. He wanted this marriage. It must become a reality. He demanded Richard remain part of his life, one way or another. Neither Mercedes nor the duchess suspected the ulterior motives hiding within their beloved Cosimo.

———

The crown prince knew how to accept hospitality. He danced, hunted, shot, and rode expertly. What attracted Mercedes most was his self-awareness and commitment to fulfilling his royal duties. To her, inner strength was the essence of a man. Richard had had the same effect on her as he did her twin, Cosimo.

Indeed, the English prince was as taken with Mercedes as he was with her brother. Noting the newfound chemistry raging between his sister and his lover, Cosimo made excuses to absent himself from the villa, disappearing for days at a time.

"Cosimo, why are you always absent? I never see you. It is as if you are running away... avoiding me." Richard and Cosimo stood facing one another in Cosimo's rooms.

"I am. I am running away. And yes, avoiding you − and Mercedes." "Avoiding me? Why?" Richard pleaded.

"I cannot bear to be with you, you with Mercedes. I still want you. It is tearing me apart."

"Cosimo, I am sorry. What am I to do? You introduced us. What do you want from me? Our love is forbidden."

Richard pulled his lover close. They wrapped their arms around one another and buried their faces in each other's shoulders.

"Nothing. I want nothing. There is nothing you can do."

Cosimo, wounded and alone in his misery, knew he would not stand in the way of the growing bond between his lover and his sister.

———

One afternoon, Cosimo heard his sister singing in the woods. He followed the sweet melody deeper into the forest. Her singing turned to laughter, then giggling. Cresting a hill, he looked across a narrow field abutting the water's edge. His head drew back quickly spying Richard's arms around Mercedes. Their lips soon met in a deep kiss.

Witnessing their passion, Cosimo's heart constricted in an

agonizing scream. His head swam, he stumbled backwards vanishing into the tree line. He felt as if a spike had been driven into his heart. He ran blindly into the forest. Branches tore at him, cutting his face and slicing into his clothes. Sweat poured out of every pore as his heart raced and his muscles numbed. Stumbling over a fallen tree he landed and rolled in agony.

As the days wore on, he came to terms with this new reality. He had created this world by conspiring to keep Richard close. Now, he would have to learn to live in it.

12

A CHIACONTELLA EDUCATION

Over the twenty years following Mercedes' and Richard's marriage, Richard and Cosimo stole time together. The families saw each other every two or three years. Sometimes it was in Italy, sometimes in England. The best had been when the families cruised the Mediterranean on the royal yacht or stayed at the ancient Roman Chiacontella villa on the isle of Capri.

But by this time years had passed since they had all seen one another; and not since Braxton was four years old had Richard and Cosimo held each other. Richard and Mercedes youngest son did not remember much about his uncle, or the young Chiacontella heir, Count Aramis.

Braxton's cousin had accompanied his father Cosimo to the Aurelio Palace. Aramis and Braxton, only a year apart, could have been mistaken for twins, had the prince not stood two inches taller than his cousin.

The Italian duke and young count stood resplendent in their court attire. It was not lost on either of them that the palace in which they were now guests had been built centuries ago by their ancestors.

The pair stepped into the Aurelio Palace's magnificent hall.

Thumping the floor with an ornate oak staff bearing a gilded lion head, the major domo bellowed, "The Duke de Chiacontella and Count Aramis de Chiacontella."

Daylight bursting through the wall of glass the length of the onehundred-fifty-foot-long hall illuminated their noble regalia shimmering in the sunlight. The father and son strode confidently the length of the room.

Reaching the dais, the Italians bowed to the Prince and Princess of Wales.

The princes nodded and the princesses offered shallow curtsies.

"Welcome to Aurelio Palace," Prince Richard said, extending his hand to Cosimo. The duke kissed the hand of his long-time lover.

"Welcome, brother, nephew," Mercedes said, beaming and extending her hand.

Pleasantries were exchanged and protocol observed. The family descended from the dais and to the main floor, warmly embracing Cosimo and Aramis.

On cue, a small orchestra played light music as footmen carried beverages first to the family, and then to courtiers and guests.

Braxton had heard of his young cousin and had only faint memories of him when his family had visited their villa in Capri years earlier. The similarity in age and appearance made their initial meeting easier.

"I am Braxton," the young prince said. "Do you remember me?"

"I am Aramis, and yes, I do."

"Excellent, now let us get out of here," Braxton said motioning to Josh, watching from the other end of the hall, to join them.

Josh made his way over to Braxton and Aramis.

"This is my friend Josh."

"Hello, my name is Aramis."

"A pleasure meeting you, your lordship," Josh said bowing to the count.

Impatient, Braxton said, "Come on, we are leaving! To the stables, Aramis. We shall have considerably more fun."

Josh piped in, "I have a couple of pints and cigarettes requiring our attention."

"Count me in!" Aramis said slapping Josh on his back. The three disappeared behind the dais and out of the hall.

————

The Duke de Chiacontella saw this visit as an opportunity to become more involved with his English family and strengthen his economic and political interests. The banks in Italy were falling further and further away from the evolving economies of the industrial revolution.

Cosimo had his eyes on the Americas. He considered New York, Chicago, and San Francisco ripe for opportunity.

As he always did, Braxton caught Cosimo's attention. Like everyone else, the duke saw unbridled potential in the prince. He wanted his son Aramis to develop a friendship and establish a bond with Braxton. He knew all he could do was encourage and not force such a relationship. The duke had created the natural opportunity for lasting friendship by bringing the cousins face to face. To further facilitate the cousin's friendship, Cosimo would spend time getting to know Braxton better, who likewise seemed equally interested in getting to know his uncle.

Both Cosimo and Braxton anticipated the other would be a useful resource. Braxton noted the serenity and confident bearing exhibited by his uncle, imagining him not only confident, but perhaps wise. His uncle knew things Braxton wanted to know. Importantly, Cosimo was a banker.

Thanks to The Unbeatables, Braxton had over £140,000 on deposit at his uncle's bank. The four priceless masters left to him by Ekaterina were stored in the bank's vaults. Still, the young prince really did not comprehend just how valuable a client he was, financially and politically.

Three days into the Chiacontella visit, Braxton and his uncle met in the library as the young prince was searching for the morning papers. While sitting across the room, Cosimo spied his nephew sifting through the newspapers lined atop a Louis XIVth commode.

He startled the unaware Braxton by saying, "My Lord, Prince Braxton, are you looking for this?" and held up The London Times.

Walking briskly to his uncle, Braxton responded, "Why yes, Uncle. Have you had an opportunity to finish reading it?"

"Yes, I have."

Cosimo neatly folded the daily and handed it to Braxton.

"Thank you, Uncle." Braxton said, intending to remove himself to another part of the room.

"Join me," Cosimo said pointing to an adjacent armchair.

"I would be happy to, Uncle," Braxton replied, seating himself in the chair.

In his short life, Braxton had been regaled with stories of his father and uncle meeting in Rome, along with bits and pieces of the adventures Richard and Cosimo experienced on their journey from Rome to Chiacontella.

Mercedes had shared with Braxton the long Chiacontella history, meticulously detailing the family and its monetary interests. Braxton saw money as a way to accomplish his dreams. Cosimo could help him understand how the Chiacontellas conducted banking and trade.

He reached over to his uncle, grabbing both Cosimo's hands in his, pleading with his eyes, his heart pounding, said, "Uncle, would you consider mentoring me in banking and trade?" Cosimo's chin dropped.

"Specifically, Uncle, I would be honored if you would impart to me what one must know regarding money. Help me understand how I can best use it in my life."

He released Cosimo's hand and stood. Braxton placed a hand on his hip and the other used for emphasis, tapping his chest, said, "As you know, I am as much a Chiacontella as anyone, and I learn quickly."

The intense purposefulness of the young prince charmed and moved Cosimo. The Chiacontella patriarch had found a true descendant of the ancient cardinal-duke de Chiacontella.

———

Cosimo turned the lessons into an adventure for Braxton and Aramis. The three spent part of everyday unfolding the history and teachings of trade and finance

"Money is a science," he told them, and if they allowed him to, he would make monetary scientists out of them both.

First, he had them read current economic treatises on the science of money. He arranged for his more astute young bankers to travel to Aurelio Palace and tutor the boys in modern day banking. It took ten months for the young cousins to complete this training. Cosimo then escorted them to the London Stock Exchange and had them schooled in trading stocks. They learned how to value equities and were introduced to people who knew people. Only in politics did who you knew matter as much as it did on the stock exchange. Knowledge was power and having that knowledge was vital.

———

The years passed quickly while Braxton and Aramis were being schooled in economics. As both boys celebrated their 16th birthdays, Braxton's celebrity had continued to grow. Because of the immense wealth he had acquired at the racetrack, the tabloids christened him the "Crown" Prince, referring to the currency used in Scandinavia and some

Eastern European regions. The real Crown Prince and England's heir, His Royal Highness Richard, Prince of Wales, found the moniker amusing.

Cosimo continued to take the youngsters around to his business meetings allowing them to observe. If his business associates seemed uncomfortable, the duke excused the boys, only to fill them in on details later. After each meeting, the three would review the meeting's discussions with one another. This detained them an additional three months in London. With the permission of his grandparents, the three lived at Buckingham Palace during this time.

13

THE FOUNDATION OF AN EMPIRE

The Prince and Princess of Wales and Princess Carmen departed on a European tour. Braxton took this opportunity to put a plan into place. He invited his Uncle Cosimo, Prince John, Viscount Ramsey, and cousin Count Aramis to lunch aboard His Majesty's Yacht, Elfin. Two clerks accompanied them.

The morning fog lifted, revealing a swollen river Thames. The autumn day was bright and crisp. Yet an odor of fish and decay lingered in places along the docks.

Numerous vessels of varying shapes and sizes crowded the river-bank. Chimneys along the shore and stacks crowning ships plying their way along the estuary emitted dark plumes of coal-fired smoke. Dockworkers scampered feverishly, manipulating lines, and shifting mountains of cargo to and from the dock. A light wind fueled the clanging of lines against masts tossed by water slopping against unyielding hulls. The muffled crack and snap of flags and pennants framed the occasional whistle or horn emerging from nowhere and everywhere.

Two teams of horses pulled large broughams carrying Braxton's party. They stopped on the dock alongside the sleek shimmering royal yacht, its lines long and low in the water. The king's Coat of

Arms was emblazoned on the bow and stern. Pennants flew rising from the bow and up the jib line to the masthead and back to the stern. The aft deck was covered in an ornate open-sided cloth pavilion. Every winch, ladder, turnbuckle, and all things metal were highly polished and glistening in the morning sun. The crew was immaculately uniformed in blue and white.

A whistle sounded as Braxton and John climbed out of their carriage and approached the gangplank. "Your Royal Highnesses, welcome aboard," the captain said, saluting.

"Thank you, Captain. My brother and our associates and I are pleased to be placed in your hands for the duration of our time aboard the Elfin," Prince John said, both he and Braxton tipping their hats.

"My honor and pleasure, Sir. We will do our best to meet and exceed you and your guests' every expectation." The captain again saluted the princes.

The others had exited their conveyances and followed Braxton and John aboard. The party worked their way toward the stern and found seats beneath the pavilion cover.

Braxton addressed his fellow passengers, "Thank you, everyone, for accepting my invitation. I must confess, I have not disclosed the reason for our meeting. I appreciate your indulging me." Braxton took his seat and surveyed his guests seated in large rattan deck chairs situated atop the gleaming teak deck.

Braxton opened with, "Cosimo and Aramis are well aware of my intentions and will assist in the presentation."

"Well, little brother, that leaves Ramsey and I in the dark. What use could two dilettantes have to three scheming financiers?" John inquired, folding his arms across his chest, looking askance at his uncle and cousin.

"Railroads," spouted Ramsey. "That is the thing, or rather the only thing that has captivated Braxton's attention for years. Well, other than horses, of course." He paused and looked over at Cosimo. "The duke has access to money. My family is waist deep in railroad debt. These two want something."

All eyes focused on Braxton as he said, "Excellent, Ramsey. I commend you on your grasp of the situation. That is precisely why we are here. We have something your family desperately requires. Cash!"

Ramsey's eyes opened wide, stammered, pleading, "Why all the secrecy? Intrigue? This is beyond even you, Braxton!"

Braxton glared at Ramsey, stating in a low hard monotone, "Your firm is vulnerable. Vultures are circling, those that wish to purchase it at a fire sale price and then pick its bones clean, ruining you, your family, and stockholders."

Ramsey swallowed hard and hung his head.

A rumbling from the steam engines below deck alerted those on board they were departing. A crisp autumn breeze washed over the passengers as the craft gently rocked. The ship had pulled away from the dock and was now plowing steadily against the current. Shouting dockworkers and the cacophony of loading and unloading cargoes faded as the elegant coal-fired cruiser distanced itself from the shore. Entering the channel, the powerful yacht picked up speed and steamed down the River Thames.

Stewards placed small writing tables in front of those seated on deck. Crystal tumblers filled with port were laid before the passengers.

The crew disappeared below deck.

"Ramsey, please forgive me for characterizing the state of affairs so bluntly. Trust me, we are here to help." Braxton took a sip from his glass and continued in a kinder tone, "Last year, Cosimo was approached by two of your company bankers. They wanted to sell him, or rather the bank, loans. Your family's debt."

John turned to Ramsey, "Why would they want to do that?" Ramsey looked away and out over the river.

Cosimo volunteered, "Because they feared the debtor was in trouble and would default."

"Ramsey, why didn't you tell me? Is this true?" John demanded.

Ramsey turned and looked at John, confessing, "My family and the board of directors insisted that our situation remain secret. I was, and am, devastated. The company is over-extended. It remains a grave situation."

Addressing Cosimo, Ramsey said, "Did you take the paper off their hands?"

"Yes, after thoroughly researching the situation, I did. Rather, the bank and Braxton did."

All eyes shot over to Braxton. He sat motionless; his hands folded in his lap. "We bought the notes we felt most likely to be called. It was our intention to hold on to them, as they were deeply discounted. We believed the notes would eventually be made good. We hoped, for your family's sake, Ramsey, that relieving your company of the burden of paying on the note would make it easier for the railroad to become profitable again."

Ramsey shifted uncomfortably in his chair.

Braxton added, "You are aware your family and the board surely must have questioned the notes not being called when they had defaulted."

John observed Ramsey swallowing hard and answering, "No one spoke of it. It was if they did not exist. Very surreal, but again, no one spoke of them. If the notes had been called, we would have been ruined. We found ourselves in silent but blatant denial."

With a resigned look, Braxton said, "We thought increasing your cash on hand would turn things around. That has not happened. As you know, for all intents and purposes, the firm and your family are insolvent. Of that I am very sorry. We tried."

"And now?" Ramsey asked, his eyes red and raw, downing his port.

Aramis folded his hands in his lap and cryptically answered, "We were overly optimistic. Now, the notes appear to be little more than junk, and more of your firms' loans are coming due.

Ramsey said angrily. "Yes, I am of course aware of that. I want to know why we are here. Why we are sitting on this stinking river discussing my family's foul finances?"

John growing visibly agitated watched the exchange; placing his hand on Ramsey's shoulder and in a calming voice said, "Surely you have been asked here as part of a solution. You can trust my family."

Cosimo joined in, speaking gently, "We are here to provide

capital for your family's failing venture. It is a business deal that will save you from ruin and hopefully pay dividends down the road for everyone."

"Let me be frank," Braxton said. "We are here to restructure the railroad's debt and provide funding for expansion."

"How in God's name can you do that?" Ramsey murmured. He stared down at his palms as if they could reveal the answer.

Cosimo said, "Braxton has agreed to secure the debt with one hundred thousand pounds sterling and seven hundred thousand pounds from my bank collateralized by the paintings left to him by the Grand Duchess Ekaterina."

"Why would you do that, Braxton?" John asked.

"I am fond of Ramsey and his family. He has been like a brother to me, and you." Braxton paused. "But this is purely business. It is also a way to, like was said earlier, get involved in the railroad business, eventually benefiting us all."

Aramis interrupted, "This is how we think our arrangement can work. After paying off the railroad's debt, cash flow will significantly improve immediately. We will have a substantial cash reserve. Funds will also be available to build one, maybe two more lines."

John sat back in his chair and said to Aramis, "Expand? How can you want to expand with finances such as they are?"

Braxton held up his hand halfway, catching everyone's attention. "I have a specific line I want built. I require your firm's expertise. It is as simple as that."

"Where to?" John asked.

"The Aurelio Palace."

"But there's nothing along the route to support it," Ramsey sputtered. "Certainly, it would be convenient to have a private line to one's country estate, but not even you can afford that, Braxton."

The ship's whistle blew, startling the aristocrats, black smoke billowing from the funnel.

"It is not that simple, much more involved. It is my offer, nonetheless."

John fidgeted in his seat. He stood up. "That may very well be, but you are a minor." John wagged his finger at his younger brother.

"You have no status, no position to conduct your own affairs. Should you succeed in your scheme, you cannot vote, so who will vote your shares?" John then sat down and crossed his legs.

Braxton, with a tight jaw and searing gaze, was stunned by the simple-mindedness of his brother. *How could he think I have not taken all this into consideration? Perhaps I have made a mistake including him in my future.* He maintained his focus on his older sibling, reigning in the anger surging within.

In a calm voice Braxton said, "John, I was hoping you would serve as my proxy. You would, of course, also serve as my agent. I will compensate you. But, rest assured, direction will come directly from me and no one else. I will seek counsel from everyone present here.

However, ownership requires leadership. I will provide that leadership."

John stuttered, "I see. Very well. What does father say to all this?"

"We shall address that later. I think it best Ramsey gives this some thought."

John and Ramsey excused themselves, leaving the deck through the door to the main salon. During their absence, Cosimo and Aramis engaged in small talk, never touching on the subject at hand. Braxton remained immersed in his own thoughts.

Returning to the group, Ramsey remained standing. John returned to his seat.

Ramsey said, "This is a very interesting proposal. I think it is worthy of further discussion. I will take it to the board of directors. My guess is this voyage was planned with that in mind. The board is scheduled to meet this evening. Of course, you knew this." Ramsey looked over at Braxton.

Braxton did not acknowledge what everyone assumed to be the truth.

Ramsey inhaled and continued, "Perhaps we will have a response to interrogatories as early as this evening or tomorrow." He paused surveying his listeners. "You understand of course, I cannot commit the firm's board to anything."

A sigh was heard, tension lifting. Cosimo and John helped themselves to port and cigars.

"Very well. Please take a seat. We have a lot to share and discuss," Braxton said and continued. "I have purchased options on three large parcels of land between London and Aurelio. You see, I have had a plan all along to make the line quite profitable. I have laid out a scheme to develop the land into manufacturing plots. All it needs is track and trains to carry raw materials and finished goods."

Stunned silence consumed the assembled, as Braxton had not shared this plan with anyone but his lawyers.

The young prince signaled toward the salon. One of the clerks appeared carrying a large portfolio. He placed the case on the floor whereupon Braxton unlocked it and removed a ten-inch pile of papers.

"I have here a proposed contract and privilege agreement. All shall sign the privilege agreement prior to reading the contract. It is important that all be bound to not revealing the terms of the contract, ever.

The second clerk appeared and distributed a copy of the privilege agreement for their signatures. He collected the signed agreements from each attendee and placed them in the satchel.

Meanwhile his coworker provided each participant with a copy of the contract. The clerks disappeared.

A steward came on deck and refreshed everyone's glass. He presented a humidor stocked with cigars. After lighting cigars, he placed pens and ink wells in front of the men and returned to the salon.

Once the servant had departed, they began the process of reviewing the contract page by page, making notes and offering comments.

Aramis served as secretary, logging changes, and making annotations on his copy. Three hours later they docked again at London Bridge.

"Gentlemen, thank you for your valued support and input," Cosimo said.

All proposed contract copies were collected and placed in the satchel.

Braxton handed the locked case containing the contracts to one of the clerks. Cosimo instructed the clerk to take the changes annotated by Aramis contained therein and revise the contract. Once completed, he was to deliver the revised proposal that evening to Ramsey and the firm's board of directors.

Viscount Ramsey and the clerk disembarked the yacht.

As evening arrived, Braxton wanted to keep everyone together should Ramsey return with word from his board of directors.

Cosimo had located a proper dining establishment. Wilton's was one of the few establishments that respected respectability. Upon disembarking, the party found their way there

Not once during the evening did the gentlemen discuss the afternoon's topic. The men's conversation centered on the track, hunting, court gossip and women. Following dessert, all enjoyed cigars and brandy.

Prince Braxton was situated prominently in the private dining room, but remained quiet and observant, mentally occupied working out the various scenarios he might face upon Ramsey's hoped for return.

At a quarter past ten, Viscount Ramsey entered the room attended by a well-appointed, but unimpressive short, round man. The uninspiring accomplice carried a satchel similar to the one used earlier in the day. Braxton requested the restaurant staff remove themselves from the room.

Lord Ramsey spoke as the impish man distributed papers hitherto contained in the satchel. "Gentlemen, as you will see, the documents are being returned to you signed and sealed by each member of the board of directors. Please take a moment to confirm what I have represented." Thirty minutes passed as the men reviewed the papers.

Not a word was spoken.

The sound of pages turning, cigars being relit, and crystal against silver as beverages were sipped was all that broke the silence. Cigar smoke wafted through the room graying the light.

Braxton was the first to complete his review. He placed the contract on the table in front of him and waited patiently as each person in the room completed their study.

"Congratulations, Ramsey. It appears you have been successful in your mission," Braxton said picking up a glass. "Let us toast our friend, our new business partner, and his accomplishment." "Hear, hear!" reverberated throughout the room.

Braxton signed the original and all copies.

Cosimo said, "Gentlemen, please place your signatures on the documents as witnesses."

Braxton now owned thirty-six percent of the railroad and fifty-one percent of its voting shares. If his calculations were correct, he was now one of the wealthiest men in England. This evening he had amassed a fortune worth at least two million pounds. He had, indeed, learned how to leverage money and now controlled a railroad that, moments earlier, had been teetering on insolvency. With the stroke of a pen, he had realized one of his dreams.

———

The contract had required each member of the railroad's board to personally guarantee the note issued by the Chiacontella Bank. While he had invested heavily in the loans previously purchased from other lenders, the young prince did not guarantee the note consolidating the debt and had assumed no additional financial liability.

The paintings which had initially served as collateral for the first note were released with the signing by board members for the merged note.

The four pieces of art were then collateralized on a second note. This loan was unknown to the other parties and had been made to Braxton by the Chiacontella Bank's London branch.

This second note was to be utilized to purchase and develop land on which Braxton held the options spoken of earlier in the day. He motioned to a footman and handed the servant three sealed envelopes. These packets contained letters and drafts exercising the options on the properties straddling the new railroad line, of which he now owned a large share.

As Braxton rose, he appeared taller to those in the room. They knew they had just witnessed an ingenious financial transaction. His Royal Highness Prince Braxton was no longer a boy, but a man with whom to be reckoned.

"Thank you everyone for your patience. I appreciate your counsel given to this worthwhile endeavor."

Exhausted, he bowed to his guests, and said, "Gentlemen, if you would please excuse me." He departed the room. Before anyone could join him, he climbed into his carriage and was driven away.

———

Late the next morning Braxton gathered Josh, John, Ramsey, and Aramis and proposed a trip to Davos, Switzerland.

Arriving in the Swiss Alps, they spent the next month discussing business and indulging in pleasure. Dreaming of their futures, they relaxed. Braxton had never taken time to experience a true holiday other than those spent with his family. He had always been too busy.

Unwinding in Switzerland had initially been physically painful. Suddenly, with nothing demanding his full attention, headaches and anxiety gave way to a reinvigorated Braxton. The older Josh introduced Braxton to a bier haus and the entertainment within.

———

The young prince had written and posted a letter to his sister Carmen several weeks into their holiday.

My Dear Sister,

Thank you for your recent correspondence. It took a while to reach me as we have knocked about Switzerland.

It pains me knowing you are experiencing unhappiness on your trip with Mama and Papa. Despite your betrothal to the czarevich, I

thought for sure a trip on the continent would be fun and exhilarating for you. Neither Grandfather nor Grandmother had shared
with me the underlying reason for the European excursion.

Your misgivings have credulity. Marrying the czarevich will
totally change your life and remove you from us and our enchanted
Aurelio existence.

That is reason enough for me to oppose the match. I desire only
the best for you and that which will ensure your happiness. Alas, our
lives are rarely our own.

Unfortunately, as the eldest daughter and The Princess Royal,
you do not have the luxury of choosing whom you shall marry. It
begs the question, what choice do you have?

I suppose you could find someone to run off with. Of course, I
jest.

Seriously, I hear the Russian heir is a monster and not possessed
of a golden heart. I know this is not comforting.

Have Mama and Papa heard about his philandering and the
blackguard's rather sadistic nature? It is common knowledge in our
circles, so I have been told.

I have heard one interesting tidbit. His royal nastiness is reputed
to be quite a handsome sod. I pray the latter is true and the former
only vicious gossip.

Come to think of it, Auntie Ekaterina thought him a bit off. You
realize, he is thirty-five years younger than his dear departed sister,
Ekaterina? To think they were siblings. They rarely corresponded
after Peter's death and her departure from St. Petersburg.

John and I, et al., are in Berne. We are having a grand time.
Again, I wish you were enjoying your journey. Not that I wish you
were here, as then you would supplant the conscience which I have
recently tucked away somewhere. I have started drinking a bit, and I
like it.

Aramis and Ramsey are out riding. Aramis and I are becoming
close. I like him. He, Ramsey, and Josh make wonderful
companions.

Josh has been quite successful broadening my education with the
ladies

Have you heard anything from father regarding my rumored business dealings? The rumors are wonderfully delicious, and in large part, true. I shall wait to share details with you when we all return to England.

I so look forward to having you back from Vienna unbetrothed to that Cossack!

Your favorite brother, I am sure. Brax

————

During the fourth week in the Swiss Alps, John received a letter.

Braxton asked, sitting in his dressing gown perusing the paper in the villa they had rented on the outskirts of Berne, "What does it say, John? Who is it from?"

"It is from father. He is quite vexed."

"Whatever for?"

"Mostly at me, I think. It seems he has gotten wind of your scheme to help Ramsey."

"Oh. Do not concern yourself. I saw this coming. And so, did you. It is our good fortune he remains hundreds of miles away and will cool down in due time."

Braxton again focused his attention to the newspaper.

John, sporting a pallid countenance, look up and exclaimed, "He has summoned us to Vienna!"

Braxton tossed the paper on the table, folding his arms across his chest and throwing his head back gazing at the ceiling. "Damn! We have been having such fun. Josh, the bier haus ladies and I have plans!"

He then rose out of his chair, walked over to where John was sitting, placing his hand on his brother's shoulder, said, "Well, I suppose we should respond. Let us give it a day or two, then reply we will be on our way soon. We have 'appointments' to keep this evening and perhaps the next. But then again, I have yet to experience Vienna."

————

Four days later Braxton booked a train to Basil where he and John boarded a luxury riverboat on the Rhine heading north to the Danube and on to Vienna. The time it took to take the somewhat circuitous trip provided them the opportunity to prepare themselves for meeting with their father.

During the voyage, Braxton cajoled his older brother on how they both had every right to pursue their own interests.

"John, think of it this way. Neither you nor I will be king. What are we supposed to do with our lives? I certainly have no chance of wearing that uncomfortable load of gold and jewels. You do not even want it. You have said it yourself, many times, how glad you are Dominic is the older one."

John breathed in, stating, "Perhaps you are right, brother. I will leave it to you to convince Papa. After all, all I did was support Ramsey and sign as a witness."

"Ha! You see! You have nothing to worry about," chortled Braxton.

———

Braxton had never visited another royal court, much less an imperial court. Vienna was an imperial city and its monarch, the Emperor of Austria-Hungary, an autocrat. Austria was an ally of Russia and the Austrian emperor ruled a splintered nation.

The awe-inspiring history of the Holy Roman Empire was on display when John and Braxton arrived in Vienna. They were relieved to find they were no longer the focus of their father's interests. The Russian czar had arrived along with his court. Carmen's future father in-law had come to inspect his presumed future daughter-in-law and one-day empress of Russia.

Vienna welcomed the wunderkind Prince Braxton and Prince John with great fanfare. Bunting, flags, an eighteen-gun salute and a guard of honor escorted Braxton and John from their ship through the streets of Vienna to the Imperial Palace. Vienna's populace needed relief from dealing with anarchists and insurrection. Feting the world-renowned winner of the Queen Anne Stakes was a welcome diversion.

The Viennese loved to orchestrate parades with the prerequisite pomp and circumstance. The youth, vigor, and magic created by His Royal Highness Prince Braxton was exactly the tonic needed to distract them from affairs of state, treaties, and marriage negotiations.

The three emperors, Austrian, Russian and his parents received the brothers at the Hofburg Palace. Braxton and John quickly acclimated themselves to the Viennese imperial society, taking part in much of the gaiety.

Braxton had a quick introduction to international politics and intrigue, carefully observing, processing, and committing to memory all that he saw and experienced.

The subject of the brothers' financial dealings was never broached as all eyes were on Carmen. Her Royal Highness Princess Carmen was immensely successful, beautiful, graceful, and charming. Her grace distinguished her on the ballroom floor as did her athleticism afield on horseback. Her judgment and intuition served her well as she purposely reigned in her intellect. Intellect was not prized in a consort. The elegant beauty comported herself as though she favored the match.

———

Prince John and his sister Carmen sat in her boudoir. Her voice cracked and her eyes filled with tears. "It is done. I am shackled to the Russian bear. Father and the czar signed the contract. There is no hope for me." Carmen sagged back into her chair.

"Carmen, dear," said John. "It cannot possibly be that bad, really."

"Really, John? Have you no sense of history? These people are tyrants! Look what they did to Ekaterina! Her sons! And then there is Peter III. All of them are bizarre. They are right out of the old testament. Eye for an eye and all that rubbish! I could be poisoned or shot for just stating my opinion, for God's sake!"

"That's a bit much!"

"No, it is not, John!" Carmen said, her chest caving, her head falling into her hands.

Braxton, standing at the door, had heard the conversation. He went over to his sobbing sister and knelt before her. Gently placing his hand atop her head, "Carmen, you have every right to be upset. Both John and I love you." He took a moment and then in a hopeful voice said, "Carmen, you know you are to return to England for six months to prepare for the wedding and leaving your homeland for a life in Russia. You have six months. Perhaps you will grow more accepting of the arrangement. Six months is a long time. Things could change for the better."

"Oh, Brax, I wish that were so. I just do not understand why father would allow it. Or grandfather. Why?"

John interjected, "It wasn't father. He and mother fought it. Grandfather did his best to explain the family's position to the prime minister. Parliament is strongly in favor of the match. It is the government that has forced this."

Carmen sat up, wiping her tears away. "So, as you said in your letter, Brax, I am a mere pawn. We are all gilded pawns. Princes and politicians move us about their chess boards, furthering their schemes."

———

Returning to England, Braxton spent the next year and a half at Aurelio Palace. He did not join his family in London for the season, intent on furthering his own education and attending to his railroad and horses. His absence from society and London worked in his favor, the entrepreneur not distracted by idle entertainments and frivolous pursuits. Following his previous year's celebrity, his absence inadvertently fostered an aura of mystery, rumor, and speculation.

———

Age 18, Braxton did not feel the need to venture forth to London. London came to him. He summoned his solicitors for monthly meetings and as was his station, his board of directors attended him quarterly at Aurelio Palace.

He closely supervised his racing stables and utilized Josh to execute his orders. Braxton was content to be the first among equals in all his ventures. The new railroad owner personally inspected the railway under construction from London to the local village. Attention to detail and demanding accountability, finite audits, and regular inspections, fostered progress. The railroad was built in less than half the time allocated and came in under budget. Braxton arranged for a separate spur to be built from the main track within a quarter mile of the Aurelio Palace.

Before the first rail was laid, Braxton hired engineers and a team to design and build a private train which would ferry his family to and from London and anywhere track existed. Braxton directed the cars not be built entirely of wood. The outer shell of each car was to be constructed of steel and glass. Gilded lamps, hand-crafted railings, velvet, and silk complemented the window treatments and upholstery. Leather furnishings, parquet floors, and chintz enhanced the overall decor

Mahogany, cherry, oak, and burlwood dominated the interiors.

There was a salon, a dining car, a lounge, the ladies' sleeping car, the gentlemen's' sleeping car, the prince and princesses' car, a kitchen, two baggage cars, three cars for horses and accouterments and the servants' sleeping car and lounge. Two engines were provided; one pulled and the other traveled in reserve. The train was designed to operate independently of trackside support. Instead of usual one coal car to carry fuel, two were provided. A third car carried backup water for steam.

Braxton also included a car for his exclusive use and one for use by his entourage. Braxton's car had a sitting room, a small dining room, a study, and one bedroom. Each car had exterior mounts for panels showcasing the family coat of arms. They were colorfully displayed on both sides of each car when Braxton's parents were on board. The cars' exteriors matched the others' metallic maroon color accented with gold piping painted bodies. Car roofs were painted a metallic black.

The extravagance of a private train on this level could have severely embarrassed the family had they not recently engendered great popularity and support. As far as the public was concerned, if it involved Braxton, all was well.

14

THE SPIRITUAL JOURNEY BEGINS

Early one morning, Braxton detected the scent of paint mixed with indistinct fumes of adhesive or glue. The odor appeared to be emanating from behind a concealed panel leading from the secret passage into his rooms. Years earlier, the nursery had been transformed into a room suitable for a young gentleman, something he had asked his parents to have done. It had been easy to convince his parents that neither he nor the tutors belonged in a nursery. Fortunately, his argument was championed by the Grand Duchess Ekaterina's encouragement and her offer to pay for the refurbishment as a gift from her to Braxton.

The prince sat alone in his rooms. He was working on plans for development of the land through which the train tracks would traverse. The prince was intent on creating an environment where manufacturing would be augmented by an infrastructure facilitating not only supply and distribution but providing a livable community for employees and their families. Braxton had conceived creating a cohesive working community while visiting various railroad manufacturing yards.

He had taken note of the jumble of factories, train yards, and squalid housing. It was obvious there was no rhyme or reason to the tangible chaos created in those environments. The concentration of humanity housed next to construction and manufacturing was confusing, dangerous, and unhealthy.

While Braxton was enthralled with everything that had to do with railroads, he had recoiled when witnessing the worker's horrendous living conditions.

His designs allowed room for expansion. There was no doubt the growth, and the needs of occupants working in them, would quickly absorb all the spaces. Infrastructure was paramount to his design. The cost would be exorbitant. It necessitated his taking another loan against Ekaterina's paintings to underwrite his costs.

Braxton lost his focus on the task at hand as the strange odor wafted into the suite. He was puzzled, then irritated, and finally curious as his quarters were far from any other inhabited rooms. He cherished his privacy.

He rose from behind his worktable and inspected the wall from which the noxious fumes emanated.

Jerking his head to one side, looking directly at the hidden panel he had used so often in the past, the hair stood up on the back of his neck. The alarmed prince experienced a sense of lack of control, a fear not unlike the one he had endured the day the crowd had carried him through the streets on race day years ago. Perspiration peppered his brow.

He looked around the room for a candlestick but was hard-pressed

to find one as the palace had been plumbed for gas while the family was in London. There was little need for candlelight in the new Aurelio Palace. Persisting, he located one candlestick in a cupboard not far from the entrance to the hidden passages. He lit the candle and immediately upon entering the dark passageway, overwhelmed by the odor, reacted by instinctively extinguishing the candle's flame.

During one of his many visits to the railroads, he had witnessed firsthand the devastation of flammable situations that could and should have been avoided. He had seen the bodies of the injured and dead being removed from a factory that assembled furnishings for the burgeoning transatlantic steamship trade. The recollection of this experience alerted him to the eminent danger when combustible fumes and flames collided. A lit candle could wreak havoc.

Braxton had spent enough time in these passageways to know his way around without the help of illumination. Indeed, there was faint light from above, dimly casting a glimmer on the narrow stone stairs. He deftly made his way toward the light. The odor grew stronger. Feeling nauseous and light-headed, he used his hand to brace himself along the wall as he ascended the stairs. The illumination seeped out from under a concealed panel. It led to what he had discovered years earlier, room

s the palace architect had used during its original construction. The architect and his staff had inhabited the garret for twenty years when the Chiacontellas began building hundreds of years earlier. The main room was large, tall, and augmented by several smaller workrooms off to the side. These rooms were full of natural light during the day.

Braxton slowly opened the panel and stepped into the room to find Seiko Higashino standing ten feet away poised to defend himself. He held himself in a rather peculiar stance, causing Braxton to cock his head quizzically.

They held each other's gaze for a moment until Seiko relaxed his stance, stood erect, and bowed to the prince. Neither of them knew exactly who should be embarrassed or offended.

Seiko Higashino was an enigma to many with whom he came into contact. He stood close to five foot eight inches tall but held himself in such a way he appeared much taller. His lean physique clothed in exotic embellished fabrics could easily have given him a formidable presence. It was only his well-developed sense of self and sublime spirituality that comforted and entranced the onlooker. Braxton had initially experienced this spiritual seduction when he had first met Seiko in the Japanese salon at Renaissance House.

The prince held out his hand. "Mr. Higashino, please excuse me for this intrusion. I was alerted by an odor that has been associated with unfortunate accidents which I have witnessed firsthand. It was in the interest of all in the palace that I came to investigate, though not aware these rooms were inhabited. Please excuse my uninvited and unexpected intrusion."

Executing a deep bow, then taking Braxton's hand, Seiko answered, "Your Royal Highness, it is I who owes the apology, for it is my work that causes your alarm. It is my lamentable lack of success in ventilating these rooms which has caused this inconvenience."

The prince, his interest piqued, said, "On the contrary, sir. I hope you agree that this may indeed be a fortuitous meeting." He paused for a moment and looked about the room, and continued, "Since our first encounter, I have wished to see you again. It is my very good fortune and I hope it is also yours that we have found ourselves here at this moment."

Seiko bowed and Braxton reciprocated.

The conversation soon flowed with less formality. Seiko explained how he had finished his work at Renaissance House several weeks after the family returned to Aurelio Palace. He was then commissioned by the family to work at Aurelio Palace several months prior to their encounter.

Braxton was distressed to have been so engrossed in his own activities that he had not taken note of the man's presence. In that moment he decided to get to know Seiko better. He knew Seiko could teach him a lot, but Braxton had no idea just how much he would learn.

They agreed to meet the following day.

The next morning, Braxton interrupted his customarily highly scheduled day to search out Seiko. He found him in the Japanese salon restoring the decorative panels and architectural details created over one-hundred-and-fifty years earlier. That explained the familiar, unpleasant odor Braxton experienced the night before, now present in the salon.

"Good morning, Mr. Seiko!" He shouted from across the room.

"Good morning, Your Royal Highness." Seiko bowed, matching the prince's enthusiasm.

"Honorable Master Higashino, would you have time to join me

in the Florentine Garden for a stroll and conversation?" A hint of pleading in his voice.

"Why of course, my prince, I would be honored." He set down his tools, wiped his hands, donned a brilliant white-on-white embroidered floor-length kimono over his simple cotton trousers and tunic. The two exited the salon through the luminescent framed French doors and onto the terrace. They proceeded to the classically designed Florentine Garden, reminiscent of thirteenth and four-teenth century Florence.

For the first ten minutes they walked at a moderate pace in silence. Braxton felt a growing need to bear his heart and soul to Seiko, an immense desire to unburden his fears, hopes, doubts, and dreams. The prince was a whirlwind of desire, ambition, plans, and compassion, and fearful of failing as if he were a house of cards.

Seiko sensed a debilitating anxiety in the young man walking alongside him. Physically, Braxton was still a youthful man, though he appeared to have donned the mantle of a man years older, continually piling more responsibilities and tasks upon his own shoulders. Seiko knew that a person of Braxton's innate drive, genius, and imagination would self-propel. The question was, did he propel himself in a direction that was manageable, sustainable, self-fulfilling, and ultimately purposeful? This is where their discussion began.

The Japanese master had a soft, undulating voice, thoughtful in nature. Spirituality framed his every thought and action. Seiko felt his purpose was to integrate his interpretation and understanding of divine spirituality into the lives of those around him. He accom-plished this through the way he modeled his life. Seiko would soon use the study and execution of martial arts to facilitate Braxton's instruction along his spiritual journey.

The very private prince did not often share his innermost feel-ings with his family. He did not feel comfortable in their circles, constricted by tradition, protocol and isolation from the outside world. He kept most of his thoughts and ambitions to himself, but he often felt the need to speak to someone about them. Perhaps he could speak to Seiko. Maybe Seiko had insight into how he might free himself from the confines of the royal family.

Seiko saw in Braxton a willing student, a youthful man bursting with potential. They continued walking in silence.

The youthful man's urge to share his feelings finally overwhelmed him, "Master Seiko, may I share with you my very personal thoughts?

"Yes, my prince. You do me honor."

Braxton took a deep breath. "I have many things running around my brain, the greatest of which is to get out into the world and make my mark, not as a member of the royal family, but as a private person. I cannot reveal these thoughts and aspirations because I would be discouraged and reminded of my duties. I am excited and curious. I want to…" Braxton paused and looked over at his companion.

Seiko was listening intently looking forward as he and Braxton maintained their pace. Braxton continued, "I must see the world. I must take part in that which is far removed from the confines of my family. Of course, I love my family and cherish them, but I must be able to leave them and venture out into the world."

"But my prince, it is my understanding that your family has been supportive of all you have done."

Braxton thought for a moment and said, "Yes, indeed, they have, but only those things of which I felt they could accept. They have not any idea of the plans which I have conceived and will one day pursue.

Plans they could never countenance."

The two men walked a short distance in silence. Seiko felt he could guide this young man and help him harness and maximize his many gifts. The teacher recognized that fueled with intelligence and ambition, the young prince was destined to impact his world in a very special way.

"My prince, may I invite you to come to my rooms as the sun rises tomorrow?"

Braxton came to an abrupt halt causing Seiko to stop and turn toward him. They faced one another, motionless. Braxton was not sure why he had been extended this invitation. He did know he wanted to spend time with Seiko. Braxton's eyes sparkled. He smiled, then executed a slight bow. They paused for a moment, contemplating one another, then both men simultaneously bowed. Without saying a word, the two men went their separate ways.

That evening a footman arrived in Braxton's rooms carrying a large beautifully wrapped package of delicate design. The outer wrapping was of subtle hues on hand painted oriental paper. It was tied with a silk ribbon.

The footman departed, closing the door behind him. Alone, Braxton took great care in unwrapping the beautiful bundle. Inside lay a folded, simple white cotton robe of Japanese design. Tucked within the garment he found slippers woven from reeds in the Japanese style. He marveled at the robe's subtle elegance. The minute detail in the handwoven reed slippers mystified him. Braxton inhaled, exhaling slowly. A simple but powerful serenity engulfed him.

———

Braxton awoke before sunrise at his usual time donning the robe and slippers. As the sun peeked over the horizon, the prince left his room through the concealed door and climbed the stone stairs slowly entering Seiko's rooms. He spied Seiko sitting on a finely woven reed matt—his legs folded, feet tucked neatly under his calves, hands resting on his legs, palms facing upward. His eyes closed.

Thus, began Braxton's education in all things Japanese. From that moment on he was schooled in the Japanese tongue, meditation, drawing, and martial arts. The training filled two hours every morning. Braxton embraced Master Seiko's teaching and became his devoted student.

———

"Richard," Mercedes said. "I think that our concern with Braxton's spending so much time with Master Seiko may be premature."

Richard put down his newspaper. "Are you sure, my dear? I think his behavior is odd. Hours each day with that mysterious man. It is peculiar behavior, at best." He retrieved the paper, rattling it, raising it to read again.

Mercedes sighed and leaning forward in her chair, "Richard, please give me a moment. I need your full attention. This is important."

"All right, what is it?" Richard said laying down the paper then tapping the nails of one hand on the table.

"I've noticed a change in our son."

"My goodness, Mercedes, what on earth do you mean? Braxton is special. We have known that for years."

"You are correct. But have you not noticed a bit less intensity? Not to say he is any less active. He is less difficult, or shall I say easier to be around. Less exuberant and possessed of a more pleasant manner when regaling the family and others with his goings on."

"Perhaps. Is that what is bothering you? This maturing?"

Mercedes' voice tensed and her posture straightened. "Obviously, this must have you concerned Richard, or you wouldn't be so impatient with me. I think you know exactly what I am saying. You must have observed it, of that I am certain."

Richard ceased drumming his fingers and reaching for Mercedes' hand just out of reach, she hesitated, then offered it to him.

Squeezing it gently, he said, "Forgive me dear. You are correct. I have noticed what I would call an improvement and as I said, a maturing behavior. Even Josh mentioned the other day that he has seen a leveling in his friends' temperament. Perhaps it is not only spending time with Master Seiko, but all his responsibilities with the railroad and the horses..."

Leaning forward again, Mercedes whispered, "Do you think he is well and healthy? Perhaps he is not prepared for all that he has undertaken."

"I think he is fine, my dear. Josh shared that our son is eating and sleeping as he always has after eighteen-hour days of non-stop activity. Nothing has really changed. Braxton is growing up emotionally, finally catching up to the genius he is." Richard smiled broadly at Mercedes.

She returned a shallow grin, nodding her head, murmuring, "I surely hope so."

―――――

When Seiko had completed the work for which he had been hired, Braxton retained him for tasks related to an upcoming trip to Europe.

Seiko took on the duty as Braxton's "Curator of Art and Culture." His responsibilities included educating himself in all areas of western art.

His first task was to catalog the family artwork, sculptures, manuscripts, and jewelry. The job encompassed spending long periods of time at Aurelio Palace, Renaissance House, Windsor Castle, Buckingham Palace, and Balmoral Castle. The prince, knowing that Master Seiko's understanding of Eastern art would complement the study of Western art, financed Seiko's studies. This included trips to London, Paris, Rome, Vienna, St. Petersburg, and Moscow. The Japanese artist was an able student and in short order accomplished the tasks to which he had been assigned. When family members queried Braxton regarding the purpose of Seiko's duties, he was bold and transparent. "Seiko is opening a window to the legacy of man's highest form of labor: art. Seiko will help me one day preserve and advance man's creativity and productivity in and beyond art."

―――――

The Prince and Princess of Wales, along with his brothers and sisters, departed Aurelio Palace for an extended holiday at the Chia-contella villa on the isle of Capri.

Braxton had declined the trip, claiming he needed to remain

behind to attend to his studies and horses. He had additional plans he did not care to share with his family.

The prince had always kept in the back of his mind his mother's attempts to draw attention to inequalities in education. He acted.

The week prior to his family's departure, Braxton had contacted his family's solicitors in London requesting they advertise for two teachers capable of instruction for children between the ages of six and sixteen.

Prince Braxton then asked his former tutors to assist him in designing a curriculum. They were also tasked with purchasing multiple copies of books covering literature, philosophy, math, science, history, and economics.

Prior to leaving for London, he asked the palace housekeeper to draw up a list of fabrics, sundries, and such, needed to make school uniforms.

He then journeyed to London to interview the individuals his solicitors felt were viable candidates for the teaching positions. Having filled the positions, Braxton returned to the palace laden with uniform fabrics, books, and school supplies. The aspiring educator felt it important that all vestiges of class distinction be removed in the classroom. What better way to achieve that by than having everyone look alike?

Two newly engaged educators attended Braxton at the Aurelio Palace one week following their hiring. Braxton commandeered the top two floors of an unused wing of the palace and had put estate workers to the task of converting it into classrooms for students and sleeping quarters for the teachers.

"It is the first day of class, and only four of the household staff's children have indicated any interest in attending the Aurelio Palace Academy," Braxton fumed, his voice echoing in one of the empty classrooms.

"Yes, that appears so, Sir," answered one of the instructors, Mr Everson. "Perhaps in time more will show an interest. If we have only one or two to work with, it is a beginning. One mind improved, one child's future brightened is a victory."

The prince paced the room, his hands clasped behind his back.

"I suppose you are correct. A small beginning, but a beginning, nonetheless."

"I beg your pardon, Your Royal Highness." Mr Hart, the other teacher said, standing in the classroom doorway. "We have a small problem."

Frustrated, the prince asked, "Yes?"

"The students have arrived."

"Pray tell, why is that a problem?"

Mr. Hart moved out of the doorway and let pass twenty-four boys and girls of varying ages.

15

THE JOURNEY OF THE BRIDE-TO-BE

Carmen's time was up. Six months had passed. She was to precede the family's arrival in Moscow. Carmen had deftly negotiated with her family and the government to alter her travel plans, insisting that she and the czarevich meet on neutral soil. The Austria-Hungary Empire was a friend to Russia more so than England. Vienna, the gateway to Europe, was selected as the meeting place. The betrothed would first set eyes upon one another at the Imperial Schönbrunn Palace. Indeed, there would be more than enough room for both royal entourages in a palace boasting over fourteen-hundred rooms.

Carmen extended her journey to Vienna by staying longer than planned at each capital she visited along the route. The British government had crafted the bridal voyage into a diplomatic excursion, representing her grandfather the king. She spent a week longer than expected in Paris. What was supposed to be a month-long journey to the various German principalities lasted six weeks.

Carmen's late arrival in Vienna would have kept the ill-tempered czarevich waiting weeks longer than planned, but the future groom also invented his own delay postponing his arrival in Vienna.

The czarevich fancied himself a warrior and champion of heroic proportions. A delusional fantasy propelling him toward one unfortunate incident after another. It had fallen on Count Maxim to keep his cousin, the czarevich, out of harm's way—to dilute and mitigate the embarrassment which could bring dishonor to the Imperial House. A taxing task ultimately proving impossible.

The young czarevich cared little for his impending marriage and thought the event an inconvenience. He did not lack for female companionship. Companionship on his terms. His behavior in matters regarding women was reputed to be rough and cruel. Many rubles were expended compensating those harmed by his indiscretions.

The self-absorbed heir to the Russian throne had reluctantly agreed to this match. His father, the czar, having threatened to imprison him at the Peter Paul Fortress if he did not honorably and enthusiastically embrace the marriage.

In a rage, the czarevich set forth from St. Petersburg, intent on reveling in debauchery, blazing a trail of illicit brutality along the way.

To his misfortune, his reputation preceded him. Ten miles outside the gates of Vienna, the czarevich delayed his arrival one more day. He instructed his equerry to secure a female companion for the evening

The officer, confident he had obtained and delivered a suitable person for his master's entertainment, took his post outside the bedchamber. All appeared to progress as was the norm, the sadistic prince, shouting commands, mocking his victim, and laughing uproariously.

The riotous night quickly fell silent following several piercing agonizing screams of pain emanating from first the woman and then the czarevich. This pain seemed frightfully more severe than previous encounters. The czarevich had never before howled out in anything but sadistic pleasure.

A groan followed, one not of delight, but of surprise—a sob followed by silence. Several minutes passed. He heard a rustling from within the room. Then all was quiet.

The chamber's double doors slowly creaked open. With both doors ajar, the woman emerged. She stood naked, clutching a knife to her breast. Her torso and legs covered in blood, she stared blankly ahead. Blood streaming from a deep wound to her neck ran down her arms, abdomen and legs, pooling at her feet. She teetered forward and fell to the stone floor.

The equerry slowly rose to his feet thinking how often he had felt the czarevich's behavior would end badly. Shaking, he braced himself against the wall, knowing full well the next thing he would see would be a dead czarevich.

Trembling and perspiring heavily, he stepped over the bloody female corpse sprawled in the doorway. He took two steps into the room. The equerry had seen violence and the mayhem of war before but had seen nothing like this. Not only was the czarevich dead, but he had also been dismembered.

———

Her Royal Highness Princess Carmen had arrived in Vienna the day before. Her tumultuous welcome by the cheering Viennese did little to assuage her angst. She had been immensely popular in Vienna six months earlier, styled as the "fairy princess" from a faraway land. She had returned to marry the man of her dreams, a future emperor, and she a future empress, or so the people had been led to believe.

The Austrian emperor and empress, along with their family, welcomed Princess Carmen. Princess Mathilde, Carmen's favorite, was also in attendance.

They held a private dinner in her honor, as the imperial family desired time with Carmen unencumbered by court protocol. The Viennese, renowned for their strictly enforced formal imperial court etiquette, were known avail themselves of any opportunity to escape the strict confines of the imperial court.

The family, through correspondence between Mathilde and Carmen, sensed Carmen's feelings of aversion to the impending marriage. Out of mutual respect and love, no one pressed her.

Sadly, Princess Carmen would perform her duties despite her feelings.

The next morning, following breakfast, Carmen and Mathilde went for a stroll in the Schönbrunn Palace's vast gardens, Schlosspark Schönbrunn. Their flowered cotton gowns trimmed in multicolored silk ruffled in the summer breeze. The ribbons adorning their bonnets fluttered as they walked, each clutching parasols in gloved hands, warding off the sun.

"Carmen, try to do your best to think favorably on the match. I know you have heard only horrible things about his imperial highness. But this afternoon you are to meet for the first time. What if you actually like him?"

Carmen stopped and turned to face her friend. "I know, Mathilde, you are right. But try as I might, I can only think the worst. I have spent six months dreading this day and the day I marry." Swallowing hard, she closed her eyes, struggling to hold back a torrent of tears.

Mathilde took her arm and encouraged them along in their walk and said, "You know, I've heard he is very handsome. He is not revered for his intellect or scholarship, but he is an accomplished horseman and hunter."

"Thank you dear, thank you for the encouragement. I will keep all that in mind and hope the people are right, that he is indeed my prince charming," Carmen said as she patted her friend's hand, looking resolutely forward.

Moments passed before Carmen spoke. "Would it not be wonderful should we be allowed to make our own decisions regarding who we would marry? Even, if we were to marry at all? Carmen smiled, turning to see Mathilde's reaction.

Mathilde cocked her head, smiling as she replied, "That would be too marvelous indeed. In an ideal world, who says I would marry a man?"

Carmen felt her chest tighten. She took in a breath, exhaling, she asked, "Mathilde, how long have you felt this way?"

"All my life. I have always felt isolated, even thinking about it. The church would think it blasphemous." She paused for a moment and whispered, "I have never revealed my thoughts on this matter to anyone. Are you offended?"

Carmen took her hand as they continued their stroll. "No, for I have had similar thoughts." She squeezed her friend's hand and said with a laugh, "We should book passage to the isle of Lesbos, don't you think?" Mathilde snorted, "That might solve your problem with the Cossack!"

They embraced each other and turned toward the palace. Carmen and Mathilde took note of the Austrian emperor and empress. They were deliberate, not strolling or meandering as was their custom, but walking briskly toward them. The girls quickened their pace to lessen the divide between them. They took notice of the couple's pained stares and that any color had drained from their faces.

The four met mid-promenade, the older couple looking directly at Carmen.

"My dear Princess Carmen," said the empress reaching for her hand.

"Yes," said the emperor slowly taking both girls' hands into his. "My dear, dear Carmen, we have some dreadful news, that which I am compelled to share with you."

Carmen shuddered, fearful that something awful had happened to a member of her family in England. She managed her emotions and said nothing, waiting nervously for the emperor to continue. "His Imperial Highness, the Czarevich, your betrothed, has met with a terrible accident and is, how shall I say it, he, has, he is dead."

Carmen and Mathilde focused on the couple and then stared at each other in total disbelief. Neither shed a tear, recognizing relief in each other's eyes. They turned their attention to the imperial couple. Carmen had not anticipated this turn of events and it was not in her nature to wish ill on anyone. She did not know what she felt, but she did know that she must present herself visibly inconsolable.

Oddly, Carmen would have to go into mourning for a man she had never met and had prepared herself to despise.

Mathilde pinched herself to repress the emerging smile rising from deep within her heart. Carmen would not marry. It was as if the heavens had opened!

———

Count Maxim, now heir presumptive to the Russian imperial throne, made quick work of covering up the truth surrounding the czarevich's death. It was not murder; apparently the prostitute had acted in self-defense. The count, first to arrive at the scene as the equerry was moving the woman's body back into the room, quickly assisted in removing all traces of blood in the hallway leading to the bed chamber.

The two men positioned the bodies on the bed, severed limbs and all. They poured the liquor cabinet contents over the bedding and the deceased, splattering the remaining alcohol throughout the room.

The count wiped clean the murder weapon and placed it on the table alongside the small dinner set for the occasion. Exiting the room, Maxim tossed a lit match on the bed where the bodies lay. He closed the door and returned to his chambers.

The equerry sounded the alarm once the flames had taken hold and smoke was billowing from beneath the door.

Fortunately for the Romanov family, all evidence of the crime was eliminated, the bodies incinerated, then crushed by the timbers supporting the two floors above. Unfortunately for their hosts, their manor house had been destroyed. Maxim would see that they were adequately compensated.

The count and equerry placed what human remains that could be recovered into a casket. Only some bones and dust were discernable from the rubble. They weighted the casket to affirm it contained a corpse within. The casket was permanently sealed, never to be opened. The equerry had repeatedly proven himself to be trustworthy, dependable, and discreet and would remain in Count Maxim's employ.

———

Carmen hoped to see Count Maxim, as they had grown fond of one another when their families had visited throughout the years. She was not to be disappointed. Maxim arrived the afternoon following the news of the czarevich's death.

Clothed in mourning black attire, Mathilde and Carmen strolled in the far corner of the Schlosspark Schönbrunn, having limited their candid conversations in the palace so as to not be overheard revealing their intimacy and being discovered. During their strolls they could speak frankly and openly to one another.

"Carmen, you know if they discover our intimacy, we may never be allowed to see one another again. Our families would not understand, and I would be devastated should we be forever separated." Carmen took Mathilde's hand in hers as they continued their stroll.

"My dear, I feel the same. We need, and must, have our private time together and be free to enjoy one another." Mathilde gently squeezed Carmen's hand.

Acknowledging the soothing affection, Carmen responded, "Perhaps this turn of fate bodes well for us both. We must get away together. We shall cite the recent tragedy as the reason we require rest and relaxation away from society."

The very idea of going away together stirred passion and excitement within their hearts. They turned to face one another, looking excitedly into each other's eyes. Moments later, they embraced, strengthened, resilient, and empowered by their mutual affections and the prospect of more time together. They began planning a hoped-for tour of the continent.

———

The palace gardens had been open to the public since the previous century. It was not uncommon to run into many familiar and unfamiliar faces.

Maxim's face stood out in the crowd. Princess Carmen took one look, then another, certain that it could not be who she thought. But it was!

"Maxim!" Carmen called, "It is you! Oh, I am so glad to see you! I thought you would be returning to St. Petersburg. Thank you, thank you, for coming!"

With that, they wrapped their arms around one another in a spontaneous act of comfort reacting to the previous day's event.

A curious crowd gathered. This was not Paris. It was Vienna! Aristocrats did not embrace in public. Princess Mathilde recognized the inappropriate display of affection. For her own reasons, she found great discomfort watching Carmen and Maxim embrace. She waved the onlookers away. Maxim and Carmen had been oblivious to the onlookers and Mathilde's actions on their behalf. Mathilde encouraged Maxim and Carmen to join her on their walk to the palace. Once inside, Maxim and the ladies removed their coats and relaxed by the fire in Mathilde's salon. The three huddled together on a sofa, Maxim in the middle, directly in front of the fire. Hot chocolate and pastries were presented, and the servants dismissed.

Maxim thought it best to reveal the details of the czarevich's demise. "I hope you don't mind, but you need to know the truth."

"The truth, Maxim?" Mathilde asked. "It was an accident. What else is there to tell?"

Carmen put one finger to Mathilde's lips, cautioning her. "Please tell us the truth."

Maxim raked his upper teeth across his lower lips and said, "It is shocking and horrible."

"Proceed, please, Maxim. There must be a reason you feel you need to tell us," Mathilde offered.

Maxim inhaled and grasped each of their hands. Speaking in a wavering voice, "The czarevich was murdered. Or rather killed by a prostitute who was in all likelihood defending herself."

Both women released Maxim's hand, eyes opened wide, gasping, bringing their hands to their mouths.

Neither spoke. As if mirrors of one another, they placed their hands in their laps, adjusted their skirts, and sat erect.

"Please go on," Carmen said in a hollow tone.

"You are certain?"

"We are, Maxim," Mathilde said.

"He had a history, one in which I am familiar and so often had the misfortune to have to cover up. A habit of wreaking havoc and pain wherever he traversed. It was my duty to hide his sins and compensate victims and their families when necessary. He was an evil man. The other night, his sins caught up with him."

"Maxim, it must have been devastating for you to see your future sovereign taken from you," Mathilde added, not entirely certain what she should have said.

"That would have been the case should he have been a worthy man. I spent many of my early years with him. We were fast friends. But he changed. I did not recognize him. He often acted deranged. I was, in fact, a caretaker to the devil."

In a consoling voice, Carmen said, "Oh my God, poor Maxim. I cannot imagine."

"It is God's gift that he is gone. The tragedy is that I am now heir presumptive."

The ladies were grateful the beast was dead and not about to enter their lives. What they had feared about the czarevich paled compared to his reality.

Exhausted and depleted, Maxim needed friendship and comforting. He had spent years fending off one crisis after another, beginning with the tragedy of war and the loss of his brother and father. Then assuming the burden of looking after his cousin the czarevich. The pressure and responsibility had been deeply stressful. As he sat on the sofa with Mathilde and Carmen on either side, he felt released from the years of torment and angst.

Carmen and Mathilde comforted him. England, Austria, and Russia's futures were physically and politically joined in that moment.

———

Prince Dominic arrived in Vienna two days following the news of the czarevich's death having reached him in Paris. Dominic had been on his way to function as his grandfather's representative at the betrothal. He greeted his sister warmly. He was devastated for all she had been subjected to leading up to the betrothal. And now, the unexpected death. He kept her company as she sorted her conflicting emotions.

Mathilde witnessed the warmth and affection for one another. She inwardly blushed acknowledging her own emotions, attracted to Dominic's kindness. She recognized the feelings she had for Carmen and now Dominic. Could he be a suitable match for her?

———

The czarevich's coffin was accorded full imperial honors and lie in state for seven days. A cable sent on behalf of the czar said he would journey to Vienna to retrieve his son's remains. His imperial train arrived on the fifth day of his son lying in state. Following services at St. Stephens Cathedral, the czar summoned Maxim to his rooms at the Schönbrunn Palace. He proclaimed Maxim his heir, creating him Grand Duke Prince Maxim.

With the death of her betrothed, Carmen had fallen from the heights of position and popularity to an object of curiosity. She was grateful for her new status. All she wished was that the funeral would end so she could go about her life, ‑a life that might include Mathilde. She had no intention of returning to England at this time. Her plan was to remain in Vienna and travel privately with Mathilde. She would find a way to take charge of her life.

The Grand Duchess Princess Mathilde was conflicted and confused. She cared for Carmen. The unfamiliar tantalizing feeling she felt distracted her. She made every effort to be with Carmen whenever she could. She asked herself, why am I drawn to Carmen? And what are my feelings for Dominic?

Giddy and terrified, the princess continued forward, embracing her confused state.

Mourning did not suit the Viennese royals. The period would be brief. Mathilde eagerly anticipated opportunities she hoped lay ahead.

16

EDUCATION & ENTERPRISE

Braxton had spent the two previous years completing his formal education, ensuring his tutors continued providing him the knowledge he felt useful. He had mastered many languages. He spoke English, French, German, Russian, and Italian daily to his family, tutors, trainers, and business associates, while also learning Japanese from his mentor, Master Higashino.

The ambitious prince continued making journal entries, improving his encryption so as not to have the journal easily read. Most people wrote about their thoughts and activities, but Braxton chronicled his plans for the future.

The prince was very attentive to his racing and expanded the breeding enterprise. His horses continued to be bred with the future in mind. He sacrificed instant self-gratifying successes for more long-term and promising financial dividends. Most of the income from the stables came from stud fees sourced from a transparent sharing of information with other owners.

Josh regularly updated a pamphlet that he and Braxton co-authored and sold to the racing set. It traced all current racing stock back generations. Its statistics were exhaustive in scope and contained copious amounts of substantiating data. As his racing competitors began to respect the information in the guide, they broke with tradition and brought their mares to the studs housed at the Aurelio Palace stables for breeding.

Once the railroad track was laid and the spur to the palace complete, the volume of stable business exploded. Braxton had his designers and engineers create railway cars catering to the transport of horses and their trainers. The boxcars were leased or sold to other horse owners. As Braxton focused more on his property development and railroad, Josh assumed the greater share and responsibility for the stables.

———

Prince Richard asked, extinguishing his cheroot in a porcelain dish, "Son, your mother and I have noticed an increase in traffic around the outbuildings housing the academy. Would you care to provide me with an update on those activities?"

Braxton had just entered the library, returning papers he had finished reading. "Yes, Papa. That would make sense, as the number of students has ballooned. It appears that not only the household staff's children, but the estate workers and tenants have been sending their children as well. It's quite amazing, actually."

"Can you afford this? It would appear the school has grown far beyond your expectations. It must require a great expenditure. Twice, perhaps thrice what you had expected. Please take a seat and spend some time with your father," Richard said, motioning to a chair.

Braxton grinned, taking the chair opposite his father. "Again, Papa, you are correct," he sighed. The young prince folded his hands in his lap. "The costs have piled high. I have had to take most of my earnings from the stable and apply them to the school." Braxton sat back in the chair and clasped his hands behind his head. "I am comfortable with the expenses. The railroad is providing sufficient revenue for me to pursue my other interests."

The generous entrepreneur originally envisioned this charitable effort as his way of providing for a useful education for those who would not be able to acquire it otherwise. He kept a close eye on each student's progress, consistently involving himself in tailoring the curriculum not just for the school, but for each student's individual needs and abilities.

The prince designed a curriculum that could produce graduates who would ultimately become the managers and supervisors needed to support his economic endeavors. He would offer well-paid employment with opportunities for advancement, and in some instances, accumulation of wealth. He was creating an education system that would serve as a feeder to satisfy his purposes. Many would prosper from this opportunity, Braxton most of all.

––––––

"Mother, may I join you?" Braxton asked standing at the door outside Mercedes' rooms.

She looked up from her magazine, removing her glasses and said, "My dear, please come in. I have just rung for tea. We shall share a cup together." She patted a cushion next to her on the sofa on which she sat.

"So, what is on that magnificent mind of yours? It must be important, as you so rarely visit me anymore. Not like you once did."

"For that, I must apologize, Mama. Please forgive me."

"I understand full well. There is nothing to forgive. You are busy harnessing the world. Now tell me, what is it that brings you here?" She smiled and rested her hand on his knee. "Please do not tell me you are here to visit. That would be so disingenuous and unlike you, my dear." Mercedes raised an eyebrow and offered a knowing grin, while handing him the cup of tea she had been preparing.

"Thank you, Mama. You are insightful as ever. I have a favor to ask of you."

"Anything else would be boring. What is the favor you know I will grant if possible?"

"Education. I want to broaden my education. You and Uncle Cosimo have the finest educations. I desire that same knowledge.

Please tell me more." He placed his cup on a nearby table and positioned himself at an angle so he could look directly at his mother.

"That is interesting. As you know, I have worked diligently to educate all my children. I have been successful with some of you, and not so successful with others. For that, I do not assume blame. One either desires and will strive to learn or they simply do not care to improve their knowledge. You are the former. Your education and your efforts far exceed your siblings."

"Thank you, Mama."

"However, your education is certainly not complete. It lacks balance. It is devoid of a deeper understanding of people. I trust Master Higashino is helping you fill in the gaps. But there is more." She adjusted her skirt and placed her hands on her lap.

"Please continue, Mama."

Mercedes inhaled, and pursed her lips, exhaling through her teeth. "When I was about three years old, I remember noticing individual colors. Different shades and hues, and how different types of light effected my senses. Instantly, I knew that color had variations and therefore, so must life. Something that I have never understood, and still perplexes me greatly, is that I can taste color. My playmates had no conception of what I was experiencing or how I thought. But Cosimo did."

"Mama, I too taste colors. I thought everyone did."

Mercedes smiled, appreciating her son even more than before.

"My brother and I were lucky to have a wise tutor. Also, as you know, the Villa Incantarre hosted a constant parade of intellectuals and knowledgeable people. Resident artists spent time with Cosimo and me. They led us through discoveries that served as a foundation for our understanding of the variations, causes, and effects of all we experienced. Today it is referred to as deductive thinking or logic. I'm not sure it had a name forty years ago."

"Tell me, exactly, how did they accomplish this?"

Mercedes relaxed in her chair, sitting back and assuming a contemplative gaze as she unfolded her story.

"I remember being fascinated by painting, complimentary colors, color combinations and primary colors. I was captivated when introduced not just to the many hues, but also shadowing and playing with different brushes having distinct shapes and textures. It was an instruction that encouraged exploration with few boundaries engendering an enthusiastic curiosity in both Cosimo and me. A desire to know more about art and exploring the masters.

As you know, our homes contained originals of many of the ancient and current masters. The family art collections are spread among various homes in Chiacontella, Rome, Venice, Capri, Paris, England, and

Germany."

Braxton placed his cup on the table in front of him, transfixed on his mother's story.

"Every two or three years our family would journey throughout Europe, visiting our homes and experiencing the respective cultures of those countries we visited.

"The Chiacontella business also maintained a sophisticated information network designed to keep Chiacontella banks up to date on all aspects of culture, economics and politics throughout their world. You see, we learned about how our family's business operated, as well as how business and art impact our world.

"That is essentially how it happened. I wish your father and I had been able to provide the same for you, but our responsibilities to the crown prevented that from happening. We have done the best we could."

"Mama, certainly, you have. However, I feel left behind. I am behind. Will you help me? Will you help me complete my education to include the special knowledge you and Uncle Cosimo received?"

Mercedes gazed with loving amazement at her precocious son. "I will, Braxton. Shall we commence with your studies? There is much to learn."

———

Braxton was approaching his majority. His quest for knowledge took on a new urgency. He was aware of his Uncle Cosimo's intelligence gathering network, though he had never seen an intelligence report.

He wanted to be trained and educated so that he too could one day avail himself of that knowledge. Braxton knew that he would require access to inside information to build his own network one day.

His studies of ancient history had exposed him to the overwhelming superior power to be had accessing information. He remembered the poignancy of what he had learned from millennials old Persian and Greek battles. The story of Troy and the gift of the horse to the Trojans was a hallmark of knowledge and trickery. So much of what he absorbed, be it myth or truth, Braxton sensed he might one day find useful in his own life.

He pondered the Medici spy network. He also marveled at what Richelieu and Mazarin had accomplished with their informants. History contained so many parallels to these stories, and the most recent information belied rumors the Rothschild banking and intelligence networks were spreading like a spider's web throughout Europe.

Braxton was confident that the Chiacontella network was comparable and as expertly embedded throughout Europe.

———

Princess Mercedes had written to her brother Cosimo asking what his thoughts were regarding Braxton's education in these matters. Cosimo had anticipated the opportunity and had provided Braxton's tutors with material for him a full six months prior to receiving her letter. It was this material that had kindled Braxton's interest in the European scene. Cosimo directed Braxton's attention to what was happening on the continent. Soon the prince realized what his Uncle Cosimo had done, and he was grateful and impressed. Braxton incorporated the knowledge of European banking and intelligence into his own studies. Insatiably curious, he required no encouragement.

Braxton and Aramis spent a lot of time together. Their education included studies in England and throughout Europe. They visited all the European countries and their capitals. They were received and hosted by the important houses, many of which were related to one or both families. They studied cultures, economies, and politics.

They engaged in daily reading of scientific journals, often meeting the authors of the journals' articles firsthand. Mercedes and Cosimo facilitated many of the more philosophical and spiritual lessons, while tutors from the Chiacontellas' vast contacts in the intelligentsia would participate in more obtuse subject matters.

Over four years, Braxton assimilated most of what his mother and uncle had learned over a ten-year period in their youth. At his age, his formal education exceeded that which any university could offer. His tutors were given an opportunity to transition to his business team and appointed to positions commensurate with their skills. He had more than enough work for the newly designated administrators.

———

Armed with experience and information, Braxton began the process of designing train cars that could carry large and heavy freight. He studied wagons, ships, and canal barges, desirous that his freight cars exceed the individual and collective freight capacity of all of them. His freight cars were designed to be easily modified to meet the transport of diverse types of cargo. They were larger and more efficient than any other freight-carrying cars and designed to load and unload faster utilizing less manpower. The train was configured to travel long distances. It was self-contained and carried sufficient spare parts to refit the train while in transit. The train carried tools, skilled men, and engineers utilized for projects on and off the train. Braxton prepared for multi-year trips originating in France taking him further than most could imagine.

The young entrepreneur's financial fortunes continued to grow. His income from the stables and the railroad sufficed to finance the operation and provide him with a very comfortable living. The revenue from the railroad had been substantial enough to build his private trains and finance his property development along the rail line from London to Aurelio Palace. A large part of his capital came from the partial ownership he had acquired in every facility, factory, and endeavor located on his land.

For three years his net income had exceeded two hundred and twenty-five thousand pounds and was still growing. As he prepared to depart for his European odyssey, he had accumulated capital in excess of two million pounds Sterling.

Only the London Chiacontella Bank was aware of the size of his fortune. His line of credit was credentialed at all the Chiacontella branches throughout Europe and as far away as St. Petersburg.

Unintentionally, Braxton had caught the attention of the government. Their curiosity had been piqued when he won the Queen Anne Stakes. The winnings were substantial and as a mere boy, they wondered, how he had accomplished such a feat at such an early age.

He once again came to their attention when he had acquired a substantial interest in the railroad. He had not won enough money at the track to afford the purchase. How had he come to control a railroad before reaching his majority?

The Prime Minister called on the Prince of Wales to discuss this anomaly.

"Your Royal Highness, I hope you will forgive me for broaching a rather delicate subject."

"What is it, Prime Minister?"

"The government is a bit flummoxed as to young Prince Braxton's activities. He seems to be all over the board with the horses, the railroad and now land development. We have heard he is planning on manufacturing railroad equipment on the continent."

"Yes, how may I assuage the governments concerns?"

The prime minister stood and paced the room. "We are concerned His Royal Highness, as a member of the royal family, could be involved in conduct that might embarrass, or even worse, compromise the royal family and the government."

Prince Richard said, "That must give you and the government sleepless nights. You need not worry. I have full confidence in my son's activities."

"How can that be, Your Royal Highness? Catching himself for what might be construed as insolence, the minister said, "I beg your pardon,

Sir."

Not visibly annoyed, Richard answered the not well articulated question, "The prince has been providing the king and me weekly reports on all his activities since he purchased his shares in the railroad.

My father and I threatened to annul the transaction and take charge of all his assets if he did not agree to keep us informed. He acceded to our terms and has remained faithful to them. Perhaps I should have informed you of our arrangement."

With a sigh of relief, the prime minister said, "The government is fortunate the crown has acted so wisely in keeping watch over the prince."

Richard continued, "What is truly remarkable is Braxton having sought our counsel. He has certainly made believers out of us in his miraculous abilities to generate profits. He is indeed a visionary. He is honest and fair. You must have heard about his underwriting the academy."

"Yes, indeed. He appears to be quite exceptional," the prime minister agreed.

"Exceptional in what way?" the prince asked.

"I beg your pardon, Sir. Please disregard my last statement."

Braxton was in residence at Renaissance House when the prime minister met with his father. Prince Richard summoned his son.

Braxton extended his hand to the prime minister as he entered the room. "It is a pleasure to see you again, Prime Minister. I believe the last time we spoke was at the races, or was it at my grandparent's garden party? Regardless, it is a pleasure." He beamed. "What may I do for you,

Father?"

"The prime minister and I have been discussing your activities, and how they might impact the crown and the government if things should go awry."

"How could my activities be of such concern to the government?" Richard grunted and said, "Suffice it to say, the prime minister has his concerns. I have taken the liberty to disclose your habit of making weekly reports to your grandfather and me."

"Excellent, Father! I suggest you share the lot with him. You have kept copies, yes? If not, I have copies."

The prime minister, standing, folded his arms and said, "You would share those with the government?"

"Why not? I share them with my grandfather, the king. We are all on the same side, is that not correct, Sir?"

"Yes, we are," the prime minister said, now pacing the room.

Braxton and his father exchanged knowing grins and watched the prime minister walk about.

"What say you about sharing those same updates with the government? What I mean is when you are traveling in Europe. Your Royal Highness could do your country a great service updating us on the things you casually observe."

"Oh, like the eyes of the government in Europe?" Braxton asked.

"Well, more like a diplomat. We could appoint you Royal Ambassador at Large, Emissary of the King. No real responsibility, but access and diplomatic immunity."

"That sounds interesting. I would appreciate your allowing me to consider your request."

———

Keenly aware the prince had no experience in diplomacy, the prime minister planned on assigning a career diplomat to the mission. He would now have a royal representative traveling throughout Europe with access to everything and everyone. Braxton's weekly reports could become an invaluable source of information for the government.

For a long time, Braxton had been providing reports that only revealed what he wanted to share; so too would be the case with the dispatches to the government. Braxton would only reveal what he thought germane.

The government had taken the bait. Years ago, Braxton had planted the seed. His regular reports to his father and the king had been the first step in securing the crown's and the government's support for his future plans.

He had hoped for diplomatic immunity. His status as ambassador and envoy was a bonus. Only the king or his father would outrank him on the continent. It was unlikely their paths would cross.

17

ROYAL ENVOY

The King seized on his grandson's popularity and made a great fanfare of Braxton's appointment as royal envoy. The people had loved Braxton from the day he won the Queen Anne Stakes and his appointment as the royal envoy only increased their fervor. With youth, vigor, and intelligence that endeared him to all, he was their young prince charming. His authentic humility and charm were the lock and key that held him in their hearts.

The papers aggrandized the marvelous train he had commissioned to be built in Germany. The English design and German engineering had created a symbiotic pride and celebration between the two countries. Once again, Braxton used this opportunity to gain favor with Germany, a powerful foe and sometimes friend to England. He had made half a dozen trips to the Ruhr Valley to monitor and supervise the construction of his dream. The newly completed train met him and his party in Calais following his crossing the channel.

Braxton was immensely pleased with his creation. Two powerful steam engines pulled forty-five cars. Because it would be home for him and his entourage for a very long time, it had every necessity and convenience they might need. Aramis accompanied the new train from Germany to Calais, the freight cars filled with German-manufactured farm equipment.

Ramsey's connections in Spain helped Braxton and his growing staff secure a large contract with farm equipment distributors in Spain. The Paris branch of the Chiacontella Bank agreed to finance the equipment purchase and inventory costs until the equipment was sold. The Chiacontella Bank and Braxton would profit from margins on the sale and interest on the loan. All transactions were handled by the Paris branch. Braxton's name did not appear on any of the paperwork.

———

Rumors of Prince John's relationship with Lord Ramsey had been making its way through royal circles in England for some time. Speculation on the continent could severely damage John's reputation and his prospects for marriage. His proximity to the throne demanded that he too produce an heir. If his brother Dominic did not have an heir, it would fall to John to help secure the future of the dynasty.

Germany's ambitious future kaiser sought a husband for his only daughter, Viktoria Louise. His need to secure a hold on German principalities necessitated him finding a match that would not offend his fellow Germans, while at the same time provide the royal household with gravitas. Prince John appeared on the surface a viable choice.

The marriage was politically and militarily expedient for England, as Germany's impending unification and growing power was perceived as a threat to the English crown's power. It was also important to England's royal family, serving to quell rumors regarding John and Ramsey's relationship.

John knew his duty and outwardly embraced the match. A hollow space took the place of his heart and he withered inwardly. The playful light that was a large part of his soul dimmed. The moment he took his wedding vows, the innocence, joy, and effervescence that framed his life vanished. To Ramsey, he promised his enduring, but doomed love. But to his credit, John did not burden his new bride with his unhappiness of spirit. He nobly embraced the marriage to Princess Viktoria Louise and soldiered on.

————

Prince John's marriage to the kaiser's daughter had been opportune for securing trading and manufacturing terms from the Germans. John was more than willing to assist Braxton in his efforts to obtain German contacts for both manufacturing the train and for future trade. Braxton rewarded John financially for his efforts.

With John now married, Ramsey had no reason to remain in England. Having endured the loss of his beloved John, Ramsey soon joined Braxton in Lisbon, as he had no desire to return to England amid the memories and anguish of his lost love.

Viscount Ramsey delegated his commercial responsibilities at home to his younger brother. Ramsey could now focus his efforts on Braxton's business interests abroad.

Outside his duties as royal envoy, Braxton set out to use the opportunity to acquire transportation assets and long-term commodity trading agreements. As royal envoy and honored guest in Europe's capitals, Braxton would have entré into valuable, influential circles.

Not unlike the first train he had built and had left in England, this second train was luxuriously furnished and the quarters for his entourage were well appointed. Braxton positioned three private cars in the back of the train. From this vantage point he could observe what was happening around him whether traveling or stationary. The last car was for personal use, containing his bedroom, sitting room, and a small dining room. The next car featured his office and the boardroom, followed by a smoking car devoted to cards, billiards, darts, even a small piano and bar. A galley and staff dining room was next, followed by cars for sleeping, baggage, and staff working areas. Twelve cars housed Braxton's entourage. The remaining cars were for freight, water, coal, maintenance, horse boxes and equipment.

Never before had a train this size been assembled. Every car was painted in red, gold, and black to project the majesty of the King of England and Emperor of India. His Royal Highness Prince Braxton's train inspired awe in everyone he passed en route, reflecting the power of his grandfather, the king.

Braxton refused Parliament's offer to fund a large part of the trip. Desiring to hold the government at arms-length, he would not countenance strings attaching him to the government's minions. He was his own man, representing the crown and his personal interests. He would keep it that way. However, Braxton had given in to one demand; that of being accompanied by a courtier and protocol advisor. Braxton let Lord Ramsey choose this officer. Ramsey made it very clear to the officer that he was to perform the duty as an advisor to the royal envoy but otherwise, he should stay out of the way.

Ramsey subsequently selected a fellow aristocrat, an experienced diplomat to advise the royal envoy and entertain Ramsey. All parties were content with the arrangement.

Lisbon proved to be one of the shorter stops. The young prince was well received by the Portuguese royal family and, of course, had gifts from his grandfather for the king. Portugal was idyllic and Braxton would have stayed longer had it not been for the trainload of equipment destined for Spain.

After a week in Lisbon, the envoy's train journeyed on to Spain. While acquainted with the country only through photographs and books, Braxton was stunned to see how the entire economy was centered on agriculture, with little emphasis placed on industry. Spain was magical, beautiful, and rich in tradition. He was grateful for the opportunity to distribute equipment to this enchanting country and was also happy to load his freight cars with the most beautiful fruits and vegetables that he had ever seen. No doubt Braxton could turn a nice profit on the produce.

One week into his four-week stay in Madrid, he wrote his sister Diedre in Paris:

·   ·   ·

Dearest Diedre,

I am in love with the Iberian Peninsula. It is so beautiful. Magic echoes down from the mountains and onto the plains. If I were looking for a place to spend my final days, it would be España.

I have been a bad boy. I have been immersed in the company of beautiful Spanish women. Ah yes, the nights are pleasant and the fragrance of flowers wafting through the warm evenings often leads to seduction.

I rather think Aramis is jealous. Until now, we have spent much time working together. He does not know what to do with his free time. I suggested he find himself a señorita. I have located several!

But that is not why I am here! I am a man of commerce. I cannot believe the laissez-faire attitude that pervades this sleepy paradise. Perhaps half the populace works a full day. None of the aristocracy are familiar or at all acquainted with enterprise. At least in England we have an upper-class that embraces commercial endeavors. In Spain, one is considered a traitor to his class if engaged in commerce!

That has created a problem, but I think I have found a solution. As there are no trusted men of stature with which to form a commercial alliance, I have called on the British Ambassador for assistance.

Through some hard work and sleight of hand, I have founded the Royal Iberian Peninsula Trading Company, chartered by the Spanish king. We have made a minor nobleman chairman, chairman in name only. I will pay him a stipend to keep out of the way. His noble ass is quite content to function in that non-capacity. The real work is done by two of my former students from the Aurelio Academy. They employ the workers and run day-to-day operations. This trading company will coordinate trade between Portugal, Spain, and the rest of Europe. We will start with produce and seafood. I believe our Shakespeare would accuse me as descending from the heights as prince to that of a costermonger, but I digress. I am leaving four freight cars to facilitate the first shipments, though more cars will be needed. I have instructed Aramis to order six additional cars. Perhaps when I am in Paris, we can make arrangements for them to be loaded with product and sent to Spain. No reason they should run the length of Europe empty.

Speaking of Paris, I shall arrive within a fortnight. I require your assistance. Would you be so kind as to spread the word that a spectacular trainload of produce and seafood will soon be on its way from Spain?

Oh, and yes, as you well know, I shall require introductions to politically and commercially influential persons. You know the type. You know everyone!

What is this gossip about you and the German crown prince? Is it true? You must fill me in when I arrive. I am concerned.

You must admit, your German is 'gibberish', and you despise that odious German staple, cabbage. It cannot possibly work! Egads!

You know I love you, mountains high, just as you are.

Your favorite brother! Brax

————

Diedre was bright, well connected, and eager to see her younger brother succeed. She went on a marketing extravaganza, spreading word of the seafood and produce's imminent arrival to all her favorite hotels, wealthy friends, and fabulous restaurants.

During their travels, meetings, and socializing, Aramis often sat and stared at Braxton. The prince, noticing the stares, would return a brief glance and half smile, embracing their friendship and growing affection. Over time, Braxton would look forward to the warmth and familiarity of Aramis's stare. Both Aramis and he felt a mutual attraction but appeared outwardly to have not given it a second thought.

Braxton was quickly becoming a man of the world, though his liaisons were complicated by an as-yet undefined attraction to his cousin Aramis. It was not so much a question of whether one attraction was right or the other wrong. Perhaps what was appropriate was the attraction that suited one best. This dismissal of socially acceptable behavior had found its roots in Chiacontella-inspired education and philosophy. This unconventional orientation was far more Eastern than Western.

———

The train, loaded to the brim with produce and seafood, headed for Paris. Diedre had prepared the city for the arrival of the storied Prince Braxton's.

The Parisians welcomed them with great pomp and circumstance. His Royal Highness Prince Braxton, Imperial Envoy, found himself thrown into a whirlwind of parades, banquets, and receptions. The news of his political, social, and commercial successes in Lisbon and Madrid had preceded him. His graciousness and charm endeared him to the French. The grandeur of his train was enough to impress even the most cynical Frenchman.

Her Royal Highness Princess Diedre had done her homework and facilitated introductions to business-oriented nobility. As the French were keen on commerce, they were fascinated with Braxton and wanted to be part of anything in which he was involved. During his five weeks in Paris and while touring France, he had many occasions to assess the economic opportunities that abounded. It was here that Braxton set about creating the Français Holdings Conglomerate. He chose not to seek a royal charter, as the French were notorious for changing governments. He kept the matter private, seeking patronage from powerful families outside the government. Braxton focused on the wines, cheeses, and textiles. He also acquainted himself with military equipment and related innovations augmented by the Franco-Prussian War. Once again, he was never directly tied to commerce. The Paris Chiacontella Bank handled all his business inquiries and transactions. When Braxton toured factories and military facilities it was perceived to be solely in his role as envoy.

During his stay in France, Braxton purchased a magnificent home in Paris, investing heavily in its refurbishment. He clandestinely constructed a massive vault in the basement, planning to eventually use it as a depository for valuable items.

The prince's weekly reports were forwarded via diplomatic pouch to his father, the king, and the prime minister. These reports did not outline his business dealings but did, however, provide detailed political, military, and economic information useful to the British government.

Braxton's photographic memory allowed him to detail facts and figures that would be useful for decades to come. By the time he departed for the Benelux countries, he had provided enough data to revise Britain's perception of Europe, exposing the incendiary anarchist and militaristic reality that prevailed throughout the continent.

As Braxton departed France, he contemplated transoceanic trading. Knowing it premature to focus on this area, he felt it prudent to formulate long-term plans to exploit his growing and profitable business.

The prince wanted to learn more about the former British colonies. He wrote to the headmaster at the Aurelio Academy and asked that a graduating student be tasked with studying American commerce and trade.

Time spent in Belgium and Germany opened his eyes to a vibrant and stimulating world of manufacturing and commerce. He employed the Berlin branch of the Chiacontella Bank to research and present data on all areas of trade and banking.

Cosimo, Duke de Chiacontella, arrived in Belgium responding to an invitation extended by his nephew. Braxton, Cosimo and Aramis began modifying the business models more in line with the methods they saw practiced in Germany and neighboring countries.

Discretion was paramount as Braxton did not want to alert the powers of Europe to his personal business goals and aspirations. He thought it best to portray himself as somewhat of a dilettante enjoying the freedoms accorded to the royal envoy. Again, he went out of his way to socialize and revel in the courts of the Benelux countries and Germany.

During his travels throughout Germany, Braxton visited important princes, focusing attention on the kaiser and his ministers. When meeting with ranking aristocrats, he conducted himself as a dependable and serious representative of his grandfather's government and was hosted as the European celebrity that he was. Braxton toured the countryside taking advantage of opportunities visiting factories and military sites.

The young English prince humored the German princes playing to their Germanic pride and vanities. He was cornered and cajoled into seeing all that the Germans cherished and in which they took pride. His weekly reports were voluminous and exhaustive. Though not commissioned as a spy for the British empire, gathering intelligence came naturally to Braxton.

Late one evening in his chambers at the kaiser's male-only palace, the famed Sans Souci, the prince was taken unaware when interrupted by his host as he labored over reports. As the kaiser entered unannounced, Braxton feared the incriminating pile of papers on his desk would compromise his activities.

Purposely, he rose from his desk, feigning surprise, knocking over a carafe of wine onto his incriminating documents, destroying them.

"My dear prince, please pardon my unannounced intrusion," bellowed the intoxicated kaiser. "I did not intend to alarm and cause havoc, only to check on your well-being."

Braxton bowed to the German king. He then smiled, waiving off the wine-soaked papers.

"Perhaps it is warranted, your majesty, as I am frustrated. I am just writing a poem to a lady of the Spanish court. She is a beauty, and I find myself at a loss. The words are hidden somewhere within, but alas, I cannot find them."

The kaiser wore army trousers and was bare chested beneath his smoking jacket. He spoke through a cigar stuck between his lips, carrying two glasses in one hand and a crystal decanter filled with cognac in the other. "Look here, handsome prince, I have brought one of my finest Hors d'Age. I know you British are fond of cognac." His unsteady hand heavily placed the decanter on the table, alarming the prince.

"How kind, Sir. Thank you for thinking of me."

As the kaiser balanced himself by placing his hand on the table, Braxton poured two glasses.

"What would you say if I undid my jacket, for I have nothing on beneath it?" the kaiser whispered.

"Well, Sire." Braxton swallowed hard and softly said, "I would reach around, gather the belt, and re-tie it for you." He smiled with closed lips, staring into the older man's eyes. "As I would hate for you to catch cold." Braxton lifted his glass, toasting the captivated monarch.

The kaiser stood dumbstruck at prince's artful response, saying nothing.

Tearing himself out of his trance the kaiser responded, "Ha! Well said, clever prince,"

The two spent the next two hours discussing military matters, politics and eventually women, particularly the terror and heart-break that is thrust upon hapless men.

The kaiser eschewed women, including that of his wife, for the company of men. Braxton avoided any physical familiarity or intimacy with the kaiser. Though the kaiser who had spent the better part of the night drinking, implied a personal interest in Braxton.

In a much more sober state than his companion, Braxton was able to spar his way around the topic and used the opportunity to ply the emperor for information on his hopes and dreams for Germany. The longer they talked, the more details of consequence were forthcoming. Fortunately for Braxton, the kaiser was too inebriated to place Braxton in a compromising position. Around two in the morning, assisted by two footmen, the kaiser left Braxton's rooms.

The royal envoy worked into the early morning hours, reconstructing his report. The report contained additional information, reflecting what had been gleaned during that evening's conversation with the inebriated and forward monarch.

———

After his conversations with the German kaiser, he thought it impolitic to set up a trading company in Germany. Imperial ambitions revealed short term opportunity and long-term devastation.

The Hun was sure to thrust his kingdom into war. The braggadocio monarch had validated his imperial ambitions foretelling political and economic instability.

Prior to their late-night encounter, the prince had enlisted the kaiser to introduce him to those who might want to use his freight cars for transport. The Berlin Chiacontella Bank entered into contracts to carry freight, a significant volume of business.

The kaiser was delighted with Braxton having ordered twenty additional freight cars from a firm in which he held a financial interest. Braxton planned on leaving ten freight cars in Germany to transport manufactured equipment around Europe. They would hopefully return to Germany bearing raw materials.

The railroad equipment Braxton ordered appealed to the kaiser's ego, as he considered himself a patron of the handsome young prince. He intended to remain in Braxton's life and participate in some level in the prince's endeavors.

A week before Braxton planned to depart for Vienna, the kaiser came to him with a peculiar proposition.

"Prince! So good to see you. I do so appreciate your accepting my invitation."

Bowing to the kaiser Braxton said, "It is an honor, Sir."

"First, I would like to share with you how impressed I am with what you and the engineers have accomplished in designing your train carriages to adapt to varying track gauges. Brilliant! Well done! Such foresight in freight car utility!"

"Thank you, Sir." Braxton stood with his hands clasped behind his back. He suspected the compliments were not the reason for his having been asked to attend the kaiser.

"I have a gift. A gift that I am sure you will appreciate."

"You are too kind, Your Majesty," the prince replied disguising his suspicions.

"Care to take a guess as to what it might be?"

"I am not sure I do, Sir. Should I guess incorrectly, I might seem ungrateful, when in fact any gift provides cause for eternal gratitude."

"Royal envoy, that you are, I shall spare you the indignity of guessing incorrectly."

The king explained that he had a gift of two freight cars for the prince. In return, all he asked was that Braxton take the new cars already attached to his train and transport machinery onboard to Vienna. He would receive compensation for this service.

The request seemed simple enough on the surface. Braxton was in no position to decline the offer. It was not an offer as much as it was a royal command. With no other option he agreed to the request, confident he was being used.

The prince could not determine how and why he was being manipulated. When he expressed interest in inspecting the new cars and the machinery to be transported, the kaiser reminded Braxton of their plans to leave that afternoon for a three-day hunting trip. It was apparent his host did not want him to get close to whatever was contained in the gifted freight cars.

The Austrian and German relations had grown stale. The machinery was slated to be delivered to factories in Austria. That evening the prince outlined his concerns in his weekly report to the British government. He also noted his alarm at the increased intensity of uprisings by anarchists in Vienna.

———

As honored guest and royal envoy, he endured nationalistic and uber race ravings extolled by the kaiser and his minions during the hunting trip. However, his superior marksmanship momentarily gave pause, providing a brief respite from the German's venal self-promoting rantings.

Braxton departed Germany feeling as though he had obtained a valuable and essential education in the economy and politics of Europe. His reports reflected concern for the fragile balance of power. He was anxious about what could very well be a looming cataclysmic conflict of power, egos, and vanities. When members of the British government reviewed the reports, they were as alarmed as their author.

The prince was exhausted as the now fully loaded, forty-seven car train headed to Vienna.

He desperately needed rest yet wanted to know what was really being transported via his train to the heart of the Austro-Hungarian Empire.

Sitting in the eastern bound train, Braxton determined that what he needed was relaxation and a sense of security. He required a friend, and as was often their custom, he and Aramis retired to his private car for cigars and cognac.

"Brax, are you as happy as I am to be leaving the Reich?"

"More than happy. That odious, lecherous autocrat makes me nervous. I am certain he will come to no good. He is vainglorious, pompous, and has Wagnerian fantasies on the brain. If we had to listen to one more Valkyrie or Götterdämmerung, I would surely have died!

The man is mad."

Wryly smiling, Aramis teased, "So, you do care for him?"

Braxton tossed a half-eaten biscuit just missing his cousin's head.

"What has happened to your aim, old boy?" Aramis taunted

"I am concerned about our cargo. Do you think perhaps we have two Trojan Horses in tow?" The perplexed prince asked.

"I'm certain your fast friend the kaiser has something buried within that he does not care for the guards on the frontier to see. He has had his seal placed on the locks securing the various compartments. If we were to break the seals, it would violate international law. We must find a way to circumvent that. As this is a diplomatic train, he could put anything on it he likes. It is an interesting feeling, being played," Aramis mused, and then lobbed a grape into the air landing squarely in Braxton's drink.

"Really Aramis, you can be such an artful ass at times," Braxton drawled, bordering on drunk, clapping his hands three times.

"Thank you, my pleasure, cousin."

Like most evenings, they discussed the day's events and future plans. The two conversed about their upcoming trip to Italy and a scheduled holiday to Capri. The island sojourn would follow the required royal envoy's stopovers in Vienna and Rome.

Surprising himself, Braxton found himself gazing at the handsome Aramis. He longed to hold him or be held by him. Was it sexual? Perhaps he just needed to hold someone – anyone. Braxton's life was focused on his economic plans and that left little room for serious relationships

Aramis rose out of his chair, intending to return to his own car.

Braxton followed him to the door. Placing his hands upon Aramis's hips, he turned him about and gently pulled him close.

Aramis put his hands upon Braxton's shoulders, then let his hands drop, wrapping them around the prince's lower back. The two men caressed the other's eyes with their own. Their gaze remained unbroken pressing their bodies together.

With his eyes locked on the face just inches away, Braxton said, "I am going to kiss you, Ari."

"I shall kiss you back."

Braxton caressed Aramis's lips with his own. Exchanging breaths, they lingered. Tongue tips touched. First shyly probing, then both chests heaved as they explored each other's mouths. Passion rising, perspiration soaking their faces, light moaning turned into groans as they thrashed against the wood paneling.

Alarmed by the sound of creaking wood against wood, they stopped. Fogging the other's face with deep breaths, they exchanged one more kiss, deeper, harder, longer.

"That was nice, Brax."

"Yes, it was more than nice"

After what was but a moment, they disengaged and bid each other good night.

18

ESPIONAGE & VIENNA

Blue skies and verdant rolling hills stretched as far as the eye could see. Approaching Vienna, the heaviness of Germany lifted from their shoulders. Vienna would be so very different, society, theatre, and dancing!

The effervescence and grandeur of Vienna welcomed them with open arms. Braxton was well known and celebrated throughout Europe. Rumors flew in all directions he was on a quest to find a bride.

The Austrian emperor had sent a carriage carrying Princess Carmen and the Imperial Guard to escort the prince to the Hofburg Palace. Embracing his sister, Braxton whispered into her ear, "Darling sister, I have so missed you."

"Hi Brax," she murmured, squeezing him tight. "So happy you are here."

He smiled, stepped back, admiring his sister dressed in the very latest fashion of colorful silks and lace. Her broad-brimmed hat was festooned with feathers. "I hope you wear these beautiful things when you finally return to England. You will assuredly make London more attractive!" Braxton smiled and bowed.

"Really Braxton, now I know you are indeed a tonic!" Carmen

blushed offering her hand; her brother assisted her into the open carriage.

Their ride to the palace took considerably longer than anticipated, as the crowds were enthusiastic. Carmen had grown a little taller and more beautiful. She had adopted Viennese fashion, as she was elegantly but not overdressed in a drapery of multi-colored pastel chiffon, emphasizing a young and winsome figure.

She personified the grace and beauty of a royal princess. Her Chiacontella light olive complexion and sparkling blue eyes framed by blond ringlets about her face captivated all who gazed upon her.

Braxton too, had grown taller. He was now six feet tall. While his attire was fashionable, it was not Viennese. His similar facial features and blond wavy hair complimented his sister. He approved of the Viennese style. Waving to the crowds, Braxton said, "You know Carmen, I love the Viennese couture. Perhaps you can locate a tailor for me."

"My pleasure dear brother. The court is full of gadflies. Though the well-dressed gentlemen will most certainly desire to not be outdone by my handsome brother," Carmen giggled.

"Well, I shall embrace the challenge and risk being ostracized, risk it, for fashion's sake, of course," Braxton said, laughing as he spoke.

The English duo arrived at the Hofburg Palace amid military bands and flourishes most often reserved for a head of state. An eighteen-gun salute signaled to all that His Royal Highness Prince Braxton had returned.

The young prince was somewhat taken aback with the commotion created by his arrival. "Carmen, what is this all about? They are cheering as if I were king, which I am not." He squinted into the sun and held his hand shielding his eyes. "It appears as if the entire palace household has turned out."

"Brother, you are his royal highness and royal envoy. You are our king, at least in Vienna. You are also a distraction. Austria-Hungary, and particularly Vienna, are not past the horror and embarrassment brought on by the death of the czarevich. And now they have the anarchists as well."

The prince mused out loud, "That stands to reason, I suppose. Rather thrilling, all the same. It has been a couple of years since his death. Interesting. I have a lot to share with you. Please find time to talk as soon as all this folderol has passed."

"I'll come to you after you have settled in."

The facade of the oval-shaped grand entrance was festooned in the Imperial Austrian-Hungarian black and yellow national flag, alternating with the English Imperial Union Jack of red, white, and blue. Trumpeters lined the rooftop balustrade in splendid uniforms trumpeting the royal envoy's arrival.

Disembarking from the carriage, the prince and princess stood at attention as the Imperial Guard Band played the British national anthem.

The prince and princess continued on to the imposing entrance of the Hofburg Palace, traversing a crimson carpet bordered with a gold Greek Key pattern.

Entering the palace, Princess Carmen whispered to the prince, "Brax, just to remind you, the Viennese are wed to formality. Please keep that in mind. Remember, you are grandpapa's representative."

He acknowledged the warning, his heart sinking. He remembered how he had dreaded experiencing the stifling Viennese court once before. But alas, he was buoyed by the thought of spending time with his dear Carmen.

"Really, Carmen, you are treating me like a schoolboy."

She took his hands in hers and kissed him on each cheek. "I will see you soon."

They were received in the entrance hall by the Grand Master of the Court. He brought greetings from the emperor. Following a brief ceremony, the prince, accompanied by his sister and an adjutant, was ushered to his suite of rooms.

———

Braxton stood at the window, alone in his suite, overlooking the parade grounds. A knock sounded on the door. A footman entered the room.

"Her Royal Highness, Princess Carmen."

Carmen swept into the rooms. She curtsied and said, "Hello, dear brother. Alone at last. Come, let us find a corner where we shall catch up, far away from prying ears."

Carmen's face glowed. No sign of mourning, and no sign of loss. "Finally, I can discard this charade of mourning the demise of the monster. You and Mathilde are the only ones, well Dominic too, who know I am celebrating my loss. How terrible of me," she sighed.

"Again, Carmen, it has been over a year since his passing."

Fanning herself Carmen said, "Let us change the subject, shall we?"

She continued, "You know, our dear Ekaterina's Maxim has been so wonderful. We correspond often. You do not remember him much, but he has been a dear. You must find a way to spend time with him." She giggled and continued, "He is almost a generation older than us. It is hard to believe. He has been like a brother to me." She paused for a moment and looked down at her hands. "I really do not want to get into the details, but he'd had quite a burden looking after, well, the deceased."

"I understand. I look forward to seeing him. Now, tell me. What are your plans? Are you going home to England?" "No!" Carmen said, defiant, sitting up.

Braxton too, sat up straight. "What? When are you returning?"

Clenching her fists in her lap, Carmen said, "I am not returning in the foreseeable future. Father cabled his permission. Of course, I would have remained regardless. Dominic must have warned him of my mindset when he returned to England."

"What are you going to do?"

"Just as I have been doing, traveling. Traveling with Mathilde. We might meet Dominic in Paris. You should join us if you can. We would so enjoy getting back together in that marvelous city."

"Well, sister, it appears you have your mind made up."

"I have, now shall we move on to other matters? I am particularly interested in hearing about all your romances and the damsels you have left in your wake crossing the continent," Carmen smiled, her eyes gleaming.

Braxton moved closer to his sister. "Carmen, I had a most unusual experience in Berlin. The kaiser behaved strangely the week before I left. He acted a bit peculiar most of the time. But this was different."

Carmen confided in a whisper, "You know, I have heard he is odd. The Austrian emperor and court despise him and certainly do not trust him. He has spies all over Vienna."

Braxton went on to explain the mysterious gift of two freight cars he had not been allowed to see before or after having been loaded with the consignment of machinery for delivery to Vienna.

Carmen stared wide-eyed at her brother. "While strolling with the emperor the other day, he shared his concern that the kaiser was supplying guns and ammunition to the anarchists here in Vienna and elsewhere. Do you think the freight cars might contain guns for the insurgency?"

Braxton looked nervously around the cavernous, gilded room, returning his gaze to Carmen. "That, I do not know. I guess whatever he may have had me inadvertently smuggle into this country is hidden amidst the legitimate cargo."

Carmen explained that if he had in fact used Braxton and his royal envoy status to pass through customs, they were in great danger. Should the emperor find smuggled weapons on Braxton's train, it could be considered an 'Act of War,' one perpetrated by their grandfather the king and the British government.

They both experienced a chill contemplating the potential ramifications of their predicament. Austria-Hungary at war with

England! A conflict created by Prince Braxton and Princess Carmen. There was a high probability it could also lead to fueling the antimonarchist movement. Such perceptions could, at best, disgrace the family, or perhaps topple the British monarchy.

They sat silent for several moments.

"Carmen, do you have anyone you can trust to take a message to the train?"

Carmen thought for a moment. "I have with me an army major

who has been assigned to protect me and supervise the small contingent sent with me by grandfather. He appears quite trustworthy. Why?"

"Please have him come to my rooms. When you speak with him, make certain others hear the purpose of my invitation is to familiarize me with court etiquette and opportunities to explore Vienna."

Within an hour the major arrived at Braxton's rooms. He epitomized the classic British officer. He was tall, handsome, confident, and polished. He gave the impression he had been battle-tested, projecting the capacity to handle any task.

Braxton breathed a sigh of relief. "Major Barret, thank you for responding to my invitation."

Bowing, the major answered, "It is my pleasure, Sir. I look forward to fulfilling any requests you may have."

The prince and the major devoted a considerable amount of time discussing those topics which he had told his sister to spread throughout the palace. He also inquired of the Spanish Riding School of which he wished to familiarize himself. His love of horses left him intrigued and enamored with the Lipizzaner stallions.

"Major, my uncle, Cosimo, Duke de Chiacontella has often spoken of the Imperial Library."

"Yes, Your Highness, it is, in my opinion, one of the wonders of the continent. I spend many hours there. Her royal highness, the princess, makes that possible, as she also spends entire days in the library." "Excellent! Please let me accompany you during your next visit. Now for the more mundane." Etiquette, Vienna-style, and so much more was discussed. Two hours into their conversation he led the major onto the terrace adjoining his rooms, out of earshot of potential eavesdroppers. They spent another hour quietly talking, formulating a plan they would soon execute.

Braxton whispered, "As royal envoy and on the authority of the king, I command you to perform the specific tasks which we have discussed."

The major whispered, "Yes, Your Royal Highness. God save the King."

———

Carmen and Braxton were standing in the marbled hall outside the entrance to the imperial throne room. Carmen, crowned with a shimmering tiara of blue sapphires and white diamonds, was exquisitely dressed in an off-the-shoulder gown exposing her olive skin, adorned by a brilliant necklace of three hundred small diamonds cascading from the top of her neck to the top of her low-cut gown.

Her stunning gown of shimmering pearl-white silk was embroidered with silver and spiraling blue threads accentuating her waist. The silver embroidery bursting outward from her waistline looked like a star radiating outward and down to the floor. The matching six-foot train enhanced her stature as princess royal, sister to the imperial royal envoy. Long pearl-white gloves completed the ensemble.

Braxton was dressed in the official court attire of the Court of St. James. The tailcoat was embroidered with a heavy gold thread covering the front of the jacket from the tall, stiff tight-fitting collar to the waist and extending to the bottom of the coat. The coat's wide cuffs mirrored the heavy embroidery on the jacket. A ceremonial sword, plumed cocked hat, and white gloves accentuated this masculine couture. Braxton's height enhanced the impact of the British imperial court attire.

Forty-foot-high doors leading to the imperial throne room opened slowly, revealing the glamourous pair standing side-by-side. A trumpet fanfare sounded, accompanied by, "His Royal Highness, Imperial Royal Envoy, Prince Braxton!" Braxton stepped forward. Following a slight pause, "Her Royal Highness, Carmen, the Princess Royal!" Carmen followed two steps behind Braxton and to his right. The courtiers, lined up in the throne room, gasped in admiration of the royal siblings. At that moment, Braxton and Carmen personified the British Empire, the most powerful nation on earth.

After the Emperor had received Braxton's credentials and he had been formally welcomed to the imperial court, there followed a state ball and banquet. Braxton and Carmen represented their grandfather, the king, with aplomb and sophistication that was appreciated by this formal assemblage of nobles and notables. The Viennese imperial court prided itself on their renowned formality. They eagerly embraced the young royal siblings as their own. The evening continued into the early morning hours.

As soon as the emperor and empress had retired, Braxton returned to his suite of rooms, dismissed his valet, and changed into dark traveling clothes. Major

Barrett, similarly dressed, let himself into the suite. Braxton spoke not a word motioning the major to lead on. Major Barrett led the prince through the dimly lit back stairs and passages emerging into the open air at the back of the palace's service wing. All was quiet, excepting the gentle pawing and snorting of four large black horses held by Master Seiko and Count Aramis. The four men mounted their steeds and quietly walked the horses along the gravel path exiting the palace grounds

The men were ignored by the guard as they passed through the gate. The inattentive guard had been compensated to see and say nothing. None of the four were recognizable as they were obscured by the moonless night and dark shadows.

The prince had instructed his staff not to move the train from where it had arrived the previous day. As royal envoy with Imperial diplomatic privileges, the train was considered English territory. Diplomatic status made the train untouchable. Braxton was enough of a realist to know that law and reality were not necessarily the same. In his instructions to the major earlier that afternoon, he had included notifying the train master to post a light guard on the train, far removed from the cars the kaiser had 'gifted' him.

Braxton wanted to avoid putting the lives of his men in unnecessary danger. He was not directly familiar with the level of temerity with which the anarchists might exhibit should they in fact, be involved.

Exiting the palace grounds, the four increased their pace and headed toward the train. Their path took them through winding streets and alleys. Seiko led the way avoiding the curious.

They dismounted and secured their horses in a grove a quarter mile from the train. Seiko led them stealthily through the grove and into the yard. Their movements were muffled by sounds emanating from the vast railroad complex.

Arriving at the back of the train they were startled by sounds of crates being unloaded off the train and loaded onto wagons. The sounds were not distinct. Anyone unaware of what might be happening would assume that these sounds emanated from work being performed elsewhere in the railroad yard.

Instinctively, they threw themselves to the ground. Seiko signaled them to stay in place. He then moved forward, keeping low to the ground. His cat-like grace made him less visible to the three the further he crawled towards the sounds of suspicious activity. Several minutes passed as the three motionless men wondered what lay ahead. Ten minutes into the wait their curiosity turned into impatience. None were accustomed to waiting and not being in positions of control and action. Two minutes later Seiko quietly approached from their rear. He had not retraced his steps to avoid alerting anyone that may have suspected his earlier movements.

Whispering, Seiko said, "There are four wagons being loaded with rifles and munitions. It appears the items have been concealed in false floors and ceilings in the freight cars. They are accessed from the top of the train and from underneath the train carriage. The German machinery we were asked to transport has not been moved. I had an opportunity to inspect the concealed compartments when the men were loading the weapons onto the wagons. The compartments run the length of each of the two cars. They are each about two feet high. All the rifles are bundled to fit in the concealed spaces. There must be at least fifty bundles of ten rifles each on both cars. I cannot calculate the amount of ammunition."

Braxton's worst fears had been confirmed.

Major Barret asked, "Are they wearing uniforms?"

"No, Major," Seiko said. "They may be dressed as laborers, but they are well-trained and are working efficiently. Oddly, no guards are posted."

Major Barret said, "That will work to our advantage."

Braxton had to see for himself. "Major, Aramis, go back to the horses and make ready for us to follow the wagons. Master Seiko, you and I will take another look."

As Braxton and Seiko crawled alongside the train, the gravel stones punished his hands and knees. The sharp pang was excruciating. Calling on his martial arts training, he disciplined his mind to embrace the agony. He focused on duplicating Seiko's every move. Within minutes, they reached the two freight cars.

Men unloading the train had taken time to secure two of the wagons loaded with weapons and munitions. Canvas covering the wagons was concealed by mounds of hay piled ten feet high. Teams of workhorses were hitched to the wagons.

The crew continued to secure the first two wagons. Seiko and Braxton crawled up to the cars and Seiko showed him what he had seen. Braxton marveled at the engineering involved in creating these concealed compartments. He was not sure he would have detected them even if his request to inspect them had been granted.

Seiko and Braxton quickly withdrew from their vantage point. The returned to the grove where the major and Aramis, concealed by trees, were waiting on a knoll. The four men would follow the wagons to their destination. Unfortunately for Braxton and his men, the wagons filed out of the yard taking different routes.

Each wagon was manned by one driver. Reluctantly, Braxton split up his men, assigning each to follow a different wagon. They agreed to meet at the train later that morning with information as to where the wagons had gone. The four separated, following their respective wagons.

———

Braxton tailed the wagon as it meandered out of the city and slowly made its way through the outskirts. The space between him and the driver appeared to draw closer as the buildings thinned out. He kept his distance, hugging the side of the road, using trees and side streets to conceal his movements. Buildings soon disappeared, as did side streets, giving way to rolling farmland.

The mostly cloudy night and quarter moon were a curse and a blessing. His silhouette sometimes towered, standing out, particularly when cresting a hill in the open country.

"Get where you are going!" Braxton whispered to himself, impatient, sweat staining his collar.

The wagon halted. The prince froze as he found himself illuminated by the intermittent passing of clouds and bright moon shining on the flat open space. He whispered to himself, "What the devil happened to the moonless night?"

Braxton leaned forward and placed his head alongside the horse's neck. He gently prodded with his heels letting the reins fall. He used leg pressure on either side of the animal to influence its walk, causing it to appear to meander back and forth across the road, as if its rider were in a drunken stupor.

Clouds once again hid the moon.

The distance between the wagon and Braxton dwindled. The horse's coarse mane chaffed the prince's face. His lower back muscles ached. Soon his inner thighs cramped as he struggled to choreograph the animal's walk.

Forty yards from the wagon, the clouds parted, revealing the driver tying off one of the ropes securing the cargo beneath the straw. Twenty yards from the wagon, the horse stopped. The wagon driver looked toward the slumped Braxton and his horse, bent necked, grazing on the grass on the side of the road.

"Verdammt betrunken!" The driver said, as he turned and headed toward the front of his wagon.

It relieved Braxton to know that his ruse had worked. The driver did indeed think he was drunk.

The wagon started moving again. Braxton did not have to wait long for the clouds to do their work and conceal him. Confident the driver could not see him, he dropped off the back of the horse and stretched his sore legs. He took note of a soft glimmer of light on the eastern horizon. In the dark, he could hear morning birds greeting the day.

Braxton took the horse's reins in hand and followed the load of weapons on foot. The rolling topography soon gave way to small hills and vales. Reaching the bottom of one hill, he noticed the wagon lurch forward as the driver shouted at the team and snapped his whip. The pounding hooves, the groaning wagon and churning wheels shattered the early dawn.

Braxton jumped back on his horse and followed at a distance. The wagon soon turned off the road, almost tipping its load as it disappeared into a grove of oak trees. Behind the wood stood several sizeable farm buildings. Braxton hurriedly dismounted and ran into the trees securing his mount.

In pursuit of the wagon, the prince kept low as he dashed toward the buildings. Two large barn doors swung open. A bright light shot across the yard. The prince threw himself to the ground, his head planted in the underbrush.

The screech of ungreased hinges and wood slamming against wood signaled the door had shut. All was silent. He looked up. The yard was dark. The wagon had disappeared.

He made a mental note of the surrounding buildings and terrain and then crawled toward where he had left his horse.

Suddenly, anxious whispers and the rapid trampling of feet came from the barns. Hurtling toward him like a raging tsunami, loud voices and heavy boots pounded the wood's undergrowth.

One of his pursuers tripped over the crawling prince. Not waiting for the man to regain his balance, he drew his knife and scrambled over to the fallen anarchist. His stomach flipped, as he thrust the blade into the anarchist's neck, twisting the blade.

Braxton on all fours, jerked his head hearing footsteps close at hand. Someone yelled, "Hier ist eins!" Another man charged at him carrying a bayoneted rifle.

"Yes! You have found one!" Braxton hollered as he rolled several times, avoiding the glistening bayonet. The attacker bellowed,

"Scheisse!" His momentum having caused him to thrust the end of his weapon into the ground, burying it up to its muzzle.

Braxton withdrew his Enfield revolver and shot the radical in the head. The man fell backward as Braxton shot him again, shouting, "For good measure!"

Braxton rose to a sitting position. Two more men came at him.

Braxton fired, blasting a hole in one attacker's forehead.

The prince aimed at the second man and pulled the trigger. The Enfield misfired, the bullet lodging in the attacker's shoulder. Braxton discarded the useless weapon and charged the wounded man.

———

Prince Braxton awoke and looked up to find Carmen gazing at him from one side of the bed and Aramis from the other. The emperor of Austria stood behind Carmen and Seiko behind Aramis. Major Barrett was at the foot of the bed. Braxton took note of the animal heads hung from the wall and guessed he was in the Mayerling hunting lodge in the Vienna Woods.

The wounded envoy painstakingly moved his head to look directly at each person at the bedside.

Carmen was first to speak, "Braxton dear, we are so glad to see that you are still with us. We were fearful that the physical trauma you had suffered would... Oh, Braxton!" She gently hugged him as she placed her tear-strewn face against his.

"Braxton," Aramis said, "the emperor would like to speak with you."

The emperor, in a familiar manner not often seen, came to Braxton's side and took the hand Aramis was holding and held it in his. "Prince Braxton, my country and I extend our thanks to you and your brave men for foiling a plot that could have cost many loyal citizen's their lives. Please continue to rest and recover. For the time being, we ask that you remain at Meyerling. As you improve, my officers will continue to sort out the situation."

The next morning Braxton woke in less discomfort, suffering from a mild headache. Carmen, Seiko, and Aramis were in armchairs placed close to him on opposite sides of his bed. Carmen and Seiko looked up simultaneously to see Braxton stirring. They said nothing, allowing him to get his bearing.

Aramis placed his arm behind Braxton's back to lift him so he could take water. Having recovered some strength, he slurped the water vigorously and appeared to be aware of his surroundings. This development pleased Carmen as she and Aramis exchanged knowing smiles.

"More pillows please, I want to sit up."

Carmen provided the pillows, and both Aramis and Carmen worked together to place him in a more upright position. The four of them sat there for a few minutes assessing Braxton's rapid improvement.

"Thank you to all that have been here for me." He paused. "Now, please tell me what happened."

Major Barrett entered the room. "Your Royal Highness." He bowed to the Prince. "I am so glad to see that you are awake this morning. It is indeed good news."

"Thank you, Major. Would you please be so kind as to tell me what happened? I remember a fight with the anarchists, but little else.

"Sir, many things have transpired simultaneously. But, let me first update other happenings leading to our leaving the palace and heading to the train. I had delivered the information as ordered to the emperor after our meeting, per your instructions." Looking at Princess Carmen, he continued. "Princess Carmen had met with his imperial majesty before your throne room presentation. The emperor, after listening to your proposal, took the action you had recommended. As you know, the emperor left the ball at precisely the time you had stipulated. He and his troops then assembled not far from the grove where we left our horses.

Once we had separated to follow the wagons the emperor's men separated into contingents of thirty men. One unit followed the anarchists that had loaded the wagons, eventually surrounding, and capturing them, encountering little resistance. Fortunately, three of the other contingents were able to keep sufficient distance not to alert the drivers they were following. In those three instances, they coordinated with Count Aramis, Master Seiko, and me the eventual capture of the drivers and anarchists.

Again, fortune worked in our favor as there was no real notice taken by the surrounding communities. Munitions, guns, and a huge stockpile of additional weapons were seized. The government has confiscated the farms and property where the weapons were found. Persons living on the properties have been incarcerated. Guilty parties will be imprisoned. Others will be banished in accordance with the customary

Austrian treatment of anarchists and their families."

The major stood as the room's occupants took a few minutes to absorb all that the major had said.

"Your situation was entirely different, Sir. The contingent following you was apparently seen by the wagon driver. He hid his wagon in one of the larger barns. We do not know what happened to you after that, Sir. All we know is that Seiko found you lying unconscious next to three dead anarchists. We found your horse tied to a fence post 50 yards from your location."

Braxton struggled to adjust his position. Carmen and Aramis worked from opposite sides of the bed to reposition his pillows. He settled back smiling at his helpers. "Thank you."

"Major, I can shed some light on that… I followed the wagon to the area leading up to the barns." He exhaled and rolled his lips. "It was obvious that somewhere, somewhere among the farm buildings the driver would conceal the weapons. I felt it important for the emperor's police to know where the munitions were located among the ten or more buildings.

"As I followed the wagon on foot, I noticed an abrupt increase in wagon speed. I was not in the position to see what the driver had seen, but evidently that is when the driver discovered the emperor's contingent following. I took cover to evaluate the situation. I froze in place for not more than two minutes and observed the wagon enter a sizeable barn. The doors closed behind it.

I laid low for several minutes. At that point, I moved to return to my horse. Suddenly there was the sound of trampling feet coming at me. At least twenty men armed with rifles were headed in my direction. They could not have known I was there, but they must have known the soldiers were close. I had not gotten far when a man tripped over me. I defended myself. The last thing I remember was, well actually, I recall nothing. I think I fought, but I remember nothing more. Maybe that's why I have this welt on the side of my head."

Aramis volunteered, "The three men found next to you were dead. The fourth was badly injured. It appears you must have been paying close attention to Master Seiko's training."

Braxton and Aramis smiled at each other. Then Braxton's eyes closed.

————

The emperor had the Vienna social schedule rearranged to allow time for Braxton's recovery. Excuses were made that he had suffered a reaction to a food allergy the night of the ball. It was also offered that he had official duties to which he need attend. His affairs would occupy him for a week.

In the meantime, the emperor's secret police had rounded up the participants in the transfer of weapons and munitions. The leaders had been culled from the group. With persuasive techniques not unique to the police, they learned the scope and details of the mission. The interrogators had also determined the methodology in which the kaiser would have been notified once the mission had been completed. The Emperor's police followed the procedure. Eventually, the 'news' reached the kaiser, who was therefore led to believe his plan had been successful.

Braxton remained at Meyerling for seven days. During that time, he nursed his wounds and appeared to have been only temporarily incapacitated. His headache continued to diminish as his bruises and cuts healed. He used the time managing his economic and political interests as best he could and filed his report with the British government detailing the events.

Returning to the Hofburg Palace eight days following the accident, Braxton resumed the delayed series of parties, dinners, concerts, and balls previously scheduled.

————

"Brax!" Dominic said, surprising his youngest brother.

"Dom!" Braxton said spinning around from his desk in his Hofburg Palace suite. "Great to see you. It appears as though you have brought a great deal of excitement to the Viennese!"

Dominic clapped Braxton on the shoulder. "Maybe that is what they need. Some distraction from the anarchists. Anyway, glad to see you are in one piece."

"What brings you here? This is a long way to come."

Dominic answered, "The prime minister and the king, actually."

"Why? What for?"

"Carmen sent a courier updating grandpapa and the government on your escapade with the anarchists. First, they wanted to ensure you were going to live and then whether or not the government had been hurled into the middle of some sort of diplomatic crisis."

Braxton stuck his hands in his pockets, "Did Carmen apprise them of what had transpired?"

"She communicated as much as she knew. You were not well and had not been conscious much of the time when she posted the letter."

"Very well, brother. I appreciate your being here." Braxton paused. "Maybe you can step in for me a bit. Some of these social occasions are quite tiring and I am not totally back to myself."

"I am at your service, little brother. Happy to assist in any way I can."

"Dom, did grandfather and the prime minister read the report I sent several days ago?"

"I believe so. The report must have arrived after I had departed London. I received a cable when in Paris. It did not say anything other than the government had been updated and that you would provide me with the details."

"Hmmm."

"Take your time. Carmen brought me up to date on much of what happened on the way here from the train. Details can wait. In the meantime, our sister recommended I renew my acquaintance with Mathilde." Dominic smiled and cast furtive looks towards the door. "I do not know if you remember, but the grand duchess and I get along quite well."

Braxton chuckled. "I do remember. You two ought to get reacquainted." Braxton placed his hand on his brother's shoulder and walked him toward the door. "Yes, go find Mathilde. No doubt she will be happy to see you."

As Braxton saw his brother out, he said, "Dom, did Carmen say anything about her joining me and Aramis on our trip to Rome?"

"No, she did not."

"Well, I promised to get her away from here for a while. She will let you know of all we have discussed."

Carmen arranged for her older brother, Prince Dominic, to spend time with the Grand Duchess Princess Mathilde. Court gossip had been seeded with the story that Braxton and Carmen had encouraged the English heir, the second in line to the British throne to come to Vienna to further his friendship with the grand duchess. Thus, began their courtship.

Weeks passed; Braxton spent much of the time preparing for his trip to Rome. He continued to solidify his commercial trading interests in Europe. The entrepreneur placed orders for more engines and freight cars from Germany.

Concerned with the volatility of the anarchist-led resistance, the prince also decided it was wise to limit his interest in commerce in Austria-Hungary. He chose to focus his efforts on investing in countries having more political and economic stability. He also did not want his commercial interests threatened by a potential conflict with the German kaiser and Austrian emperor. Braxton felt ordering more equipment from the Germans would assuage any suspicion the kaiser might have, should the undoing of the kaiser's scheme be discovered.

19

ROME & A SURPRISE VISITOR

The train journey from Vienna to Rome in Braxton's luxuriously appointed cars was uneventful and pleasurable. Mathilde and Dominic had invited themselves to accompany Aramis, Carmen, and Braxton to Rome.

Princess Carmen joined Braxton and Aramis in his private car one morning as the trained wove through the Alps.

The threesome had worn out discussing their experiences in Vienna when Carmen changed the subject. "Aramis, it appears that you and my brother have acquired a deep friendship."

"Of course, we are cousins and excellent friends," Aramis said, his eyes widening behind the paper he was reading.

"Carmen, how long are you planning on staying in Rome?" Braxton asked, his head in a book, avoiding eye contact with the other two.

"Oh, not sure, and you two?" Carmen asked, probing shyly.

Braxton continued to stare down at his book, "I haven't any idea. It depends on whether we are enjoying ourselves and perhaps is dependent on you and what you decide to do."

Aramis peered from behind the paper, "I am taking Braxton to our villa on Capri, just the two of us. We are taking a month away from everything. You remember, you have been there with my family." He returned to his paper.

Carmen sipped her tea, raising the cup, balancing it as the train rocked on a curve prior to entering a mountain tunnel. The room darkened for several minutes as the train raced through the tunnel dug through a mile of rock. Wheels clipping along the track and the echoing sounds of the engine stifled all conversation. The readers placed their papers and books in their laps lost in their own thoughts.

Without warning, glaring sunlight startled the three as the train emerged from within the tunnel.

"Why that sounds lovely. Interesting, though," Carmen said continuing from where she had left off, placing the cup and saucer on the table in front of her. She smiled without separating her lips. "How so?" Braxton asked, his face a mask of concentration.

"It seems odd to me that two men would want to be alone on an island, far away from women, song, and dance." She cocked her head, smiled, and picked up her book.

————

Upon arriving in Rome, they were well received by the crowds and the pontiff. The nobility of Rome was more than enthusiastic and generous with their hospitality. It took every bit of the visiting party's strength and stamina to keep up the appearance of well-being and health, still recovering emotionally from the events in Vienna.

Aramis opened his expansive Chiacontella's villa in Rome to Braxton, Mathilde, Carmen, and Dominic. The camaraderie of this collective of aristocrats was warm and congenial. Aramis served as host until Cosimo arrived following a lengthy tour and inspection of various family bank branches throughout England and Europe.

Braxton stepped onto the loggia outside their suite of rooms overlooking the Spanish Steps. "Carmen, I have very interesting news. It appears Grand Duke Maxim is in Civitavecchia, on his way to Rome."

Carmen sat up in her chair and gasped, "Maxim? Oh my! That is interesting news. Do you know why?"

"Why what, dear sister?" he responded in a placid uncurious tone.

Carmen almost shouting, "Why is he coming here?"

"My dear sister, you are a bit overwrought," Braxton said, smiling impishly.

"Braxton answer the question. What do you know?" Carmen demanded, coming to her feet.

"Oh, just that he is coming to see you. In fact, I know that because he has written, asking my permission to call on you."

"Why would he ask you and not me?"

Annoyed, Braxton responded, "Carmen, because he respects you and our family. Quite often one refers to this as etiquette." Carmen paced the loggia. "Well, I'm happy to..." "Happy to what?" Braxton asked.

"Never mind, nosey brother."

Braxton had met Maxim on several occasions when his deceased mother, the Grand Duchess Ekaterina, had stayed with them at Renaissance House and the Aurelio Palace. Their age difference was such that he was more a contemporary of Braxton's older brothers, but time had all but erased the age difference.

Experiences the two men had lived through in the meantime had altered many of the beliefs and attitudes embraced in their youth. Both were now men of the world and keenly aware of their place in it. While Braxton was further removed from a throne than was Maxim, they thought much alike. Politics, economy, and military topics occupied them. Their friendship would grow, and they would learn much about the other.

The bond was such that Maxim was successful in convincing Braxton to extend his royal tour on the continent and visit him in Russia following his stay in Capri. Braxton wrote to the British government.

The king, his father, and the prime minister encouraged the royal envoy to accept Maxim's offer of hospitality. The government saw the opportunity was one not to be missed. Braxton's reports could be invaluable.

The English prince eagerly made time to return to his studies and training with Seiko. He also summoned his former Russian tutor, Count Konstantin Volkov from England. Prince Braxton and Konstantin spent a great deal of time with Maxim's entourage, wanting to improve his knowledge of all things Russian.

Braxton's interest in Russian culture caught Maxim's attention. The Russian heir apparent did all he could to further Braxton's education about his country and countrymen.

Both Prince Braxton and Princess Carmen enjoyed the Russian's company. Most mornings they would take walks in the Chiacontella Palace gardens to compare notes. The entire party would go for rides in the hills overlooking Rome, outings not unlike those their father, Prince Richard, had experienced over thirty plus years earlier.

Braxton's reports were full of information useful to the British. There was also plenty of news that he could use as he strengthened and expanded his trading companies. It was during this period he commenced purchasing interests in various manufacturing concerns.

Aramis was the liaison with the Chiacontella banks. Braxton's increased interaction with the banks was a byproduct of the banks serving as trustee of all of his interests throughout Europe.

The prince had another preoccupation. His grandfather, the king, was in declining health. He anticipated his father becoming king in the very near future. Only his two older brothers stood between him and a crown he did not covet. While he would not shirk responsibility, he dreaded the prospect of a life that would imprison him should he have the misfortune to be crowned. Prince John's German-born bride was taking her time producing an heir. Braxton had an odd premonition John would never be king.

His oldest brother, Crown Prince Dominic of Wales, had not yet married. Braxton felt compelled to do everything he could to support Carmen's matrimonial scheming advocating that their brother and Mathilde wed. He had lobbied the king, prime minister, and his parents to support the marriage. In his heart, he felt the match was good for the couple personally and advantageous for the two empires. Importantly, for his own sake, Braxton wanted the marriage to produce an heir.

Not long thereafter, news arrived that parliament and the king had tentatively approved the match. Braxton's fears of succession were assuaged.

Braxton began to have second thoughts pertaining to the growing friendship and intimacy between Carmen and Maxim. He adored his sister and liked Maxim. But he was concerned for his sister and what could be a tumultuous future. Russia had a history of not dealing well with czar's consorts. Their court was grand but mired in orthodox traditions and protocol that could imprison and stifle the intelligent, ambitious, and independent Carmen. Carmen shared his concerns. She would eventually share those concerns with Maxim. She was fortunate, as Maxim was more Western in his outlook than his Russian contemporaries.

Cosimo finally reached Rome two weeks after Braxton, Carmen, and Aramis had arrived. The prince was delighted and eager to spend time with his uncle. The older man would be an excellent sounding board.

As Braxton's economic tendrils expanded, he had become one of the Chiacontella bank's largest clients, as well as its most influential and well-connected. He was also one of its most complex. Braxton's economic interests were increasingly lucrative for the banks. Both fees earned and the information his network provided, directly and indirectly, contributed significantly to the bank's profitability.

Braxton insisted on paying fees commensurate with what the bank invoiced other clients of his size and complexity. He made certain the banks earned what they were paid, as he was a demanding client maximizing their services while requiring exemplary results. Braxton was also paying for discretion and secrecy.

Bank couriers arrived daily with portfolios filled with papers requiring review and being acted upon by the growing staff Braxton had in tow. The entrepreneur was also expanding his network of spies, not unlike that which the Rothschilds had mastered. He knew knowledge was power. Braxton paid handsomely for these services, often competing for the information with other business entities.

The prince insisted that he see the information before it was shared with anyone in the bank, including Cosimo.

"Nephew, I do not see why it is necessary for you to see the reports before anyone else, including me," Cosimo said.

"There are several reasons, Uncle." He leaned back in his desk chair. "I require unvarnished information. From that I can determine where it will be directed and how it will be used, if indeed it is at all useful."

"As a director of the bank, that is my job," Cosimo insisted, his eyes hard.

"It is my money that is paying for it and it is I who have commissioned the service. Am I not correct?" Braxton insisted, commanding a civil tongue.

"I do not feel comfortable not seeing it firsthand."

"You are getting it firsthand. Firsthand from me."

"Braxton, I think I know banking better than you. This makes little sense. Such an arrangement causes me great discomfort."

"Uncle, you and your bank are in one business, banking. I am in another. Our paths are not parallel, nor are they at cross purposes. I will have the raw intelligence and pass it onto you when I have reviewed it."

Braxton struggled with the dualities of his purpose, pondering, my loyalties lay with my country. I must protect the Empire's interests over the bank's and even my own. I must remain independent. At any time, the crown or the government could demand I return to England and abandon my interests.

Braxton stood. "Let us not quarrel about this. It is my decision, and I have made it." Braxton looked down and the table and then back at his uncle. "Will you abide by it?"

"I suppose I have no choice," Cosimo said sternly. "Your royal highness, with your permission I will withdraw." Not waiting for an answer, he left the room. The next day he departed his family's Roman villa.

———

"Maxim, do you think you might join Carmen, Braxton, and me at the Villa Incantarre?" Aramis asked as the two returned from a day of hunting.

"Why, why not? Why would I ever desire to be separated from this charming company? Besides, Mathilde and Dominic have returned to Vienna."

"I am not saying you would, but with your responsibilities as heir apparent, well, I thought you would have to head back to Moscow or some other remote region of Russia."

"Aramis, you're probably correct. I have been neglecting my duties. I am certain you know why," Maxim said, smiling.

A month following Maxim's arrival, Carmen, Maxim, Braxton, and Aramis left Rome, traveling to the Chiacontella duchy.

Villa Incantarre was a beautiful locale for Maxim and Carmen to fall in love. The rolling hills were covered in orchards and the vineyards bordered by endless fields of wheat and barley, winding rivers and quiet lakes. The couple were enormously happy together; longing for one another when apart.

Ever loyal to the government, Braxton included all the developments in his reports. It was decided that a decision on the matter of marriage between Carmen and Maxim would be tabled until the question regarding Dominic and Mathilde had been formally approved by the British and Austrian governments.

They did not have long to wait, as Buckingham Palace announced the betrothal of Dominic. The British Diplomatic Corps had also sounded out the capitals of Europe and the empire to see how the match would be received.

Mathilde would one day be queen of England. The prospects of Mathilde, an Austrian grand duchess on the throne of England, did not sit well with the kaiser

The kaiser's son had married Braxton's, Dominic's and John's sister, Princess Diedre. The Kaiser assumed his influence in the Court of St. James and with the British government would be diluted should his rival Austria and its grand duchess, Princess Mathilde, wed Dominic, England's future king. He was correct.

With the various siblings secure in their marriages and betrothals, Braxton and Aramis left the Chiacontella duchy for Naples and the island of Capri.

20

CAPRI: A BEGINNING & AN END

The island of Capri is a rocky mass of mountains and valleys nestled off the coast of Naples in southern Italy. For thousands of years, it had spawned legends of Greek and Roman gods. It had been a favorite of the Emperors Augustus and Hadrian. Almost two millennia later it was a sanctuary to the literati and those choosing a bohemian lifestyle.

Long before the Nineteenth Century, the Chiacontellas had renovated an old Roman villa, the same villa Braxton had visited years earlier with his family. The villa was positioned like most of the Chiacontella homes, secluded and off the beaten path. Primary access was by sea; a packet boat servicing the remote location from Naples. There was no real contact with the rest of the island. The mountains surrounding the villa and their steep circuitous paths were dangerous and seldom traveled. A skeleton staff of servants tended the villa during the day disappearing to their local village every day prior to sunset. The staff sought to avoid traversing the rocky paths in the thick darkness that engulfed the mountainside when the sun had disappeared.

Sweeping terraces and intimate gardens surrounded the villa, an ancient monument to Roman excess. A vineyard provided grapes for wine and fruit for the table. Vegetable gardens and livestock offered much of the food for infrequent guests.

The villa was self-sufficient. Only the luxuries that had become necessities to visitors were imported from the mainland. At most, the boat trip from Naples could take three hours to half a day. This day, the winds were blowing favorably, as was the current. The relaxing trip initiated the easing of Braxton's mind he so desperately sought.

Braxton and Aramis arrived on the island with only the personal items deemed necessary. He brought with him papers and materials necessary for work-related tasks. Very little in the way of clothing was required, as there would be no soirées, lawn parties, theatre, balls, or other such distractions.

On their arrival at the eastern facing seaside pier, they were met by Pedro the estate manager. He was accompanied by two mule carts and drivers. The servants welcomed Aramis enthusiastically. Braxton was introduced as Baron Coburg. To further keep the prince's identity secret and protect their private conversation, they chose to speak French for the duration of their stay on Capri.

The prince had matured into a youthful man since his last visit. Both Aramis and Braxton were certain he would not be recognized, just another of many friends hosted by the Chiacontella family.

Mule-drawn carts carried them and their baggage slowly up the mountain road leading to the villa atop the cliffs. The mules maintained a steady pace as the carts bounced and creaked along the ancient rutfilled road. The sun beating down upon them, rivulets of sweat poured off animals and humans alike.

"I do not recall the ride up the mountain requiring so much time," Braxton said, removing his wide-brimmed straw hat wiping the perspiration from his brow.

Aramis reminded Braxton, "It was a lot more fun when we were children. I think we walked back then. We had so much more energy and would do anything to get away from the adults."

"Ah, yes. Now I remember. Look, I just caught sight of the house. Yes, there it is, see?"

Aramis sighed and wistfully replied, "Indeed. I have always treasured the long drive lined by the cypress rising to the sky. I have played, run, and laughed for hours among them. I love this place. It is my favorite of our many homes."

Braxton hopped out of the cart and walked alongside. They came upon a larger grove of trees. "Odd, how could I not remember these magnificent oaks? And the heather and myrtle blend so beautifully." He paused to pick flowers blooming randomly along the rugged drive. "These are so lovely, so colorful. And look, there are fields and fields of them!"

Drenched in sweat and invigorated, Braxton and Aramis walked the remaining distance to the villa, the carts following behind.

Verandas provided shade and protection and access to spectacular mountain and ocean views. The tall windows stood open wide, capturing the ocean breeze within the villa.

Three servants stood in formation welcoming them. Aramis greeted each warmly. Braxton admired his informality and genuineness. Fond memories of this idyllic villa emerged as Braxton took in the surroundings and the sense of family exhibited by those present. Capri, the villa, and its inhabitants were magical.

"Come Braxton, what are you day-dreaming about? Yes, everyone falls victim to the island's spell. Shall we go in?"

Aramis led him through the main entrance and to the wing furthest from the central part of the house.

"Come up these steps," Aramis said, smiling at Braxton. He gestured to wide, well-worn steps forming a circular stairway rising several floors.

"I am taking you to a very special place. Our 'sans souci', a heaven without care," Aramis said, extending his hand.

Braxton smiled softly and took Aramis's hand.

The men climbed to the fourth and final floor. There was only one doorway. A set of tall oak double doors opened into a cavernous room decorated with restored frescos and floors inlaid with multicolored tiles. Aramis whispered as if he were in heaven, "This is the only room at this height in the villa.

The sizeable room had an enormous bed canopied in muslin. Chairs and couches sectioned off parts of the room. There were tables for reading, entertainment, and dining.

Braxton stepped over to a large table and asked, "May I use this beautiful, carved wooden table for my work while we are here?" Aramis smiled and nodded appreciatively.

There stood two baroque walk-in marble fireplaces, one by Braxton's table and another closer to the bed.

"We have no running water or gas for light, Braxton."

"Interesting. I suppose candles will have to do," Braxton said, half out loud. "I can see why this room is so special to you."

The cupboards were filled with exquisite linens. Wine racks were fully stocked. An icebox resting between shelves was stacked atop with plates, glasses, bowls, cutlery, and within, packed with meats and dairy.

Aramis and Braxton changed into linen trousers, cotton shirts, and island sandals.

The prince watched as Aramis approached the wine rack and ice box. He prepared bread, cheese, and opened a decorative jar hiding a spread that appeared to be made from dates.

Aramis said, "I love the view of the ocean and mountains. For the next month, this is all ours. Come see the terrace. It is not visible to the rest of the house and opens to the sea."

Braxton's host handed him two glasses and a bottle of Uva Rassa grape wine. Aramis carried the food on a wooden tray. They walked from the room through a loggia having towering white, blue-striped curtains tied back to ionic columns opening onto the expansive terrace.

Stepping onto the marble terrace and bright sunlight, Braxton gasped, eyeing the rising rocky slopes to either side and the sparking Mediterranean Sea spreading endlessly before him.

Aramis gave his friend a moment to take in the panorama.

Then moving close, he touched his lips on Braxton's. Aramis slowly moved a step back, raised his glass, and said, "Benvenuto in casa mia!"

The prince smiled, raised his glass, and thanked Aramis with a tender kiss.

They found comfortable cushioned chairs alongside an umbrella shaded table.

Braxton inhaled and sighed, "Ahhhhh," reveling in the informality and beauty that surrounded him.

Soon they finished the cibo delizioso and the wine. As Braxton headed toward the loggia in search of a second bottle, Aramis suggested, "Shall we take a bottle and let me show you about the villa?"

"Why not? Come!" Braxton said standing up, motioning Aramis to follow, and trotting off the terrace.

Aramis followed the prince through the loggia, into the room and over to the wine rack. His guest chose a bottle and turned to face his lover standing close behind, receiving a kiss on his cheek. Aramis ran out of the room, galloping down the stairs, laughing loudly, followed by a broadly smiling Braxton carrying the bottle and glasses.

The villa was cozy and comfortable in some places, but cavernous in others. The part used by the family was over-furnished with sizeable pieces having ample cushions and pillows. There was a lot of wood and relatively little glass or crystal in the decor. Pottery adorned the rooms and walls. Bright colors leapt out of the most unsuspecting places. It might be a wall, a piece of furniture, a painting, pottery, or carvings. All was magical.

Every room stood exposed to the breezes. Doors and windows were held open by heavy hooks meant to keep them in place when unanticipated winds kicked up. Windows and doors had shutters that could quickly cover them in the event of tempestuous weather.

The charm and character of the villa embraced Braxton. The principal building was surrounded on four sides by a loggia that opened onto sweeping terraces. Pergolas of stone and wood covered in vines dotted the terraces, a home frozen in time meant for living alfresco.

Aramis placed his lips close to Braxton's ear and whispered, "My dearest, tomorrow we shall go to the sea, and I will share my most favorite place."

They returned to their fourth-floor tower and found all their things had been delivered to the room. Most of their clothing and belongings had been unpacked. Braxton was relieved to see the two trunks containing his personal and business papers had remained secure.

They washed up and, not bothering to change, headed downstairs for dinner. There was no need to dress for dinner.

The meal was served on the south terrace. Absorbed with each other's company, they savored the sun falling quickly toward the horizon. The dinner of cuttlefish was familiar and welcome. The two remaining servants cleared the table and busied themselves closing the shutters and windows on the first floor.

Prior to sunset, the departing servants provided the gentlemen with two glowing lanterns and two bottles of wine, along with two glistening glasses and a bowl of grapes and dates.

Braxton and Aramis left the terrace for an evening stroll around the grounds. This would be their evening routine for the following month.

Having finished the bottles of wine hours later, the pair headed back to the villa, seduced by the balmy night and brilliant stars falling away into eternity. Entering the villa each carrying a lantern, they secured the door behind them and found their way through the pitch black to the stairs leading up to their 'Sans Souci.'

Reaching the bottom of the stairs, Aramis gently took Braxton by the hand and led him up the ancient stone staircase, taking their time as they climbed.

Securing the bedroom door behind them, they walked through the loggia and onto the terrace. A warm ocean breeze caressed them as they gazed out over the moonlit Mediterranean Sea.

The two lanterns, left on a table within the loggia, presented an ephemeral backdrop to this theatre of beauty and romance. Standing facing one another next to the balustrade, they undid their clothing, letting it fall to the tiled terrace. They embraced, then kissed.

Turning, their backs to the sea, they walked hand in hand toward to loggia, their sinewy forms shimmering in the heavenly luminescence, disappearing into the tower room.

Braxton pulled back the bedding, dropping onto the crisp white sheets.

Aramis followed and lay down wrapping himself around his prince, murmuring, "I have endured an eternity waiting for this moment."

———

Twelve hours later, Braxton opened his eyes, it was late morning. He awoke bewildered. Never had Braxton slept for more than six hours. He was sure that something was wrong. He sat up, and spied Aramis wearing a short oriental patterned robe, preparing a tray of coffee and biscotti. A half-full cup and the remnants of a biscotti evidenced Aramis had been up for a while.

"Relax, my Braxton. The island casts a sleeping spell on the first night. You will never sleep better anywhere, than you do on Capri. Perhaps you do not remember from your childhood visits here? When your family visited mine?"

"I suppose I must still be under that spell," Braxton said, stretching his arms and legs and then accepting a cup of coffee and a biscotti from his host.

Aramis released the robe, letting it fall to the floor and slipped into bed next to the naked Braxton. Propped up on a pillow, Aramis held his cup in one hand and a small plate of biscotti in the other. He looked at his half-awake prince, slurping his coffee with a grin.

"Take care with the crumbs," Braxton said. "I am going back to sleep." He placed his cup on a side table, scooted back under the bedding, rolling over onto his side, and exposing his bottom. "Hmm, is that an invitation?"

———

Later that morning, breakfast was served under a pergola on the terrace. They had begun their day.

"Braxton, you know the first day is supposed to be a lazy day."

"Yes, of that I am aware, and am planning on taking full advantage of you," Braxton said, with not-so-innocent eyes.

"Promise?"

"Do you doubt me?"

Aramis blushed and looked out across the grounds toward the sea.

"No. I certainly do not.

"Tomorrow will be here too soon. Let us see that special place of yours. I recall you saying the packet boat will be here in five days and I have got things to catch up on before the company portfolios arrive. You know what that means. Back to work, real work. Today, no work!"

Aramis had requested a picnic and two bottles of wine be prepared. All were placed in two knapsacks along with two light blankets. The count put one bundle on his shoulder and held the other one out for the prince. "Come on! The day is wasting."

Braxton stood up, took the knapsack holding the wine and placed it across his shoulder and followed Aramis toward the cliffs. He contemplated the beautiful countryside, occasionally diverting his gaze to the panoramic ocean view. He increasingly directed his attention to their progress as Aramis led them down a rocky uneven precipitous trail. Conversation was limited to avoid falling into a ravine.

What certainly must have been thirty minutes later they descended onto a grotto surrounded on three sides by steep rock, opening to the sea. Brilliant white sand glistened in the sunlight, welcoming the gentle waves lapping the secluded beach.

"Is this your very special place you wanted to share with me my love?" whispered Braxton. "It is indeed special, but my very special place is saved for later."

The isolation, the intimate beach, and sun-filled clear blue sky charged them with exuberance and energy. Placing their belongings in a nearby shade, they disrobed and sped to the water. The pair dove into the waves, splashing, hollering, and laughing like school-boys. They wrestled and tossed each other about, carrying on for what seemed a fabulous eternity. Exhausted, they walked out of the sea and back to the beach. Wet and unclothed the men sprawled out on the sand, catching their breath and the sun's golden rays.

About to doze, Braxton jumped up and began covering Aramis

in sand from his neck to his feet. Aramis lay there laughing as he was covered in the glistening powder.

Having fully covered Aramis, he straddled him atop the sand and shouted, "I have you where I want you! I shall never let you go! You are mine forever and ever!" He then flattened himself on Aramis leaning forward kissing Aramis's lips. Laughing again, they soon returned to the water to wash the sand from their bodies.

Back at the beach they consumed most of the food and finished a bottle of wine.

"Aramis, when we were swimming under water, did you notice how clear the water is? I cannot fathom the colors. The light shining down is as if millions of tiny silver needles are piercing the sea from above."

"Yes, but wait until you see what else I have in store."

"What could that possibly be?"

"It is time to see my very special place." Hopping up, Aramis ordered, "Come swim with me!"

Braxton sprang up and followed Aramis into the water. They walked out to their waists and then swam out into the gentle surf. Their route took them around a rocky precipice facing the ocean. Picking up the pace, they swam to a secluded break in the rocks, a small cave opening.

Braxton treading water, sputtered, "Are you sure you want to go in there?"

"Oh, come on Brax, you will like it, trust me!"

"That's not what I meant. It just looks…"

Aramis swam toward the cave, looking back, gesturing for his wary lover to follow.

He followed. Entering the cave, the ocean's gentle waves encouraged him forward. Soon the dark was illuminated, the crystal blue-green engulfing him. The cavern was brightly lit in spots by indirect sunlight. The gentle pulsing water's movement reflecting from the sun and refracting from the pool's bottom created a kaleidoscopic mystical shimmering basin. Smooth stones and ledges surrounded the pool as if inviting one to repose alongside, the depth varing from inches to several feet. The cavernous ceiling reached fifty feet up into the rock, sheltering the shadows and light dancing off the walls and the water's surface.

Enchanted, the prince was drawn into the chamber of warm, circulating water and dancing light. Submerging, he swam underwater toward Aramis on the other side of the cavern. He popped to the surface close to where Aramis stood, his chest expanding, rivulets of water running down his chiseled abdomen.

"Rejoins mois, please," Aramis said, motioning Braxton to join him in a shallow pool.

"C'est beau," Braxton said, wading toward his lover, the light refracting off his glistening torso.

Aramis held out his hand. "Come closer, sit next to me."

———

The first week at the Capri villa was calm and relaxing. Their time was filled with swimming, sailing, riding, and hiking. Little thought was given to the papers, periodicals, and documents locked in the trunks.

As the week neared its end, Aramis saw Braxton growing impatient. The day before the packet boat was to arrive, Aramis awoke before the sun to find Braxton at the large table busily at work. He had apparently been working for hours, reading, signing, and writing.

Aramis shot up in bed. "Braxton, must you?" he cried. Aramis's heart ached as he internalized their magical week drawing to a close.

Braxton, startled, looked up. A strange bliss had passed over him when he had immersed himself again in his business affairs.

"What is wrong? What have I done?"

Braxton rose from the table and joined Aramis. Wrapping his arms around him, he regretted having so upset Aramis. They settled into one another and fell fast asleep.

When Aramis awoke again, he found Braxton had gone back to work at the table. The sun had risen, and this time Braxton had prepared the coffee and biscotti. He lay back staring at the ceiling, sighing to himself. He knew their stolen time was coming to an end.

Following breakfast, their routine changed for the first time. They spent the better part of their mornings working side by side on business affairs. The afternoons remained dedicated to enjoying the island and each other's company.

The packet boat arrived late in the morning on the seventh day. A trunk full of correspondence and business reports was exchanged for a similar trunk Braxton and Aramis had spent the better part of two days working through.

The following week, trunks were once again exchanged. Every seven days this routine was repeated.

The packet boat supplied necessities not available from the villa's orchard, vineyard, or vegetable gardens. There were often bundles of personal correspondence for both Aramis and Braxton.

The royal envoy did not prepare a report for the government during his stay on Capri. They had both written to their families letting them know they were well and enjoying the island and their holiday.

———

Three weeks had passed quickly. The day following the arrival of the last weekly packet, Braxton and Aramis retreated to their special place, the magical pool in the caves.

The lovers lay relaxing as the sparkling light shimmered and danced across their deeply tanned bodies. They were comfortable, reclining unclothed side by side, drinking in the quiet beauty and solitude that surrounded them.

They were sitting upright, facing the entrance to the pool, and discussing a business matter, when a slow sloshing sound revealed the shadow of a man. He was carrying a well-provisioned net over his shoulder. He too was naked. The stranger moved with confidence, obviously familiar with his surroundings.

Aramis gasped, and in a surprised and agitated voice shouted, "Father, what are you doing here?"

"Well, Aramis, it must be evident that I have come to see you and your cousin. Gentlemen, I bring you greetings from your families."

Aramis and Braxton looked at one another, astounded that Aramis's father, Braxton's uncle, had joined them unannounced in a remote cave full of water and unclothed.

"Hello uncle," Braxton said hesitantly.

"Nephew, pray you will excuse me if I do not bow, as it seems the three of us are quite naked and there appears to be an uncommon equality present."

Aramis's and Braxton's nervous laughter echoed throughout the cavern as Cosimo joined in.

Cosimo loosely embraced his son and his nephew. He then sat between them and opened the net he had been carrying. From it, he unwrapped three bottles of wine, three heavy glass cups, along with bread and cheese that had been tightly wrapped in thick wax paper.

Initially, the conversation remained stilted, the two young men having no concept of how to react to Cosimo's surprise visit.

Cosimo quipped, "Well, we are all three in the altogether, so there is nothing to hide."

Aramis snorted, "You have hit that one square on the head, Father." Braxton spewed out his wine.

"Hold on to your liquor nephew. We only have three bottles between us!" Grinning broadly, he handed each young man a slice of bread and cheese.

All three enjoyed their jovial banter consuming the second bottle of wine. No one spoke of politics, business, or family. They rattled on about the island. Cosimo regaled them with stories from his childhood. He was unexpectedly frank and personal. He opened-up as neither of the young men had known him to do. By the time they were into the third bottle, he spoke of the love of his life.

"The first person I ever loved I brought here too, years after we were lovers."

The young men looked at each other wide-eyed and then at Cosimo.

Cosimo's countenance was placid and dreamy. "We were so in

love. We fought to keep our secret from everyone. We could not be discovered.

"We still are, I think, in love." He took a long deep breath, slowly releasing it and drank some wine. "Yes, as you have probably surmised, my love is for another man."

The prince and count sat silent, staring at the pulsing water undulating in pools of emerald green.

The Duke did not provide details, but he continued to speak intimately concerning the relationship. Neither Braxton nor Aramis knew then that the man Cosimo loved was Braxton's father and Aramis's uncle.

Braxton and Aramis knew that they had been found out and that they were about to hear more.

Cosimo removed himself from between Braxton and Aramis. He slid into the pool and stood in waist deep water facing them.

"My lover and I were not in the ancient Greco-Roman world when we fell in love. We were then, and still are today, in far different times. Things accepted in times past are, as you both know, forbidden in today's world. One day that may change. For the moment those who take part in 'forbidden love' and are discovered are driven from their world."

Cosimo paused for a moment, allowing the young men to give thought to what he had said. He continued, "You both have been born into families that have significant responsibilities and power. Should your mutual attraction be unveiled, Aramis, our family, and its interests, would be compromised. Even now, the family and our banks are losing centuries-old anonymity. We are objects of envy, and through our successes, have created enemies whose interests threaten ours and are diametrically opposed. These enemies feel threatened and continually scheme to undermine us. They will stop at nothing to protect their interests, including destroying our family should it suit their purposes. You both experienced this reality in Germany and Vienna. Please reflect on that."

Braxton reached over and took Aramis's hand. Aramis moved closer to Braxton.

Cosimo began again, "Braxton, you are a member of the family ruling the most powerful empire in history. The English monarchy maintains its position through its popularity. Dare to imagine the consequences of the scandal and ridicule that could erupt and quite possibly topple the monarchy if this 'holiday' of yours became common knowledge. Imagine the ramifications worldwide if the English government could not withstand the scandal's onslaught. The turmoil of 1848 could surely raise its ugly head again.

Cosimo emptied the remnants of the last bottle equally into their glasses.

"You both have choices to make. Make them before they are made for you. You can choose to renounce your positions in the world. If you abandon your birthrights, you will in fact, be forced to live a life much as you have these past three weeks, isolated from the rest of the world."

Many who have come before you have chosen that path. In fact, this island has traditionally been a haven for those who have made such choices. Is that how you choose to live out the remainder of your lives?"

As the minutes flowed by in silence, Cosimo collected the items that remained from the wine and food. He carefully returned them to the net, swinging it over his back. He embraced both men and slid back into the water.

"I love you both and honor your love for one another. I hope you will take the next week to experience and enjoy your time together. But be warned. Your lives are not your own and the reality of our world is far uglier than this beautiful island. Be careful." He then turned and waded towards the entrance of their magical pool. The water's churning that had announced his arrival, sounded his departure.

Aramis and Braxton were once again alone.

They spoke not a word leaving their sanctuary and making their way back to the beach. Cosimo was nowhere to be found. However, when retrieving their clothing, they discovered two leather-bound copies of Niccolò Machiavelli's The Prince.

"Why do you think my father left these for us?"

"I suppose it is his attempt to ensure we learn to protect ourselves from the unseemly sides of the world."

For the remaining week, they recklessly lived a life of love and passion. Not for a moment did they separate themselves from one another. It was luck, and not discretion, that shielded them from the eyes and potential witness of others. They were lovers approaching the precipice of separation, loneliness, heartbreak, and emotional desolation.

Returning to Naples, Aramis went on to the Duchy de Chiacontella. Braxton boarded his train for St. Petersburg.

21

ST. PETERSBURG TO MOSCOW

Braxton retired to his private car. He dove into the book his Uncle Cosimo had left him on the sand in Capri. Initially, he was repulsed by what appeared to be an amoral and simplistic underlying theme attempting to validate 'the end justifies the means.'

He soon came to see the text as a treatise on guidance for those who found themselves having power by birth or were seeking to gain power in their own right. He noted the inherent differences between the hereditary ruler and the 'new' ruler.

He realized Cosimo must have left the volume to help him prepare for what lay ahead and to learn to survive in the real world. Braxton vowed he would never conduct his life as Machiavelli prescribed in his book.

He stared out the train window observing the countryside roll by. The young prince contemplated his position and the dangers that surrounded him. His encounter with the kaiser and the events in Vienna kept coming back to mind. He recalled the people he had had dealings when years ago he had begun to grow his business interests. Things he had not understood, now had clarity. Many happenings of which he had taken little notice then, now glared full-face at him.

Prince Braxton thought back to his early days in the stables when he encountered jealous and petty spats amongst the stable boys and spats between trainers. The now adult Braxton struggled as he pondered on experiences he had had when dealing with the men he had come across at the track, assuming them to be honorable. He knew even then, deep down, they had tried to manipulate and cheat Josh and him as they built their stable and breeding business. The naïve young prince had so wanted the avarice and greed he suspected not to be true.

Braxton rarely questioned his own judgement. It was easier and less disheartening to not doubt the character of those he yearned to trust. He had retreated into denial, deceiving himself with the notion they played a harmless game.

However, after reading The Prince, he concluded that indeed, life and business were not a game. The realization that he had been correct in being suspect of others was both validating and a warning.

Lacking this newfound insight, business negotiations in Madrid, Paris, Amsterdam, and Berlin had been games to him. He was fortunate he had come out ahead. Now he must work harder and learn how to separate truth from fiction, deceit from honesty.

———

During the two-day train trip from St. Petersburg, Braxton set an alternative course. He immersed himself in outlining a reliable information network that would provide him with the most up-to-date intelligence. Intelligence that would not only protect him but also strengthen his business negotiations.

Braxton determined the best person to serve as a front for this new intelligence network would be Lord Ramsey.

My Dear Ramsey,

I am sitting aboard the train on my way to St. Petersburg. I have two days with which to attend to affairs left undone during my time in Capri. Yet here I sit crafting a scheme which I would like you to take hold of and assist me in bringing to life.

The easiest way to get your head around what I am contemplating is to envision what we have heard for years to be the Rothschild espionage ring spread throughout Europe. And no, I am not ignoring the Chiacontella web. But that belongs to them. I must have my own sources, separate from my family's network.

Over the years you and I have discussed the need to have more knowledge and up-to-date information at our fingertips. Well, it is time to make that happen.

We can never lose sight of the fact that I am in a sensitive position, politically. My father's government would go into spasms should they find out a senior member of the royal family operated an independent intelligence gathering service. It would not surprise me if it was not bordering on unconstitutional. Regardless, I am determined to grow my enterprises and protect my investments.

We shall set up a triple blind network to ensure we will not be discovered, maintaining the option of plausible deniability. No one within the Chiacontella Bank, the government, our businesses, or my family is to know of its existence. Our experience with conflicts from elements within the government regarding our business interests has proven costly. As we suspected, I have confirmed that powerful business and business interests at home and abroad feel threatened by our successes. It can only get worse.

I will be the sole recipient of all intelligence gathered by our operatives. You and I will refer to the organization as the Intelligence Operation, or IO. It will limit itself to intelligence gathering. We will use field operatives who are academic researchers, scientists, and anyone else who can keep us up to date on inventions, as well as threats to our interests.

We will, of course, need people in patent offices throughout Europe and in the United States. More on that later. We will also continue to utilize information from my uncle's bank's intelligence arm.

When I arrive in St. Petersburg, I will send a packet to the

Aurelio Palace Headmaster. It is time to tap into the Academy for the talent needed to bring this to fruition.

There are many additional matters on which I need to attend.

Please plan to come to me at your earliest convenience.

I trust you will continue to remain discrete in your own personal life. By that I refer to a tidbit found in a Chiacontella intelligence report I received while in Capri. Your 'other' life is known to some. You are my friend, and I want you to have a happy and long prison-free life.

Take special care,

Fondly,

Braxton

While sealing the letter, its author took note of the hypocrisy in the last paragraph, whoever would have dreamed those situations in which decades ago I spied John and Ramsey in, then so confusing, have been recreated in my own life.

Following through on his commitment to write the headmaster, he wrote the following and then sent it via courier to the Aurelio Academy headmaster.

My Dear Headmaster,

First, I would like to thank you for your thorough and enlightening reports regarding the academy and its students. While I have taken pains to respond to them, you will not find these responses in this packet. Not wanting to confuse this subject with any other, I have sent them by post.

Now to my purpose. You will recall that you provided me with the marks and some detail on this year's matriculating class. Of the twenty or so names, I have my eyes on six, which I have annotated on another sheet of paper, enclosed. They have been chosen because they appear to be talented linguistically, innately intelligent, purposeful, and resourceful.

I ask that you use a portion of the funds enclosed to retire any personal debts these individuals may have. Provide them with suit-able traveling clothes as would befit a gentleman. Inform them they will not be returning to England for some time. Send them to St. Petersburg per the attached instructions. No one is to know of this letter or its contents. You are commanded to destroy all within and make no mention of it or its contents to anyone, ever.

Sincerely,

Prince Braxton of Wales

————

Braxton was aware the 90-year-old Czar had become somewhat of a recluse following the untimely death of his son, the czarevich. He suspected Maxim's invitation had something to do with the czar's isolation.

The prince's train arrived in St. Petersburg as planned late one afternoon. It was not hard to miss, as it was the most magnificent train of its time. Before departing from Vienna more than two months earlier, Braxton had dispatched all the freight cars excepting the two cars gifted him by the kaiser to various parts of Europe to facilitate his trading business.

Through the capable management augmented by an ever-increasing number of Aurelio Palace Academy graduates, a cohesive well-oiled commercial enterprise was emerging. Lord Ramsey continued to direct the day-to-day management of the various enterprises. The Chiacontella Banks, under the direction of Aramis and the Duc de Chiacontella, were, in fact, extensions of Braxton's business concerns.

————

Grand Duke Prince Maxim arrived at the Moskovsky railway station as the train pulled into St. Petersburg. As heir presumptive, Maxim was accompanied by a troop of the Imperial Guard.

Braxton asked stepping down to the platform, "Maxim, why are you wearing a sling? How are you hurt?"

"I got into a confrontation with my winter coat. And it won!" Maxim joked. "Come, let us go to my carriage and I will explain everything. But tell me about Capri and your trip. You have color. Obviously, you spent time basking on the Mediterranean Sea!"

"Yes, I did," Braxton said, smiling. "Remind me to stay away from whatever 'coat' got the better of you, my friend!"

Braxton and Maxim set off for Maxim's official residence, the Anichkov Palace. The palace was the former home of the fabled Empress Elizabeth's lover and favorite, Aleksey Razumovsky.

Braxton had reconciled himself to Maxim and his sister marrying. They agreed that the marriage should take place in a timely manner. The union had the potential to stabilize relations between Russia and England. Austria might come around as well. Once the marriage had been performed, perhaps time would have a cooling effect on the mercurial kaiser.

The marriage of Braxton's sister, Princess Diedre, to the kaiser's son having taken place earlier that year had not placated the kaiser's lust for power. The vainglorious agitator continued to grasp for more power and international validation.

Maxim and Braxton sat in front of a fire in the dimly lit Louis XIV style room. Gas lit sconces flickered against the walls. Silk monotone curtains had been drawn against the waning summer sunlight.

Partaking of cigars and vodka, Maxim began, "I know you must be aware of the czar's hermit-like existence."

"Yes, I have heard rumors."

"There is much more to my uncle's self-imposed seclusion."

Braxton leaned forward in his chair and said, "Are you going to tell me about your injury? What happened? Are you in danger, Maxim?"

"I will tell you about my injury. But as I said, there is so much to speak about before we get to that."

"Very well."

Maxim stood and walked over to a gilded tasseled rope hanging from the ceiling. He pulled three times. "I have ordered a dinner prepared for us. We have a great deal to discuss. Things that are best kept between the two of us."

"Maxim," Braxton said, sitting back in his chair and crossing his legs. "You have my full attention. I am intrigued."

"I promise, you will be more than intrigued before the night is over."

Braxton, not neglecting his cigar or vodka, nodded his head in anticipation.

The snap of a matchstick being struck as Maxim relit his cigar accentuated Maxims next remark, "And there is Princess Valentina, my cousin, the grand duchess."

"Ah yes, your cousin, the old czar's youngest daughter." Braxton smiled and continued, "From her photographs I can tell she is beautiful." Braxton chuckled and said, "I hear she is willful, too." He paused and questioned, "It is beyond me why she is not the czar's heir."

Maxim ignored the query, responding, "Yes, she has all those qualities."

Braxton continued, "Her older sister, Grand Duchess Ekaterina, my dear friend, was old enough to be her mother. Ekaterina was almost twenty years older than her brother the late czarevich, and around fifty years older than her sister Valentina. Three generations between them!"

Maxim confirmed the prince's narrative, "Yes, their father spent fifty years siring offspring. Valentina is special. I have arranged for an introduction tomorrow."

"Excellent! I look forward to meeting her. But tell me, why is she not succeeding her father on the throne?"

Maxim's answer bordered on curt, "You must pose that question to her yourself. And please keep in mind, my mother was the oldest daughter, and to my dismay, the czar had no other sons."

A door opened, Light from the hall penetrated the dimly lit room racing across the parquet floor. A pre-set dinner table was wheeled in. Two servants raised the table leaves expanding its surface area. Dinnerware and the silver service were re-positioned.

Two chairs were placed opposite each other. The footmen exited the room as quickly as they had arrived.

"We shall enjoy our dinner as I regale you with quite a story," Maxim said, motioning Prince Braxton to the table.

"I hope you do not mind, but I have ordered a traditional Russian meal. There is not often an opportunity to enjoy simple meals, as the court is well into its third century of trying hard to be French."

Braxton laughed. "That is perfectly fine with me. I took over running my kitchen long ago and seldom stray from the basics. So, what is it we are having?"

Pointing at various foods on their plates, Maxim said, "I imagine you have never had smoked salmon? These pickled mushrooms will light up your palate."

Braxton raised his eyebrows taking note of the strange dishes. He opened his mouth to say something.

"Ah, yes," continued the grand duke, "You will truly savor the sturgeon soup and tendon of sturgeon pie!" Maxim laughed, amused by his guest's incredulous stare.

"Trust me, after you have tasted sweet porridge, kasha and dried fruit, you will never ever ask for anything but true Russian cooking!" Maxim snorted. "Enjoy, my friend!

"And of course, the best, iced vodka my country has to offer," Maxim said filling their glasses. Holding his uplifted, he said, "Za tvajo zdarovje! To your health, my friend."

"Za tvajo zdarovje!" Braxton responded, throwing back his glass. He set his glass back on the table and picked up a large-handled silver fork and knife and said, "It looks delicious. Now, please share your tale."

Maxim, his mouth half full, began, "The czar's health declined precipitously with the death of the czarevich. He lost interest in ruling and all day-to-day activities. Through inaction and apathy, he had effectively 'abdicated' his previous hands-on autocratic rule." Maxim paused for a moment savoring his meal.

"With the czar in isolation, the imperial ministers grabbed as much power and wealth as they could. The conniving manipulative princes of the orthodox Roman Church have also shown themselves to be brazenly ambitious. They too, have joined in the feeding frenzy. The government is crumbling from within. Numerous byzantine plots and mismanagement have all but brought the bloated bureaucracy to a halt. Russia, for all intents and purposes, has been without a government. It has only an underpaid army to keep the czar on the throne."

"My God, Maxim! Does anyone outside the ministry know the depth of this debacle? Ambassadors? Foreign governments?" Braxton threw back his Vodka.

The grand duke had consumed most of his meal while Braxton sat mesmerized, hands resting on the table, having ignored his food and drink.

"No doubt they have their suspicions. The first minister had replaced the czar in what few public appearances were made. I had been pretty much cast aside." Maxim paused. He refilled both their glasses. He sat back in his chair contemplating the glass with both hands saying, "They tried to assassinate me."

"Maxim!" Braxton stood up, his eyes widening and his chair falling backward.

"Hence my arm and shoulder in this contraption."

"Is your life still in danger?" Braxton said placing his chair upright, and regaining his seat, leaning forward, elbows on the table, his chin resting on folded hands.

"Let me proceed only to answer your questions completely. The plot and assassination attempt focused mainly on the question of my legitimacy as heir. The church had its favorite candidate for the succession. I was not it. It escapes me as to why the succession would be in question, but this is Russia."

"A month ago, while attending the baptism of one of my cousin's adolescent sons in the cathedral where the czars have been crowned for 400 years, my small entourage and I were attacked as we were leaving the Cathedral of the Assumption in Moscow."

Braxton held up his hand and remarked, "You are telling me that someone tried to kill you outside a church leaving a family baptism? That is barbaric!"

"Well, perhaps in your country, but not so much in Russia, I am sad to say. "A shot fired at close range hit me. I fell, dislocating my shoulder. Fortunately, I was wearing my dress military uniform and the epaulet on my shoulder deflected the bullet. The round had struck the metal plate inside the epaulet's material. When I fell, I hit my head on the granite steps. I lay there helplessly observing my companions draw swords and make short work of the five assailants. All but two were dispatched."

Braxton took a deep breath and exhaled loudly.

Maxim went on to say, "The two surviving assassins proved useful."

"What action was taken for the attempt on your life?" Braxton asked

"My cousin and family were arrested along with his wife's family. The church's hierarchy was removed and thrown into prison. The investigation continues. Oh, and yes, their properties confiscated as well."

Braxton sat dumbstruck.

He then, with a fixed look, asked Maxim, "Have you shared this with the czar?"

"I went to him as soon as my wound was dressed; my tunic had been cut off at the shoulder. The theatrics produced the desire effect. As I said, we dealt with the conspirators. In the meantime, his imperial majesty gave me full authority to replace the church hierarchy with those friendly to our family."

"A good first step. What about your companions, those who saved your life? They could be useful, yes?"

Maxim looked at his friend, a slow smile building. "My dear royal envoy, you seem to have an in-depth grasp of the situation. These are good questions. I appreciate and value your observations." Braxton raised a brow.

The heir presumptive went on to say, "We will give those who stood beside me and saved my life opportunities within the government and the military to serve in positions commensurate with their capacity."

"That is a terrible story. I fear for you, Maxim. I fear the cancer is still present in the court and government. None of this could have happened without a deep undercurrent of disharmony and a plethora of malcontents."

"I am impressed, Braxton, that you understand the tenuous situation in which I find myself. In fact, I have uncovered and informed my uncle, the czar which of his ministers had conspired and divided the imperial power amongst themselves."

"How did he respond?"

"That may be the most unusual aspect of this entire story. I think the bastard is more cunning and less idle that any of us thought. I believe he was waiting for me to show initiative, rise to the occasion and demonstrate leadership."

Agitated, Braxton asked, "Did he not realize the harm that had been done by allowing this to fester? My God, he risked everything. He is mad!" Slamming his fist on the table, he said, "They almost killed you!"

Maxim rolled his tongue around the inside of his closed mouth, and then looking straight into Braxton's eyes, said, "It is different here. Russia is unique. There is no rhyme, there is no reason. Russians are a people that epitomize the cliché 'cutting off one's nose to spite one's face.'"

Braxton sat shaking his head.

Maxim went on to say, "Ego could not be more blatantly and foolishly manifested than in this backward nation. The czar no longer cares to rule. After my coming to him and exposing the corruption, he has made me regent. The czar has exiled his first minister and appointed me in his place. That is why your arrival in St. Petersburg may be fortuitous." Maxim swallowed hard and haltingly said, "I need your help."

———

Braxton reflected on his recent reading of Machiavelli's book. His own experiences and those of Maxim only strengthened his resolve to do whatever it took to protect himself and his family.

· · ·

Dearest Mama and Papa,

I am writing you this letter as your son and not in my capacity as royal envoy. It is a private letter, but in the end, I know you are duty bound to share the essence of what I am about to reveal with the prime minister.

There have been some rather unsavory developments in Moscow and St. Petersburg. Grand Duke Prince Maxim has asked me to help him sort out an immensely troublesome situation. In fact, for the past month, I have been doing just that.

It began with an attempt on his life culminating in the czar creating him regent. The grand duke has also taken over the role as first minister. We spend our days reviewing government documents. There are mountains and mountains of them. Most are in French. As you know, Russian is not spoken at court. Many are written in German. Thank you, Mama, for insisting I acquire foreign languages.

We are in the process of appointing members of the Supreme Privy Council. The challenge we have here is that Germans have been carrying on the most rudimentary aspects of the administration of the Russian government for centuries. As a result, there does not exist a dearth of depth to the Russian nobility's ability or interest in governing.

Naturally, I refused to accept an appointment or compensation for my efforts. That would have certainly made headlines, 'Fourth in Line to English Throne Governs Russia!' I would love to see the look on the prime minister's face if you shared that with him, Papa.

I have reason to believe Maxim will invite me to accompany him on his upcoming tour of Russia. I shall accept his invitation. This experience will provide me an unexpected opportunity to learn about Russia and its people. Who would have ever thought a businessman such as me would assist in the governance of the largest land mass in the world?

Thankfully, it is temporary. I leave for Venice in a couple of months.

Your Loving Son, Braxton

———

Prior to embarking on his tour of Russia with Maxim, Braxton still had to put his private espionage network in place and execute what he had dubbed his daring "Mars" campaign—a campaign to root out his dissenters and all threats to his business plans. During his first weeks in St. Petersburg, Braxton worked feverishly laying out the campaign that would come to fruition during the Carnivale di Venizia two months later.

The spymaster had targeted two dozen people he felt posed a threat to him and his interests. These individuals had shown themselves to be underhanded and working against him, his family, and/or his business interests. He would make every effort to ensure each of them attended Carnivale.

Weeks after arriving in St. Petersburg, six graduates of the Aurelio Palace Academy, now agents of the IO, were put to work. They began laying the groundwork for the Mars campaign.

For seven hundred years, Carnivale di Venizia had endured, renowned for raucous behavior and the seeking of pleasure. The annual event tantalized all of Europe. Anonymity provided by wearing unique and often extravagant masks and costumes emboldened the revelers.

Now, however, Carnivale was outlawed under the ruling Austrian Habsburgs. This year the entertainment would be held in private palazzos confined to Carnivale friendly areas of Venice.

Braxton's agents discreetly circulated rumors targeting those whom Braxton had singled out. Rumors that this year's Carnivale di Vanezia would be very special: the ancient god Mars would make an appearance.

The prince had rented a villa in Venice separate from the Chiacontella Palazzo. He required privacy for planning and execution. He also secured a room away from the palazzo that had an enormous fireplace and a private entrance. He planned to take possession of both residences one month prior to Carnivale.

———

Just days following Maxim's and Braxton's meeting, the English prince mounted his horse for a morning ride. The St. Petersburg sky was clear and the air crisp. The horse shivered, snorted, shaking its head eager to take off on a vigorous ride out of the city and into the countryside.

He heard a woman's voice from behind, "Good morning, Your Royal

Highness. Welcome to St. Petersburg."

Braxton turned in his saddle. His heart leapt and his gloved hands grew clammy. A beautiful young woman, riding side-saddle, drew near. Her eyes sparkled; her full lips lifted in a modest smile. She came up alongside him and holding out her hand.

"I am Valentina."

Braxton's movements remained frozen.

Flowing from beneath a stylish hat, her ebony hair tumbled in luxurious waves onto her shoulders, complimenting her penetrating amber eyes.

Valentina smiled playfully at Braxton. "This is when you take my hand and say, 'I am Braxton. So nice to meet you." She paused. "Then you ask me to join you on your ride."

Braxton's eyes locked on Valentina's. He positioned his horse close to her and kissed the back of her gloved hand and said, "I am Braxton, would you be so kind as to join me for a ride?"

Valentina stood five feet nine inches tall. Her figure was elegant and her proportions perfect. She carried herself with confidence, yet with no hint of arrogance. Her charm captivated all with whom she came into contact

She had the same effect on Braxton. He was immobilized with admiration for her beauty and the pure spirit that emanated from the depth of her soul radiating from her eyes. She had won him over.

He knew he must make her his own. Valentina, in turn, was curious about Braxton. His reputation as a brilliant and accomplished young man had preceded him. She found his western European sophistication, polish, and commanding physical appearance somewhat intimidating. His persona exceeded the two dimensional men she had been accustomed to at court.

Valentina respected the British prince's successes in business and his political acumen. Knowing that it was unlikely he would succeed to the British throne was also attractive. Grand Duchess, Princess Valentina had eschewed her line in the succession and had asked her father to exclude her. She did not want the life of a ruling empress. She was intimate with the history of Catherine the Great and the empresses' mother-in-law, daughter of Peter the Great, Empress Elizabeth. She recoiled at the thought of having to live their lives.

The grand duchess would take her time and get to know this man.

Over the following weeks, Braxton and Valentina were often in each other's company at court. Slowly, they became more familiar with one another. They discovered they had many interests in common. A friendship unfolded. Unlike most young aristocrats, they avoided small talk. Prince Braxton and Valentina defied convention and discussed politics and the world stage. They shared their thoughts on economics, sounding one another out on matters that interested them. The pair attended the theater, races, balls, and dinners, as this allowed convenient backdrops for their conversations and interaction.

———

As Braxton had predicted, Maxim came to him and said, "Would you consider accompanying me on my tour of Russia?"

"In what capacity?"

"What capacity would induce you to accept the invitation?

"Not as envoy, but as a friend."

"Well, certainly as a friend. But you do realize that everyone will know who you are and that you are your grandfather's, the king's, envoy? That cannot be avoided." Maxim grinned at Braxton.

"I think," Braxton cautioned, "The further we get from St. Petersburg and then beyond Moscow, it won't really make a difference. None of us are nearly as important in your subject's daily lives as we think we are."

"I am afraid you are correct," Maxim agreed. "We tend to delude ourselves when surrounded by sycophants. So, you see, you must accompany me."

"Very well. Together we will provide the Russian people a look at their future emperor! I am happy to join you in any capacity."

———

Dearest Papa,

Grand Duke Maxim has indeed invited me to accompany him on a trip throughout Russia. He feels the need to show the people the face of its future emperor and to familiarize himself with his country. The Russian empire is vast, and the tour will take several months.

I feel this is an excellent opportunity to befriend our dear Maxim and good fortune for me in my capacity as royal envoy to learn more about this country.

I would be less than forthright to not admit that there are economic interests that intrigue me. As an entrepreneur, I am dazzled beyond belief of what might lie in wait for business expansion. Minerals, lumber, trade, oil, and who knows what awaits me!

Of course, the trip is officially diplomatic. I have taken steps to ingratiate myself to the government at my expense. My train has been modified to display the Imperial two-headed eagle, the Romanov's Coat of Arms, alongside that of the British Royal Coat of Arms. The Imperial Russian Flag is also displayed alongside the Union Jack at the front and rear of the train. I am having one carriage refurbished to serve as Maxim's private car.

Now that official business is out of the way, let me express my sincerest sympathy and empathy for what you and the family are experiencing with Grandpapa's declining health. Please give my best to him, Grandmama, and the family. I pray he recovers, as I would love to see him when I return to England.

As for returning to England, I fear that is unlikely in the near term. It pains my heart to not be able to attend brother Dominic's wedding. I truly adore Mathilde and think her a wonderful choice for a bride and future queen. Please give them my love.

I have met a most lovely creature, Valentina, the czar's youngest daughter. I rather like her. I know a marriage is impossible, as Carmen desires to marry Valentina's cousin, Maxim, so let us keep this between us!

All my love,
Braxton

22

VENEZIA

Prior to joining Maxim on their tour of Russia, Braxton made his planned trip to Venice for Carnivale. Arriving at his rented palazzo, Braxton cleared it of all but minimal servants and staff. He determined that everything was in place for confronting those he felt did or could serve as an impediment to his work.

With only three weeks remaining before Carnivale Night his time was spent making obligatory appearances, preparing for the execution of his plan, and tending to his increasingly complex business affairs.

Braxton designed his Carnivale costume based on a statue of the long dead Medici patriarch, Cosimo Pater Patria. A centuries old marble likeness presented the legendary Florentine dressed in long simple robes. Braxton adapted the garments to accommodate his purpose: intentionally drawing attention to himself.

The costume was constructed of a richly textured black material and trimmed with small, elegant, crystal quartz beads, causing the costume to flash intriguing luminescence with the wearer's every movement. A wide brimmed black hat was fitted with a heavy veil to obscure the wearer's face. And as a last touch, he added long black silk gloves.

Every stitch and sequin perfectly placed, the regalia created an aura and presence that would stand out, but not overwhelm. Braxton had the design copied onto fine linen paper bearing his family's coat of arms, thus tying the design directly to him.

Weeks before Carnivale Braxton disguised himself as a clerk and departed the palazzo. He carried with him multiple copies of the Medici costume design. He visited all the best design houses in Venice and left a copy with each designer, asking them to review it carefully. Before making the commission decision, Braxton informed the designers he would send someone to pick up their proposals. Departing the shops, he discreetly left more copies of his costume pattern lying about in public places. He laughed to himself This is one of the cleverest parts of my ruse. I wonder how many revelers will come dressed as Cosimo Pater Patria.

Unknown to the Venetian costume designers, Braxton had months earlier commissioned the costume in St. Petersburg and had brought the finished product with him. He calculated that soon others would 'steal' his design and wear the copied costume to Carnivale.

The prince, again disguised as a clerk, also visited a one very special Venetian costumer to place a commission on an entirely different design. This costume represented the ancient god Mars, son of Jupiter and Juno. Braxton's design glorified the god depicted in Roman armor made of gold. Mars' legendary shield, the Ancile, was replicated in faux gold. The classic Roman helmet, sword, cuirass, vambraces, greaves, and sandals were all covered in the same faux gold. A gold-like mesh hung from the helmets visor, obscuring the face.

The costume was overpowering and represented unharnessed strength. It left no doubt the wearer could conquer all. Braxton paid handsomely for the costume and more for confidentiality. The designers and fabricators were instructed to not speculate or ask the name of the person who had commissioned the order.

Once the Mars costume had been completed, Braxton took it and the Medici costume to the room he had rented a distance from his palazzo. He prepared a fire in the commodious fireplace but left it unlit.

He designed and had printed, over-size cards and matching envelopes. The envelopes were of luminescent pearl paper, with the words 'Mars God of War' imprinted in gold on the back flap. The card was engraved.

'The Mighty Mars Thanks You for The Pleasure and Indiscretion of Your Company.'

The modern-day Machiavelli spent hours crafting his plan and addressing his envelopes. There must be no trace of his involvement. Addressing the envelopes and not being discovered was his most challenging task. He taught himself calligraphy to disguise his handwriting. Practice led to success. Several days before Carnivale his preparations were complete. He had twenty-four exquisitely addressed envelopes ready for delivery to their intended.

Hosted at fetes in palazzos and villas leading up to Carnivale, he kept alert, on the lookout for someone, someone familiar with Venice's noble houses. A person who might assist in the execution of the Mars plan. Through careful listening, Braxton while a guest at one of Venice's noble's palazzo, overheard enough conversation amongst the servants to have his attention drawn to one young footman, a servant who seemed to anticipate and fulfill the needs of his employers' guests.

One evening, Braxton followed the footman as he approached a tavern. The disguised prince hailed a callow boy on the street and said, while pointing across a small square, "Boy, take this letter to that man entering the tavern?"

"Aye!" answered the boy as he grabbed the note and the gold coin Braxton held between his fingers.

The young urchin ran to the tavern. He slipped in unseen giving the letter to the off-duty footman.

The footman looked around the dimly lit tavern to see if anyone had noticed the boy pass the envelope. The envelope felt heavily off-balance. It contained more than just paper within. He downed the contents of his cup and walked out to the street in search of an isolated corner with just enough light. Curious, he broke the nondescript wax seal holding the flap in place. Removing the letter, he could feel coins within the folds. He carefully opened the paper finding the equivalent of three month's wages, and surreptitiously slipping the coins into his pocket, he turned his attention to the letter.

Sir, I am in need of your services and I am prepared to compensate you well. What I ask is not illegal. It requires discretion and the perfect execution of a plan I shall share with you should we meet. The task will take little time to execute but will require planning. If it interests you in learning more, meet me at 9:00 at the Piazza San Marco. I will find you.

The footman had forty minutes to travel to the Piazza San Marco.

Braxton, watching from the shadows, observed him heading in the square's direction. The prince took an alternative route.

The footman arrived before 9. He sat on a low wall, leaning against a column shielding him from direct light.

The would-be Mars was pleased. This man knew how to be discreet. Once again dressed as a person of no rank, the prince slouched so as to not draw attention to his six-foot two-inch height.

The prince approached the footman from behind five minutes before the stroke of nine.

"Do not turn around." Braxton paused and then continued. "Thank you, Sir, for accepting my invitation. Before you speak, I will preface our conversation with some simple rules. You will not ask me who has hired me to engage your services. You will not attempt to determine my identity or my employer's identity. Is that clear?"

The footman, facing in the opposite direction, nodded, and answered, "Yes."

"You appear to be a clever man. Once the task I spoke of in my letter has been completed, nothing, I mean nothing, is ever again to be said of it. Are you interested in hearing more?"

"I am," responded the man, his back still to Braxton.

"You will engage four men to assist you in delivering letters, at a precise hour, the morning following Carnivale. It is likely the recipients will want to know who sent them. My employer demands secrecy. Therefore, it is vital you and the others do not know by whom they are employed. The task is simple. You will be provided with the letters and the names and locations of those to whom they are to be delivered.

"If you are successful, my employer will pay you four times what you received in the previous payment. Those whom you engage to assist will receive the same."

Braxton stood silent while the man mulled over the offer.

"One more thing. If this commission is successful, we will consider you for further employment."

"I will accept the commission."

"There is a general delivery post down the street from your master's palazzo. What is your name?"

"Carlo Ratini."

"Signore Ratini, further instructions will be left for you there. Remember, success is the only option. Should you and your associates not accomplish your task, there is no additional payment, and a distinct possibility exists you will lose your current position."

Nine tolled on the 400-year-old San Marco clock tower. The meeting had ended before it had been scheduled to begin. The footman slowly turned to where Braxton had been standing.

He had vanished.

Prince Braxton returned to his rooms and prepared the instructions for the footman. He included another gold coin in the envelope. Braxton anticipated the handing off of envelopes and payments to be the biggest difficulty. It must be carefully coordinated. Braxton decided that on the night of Carnivale, Mars would deliver the envelopes and instructions to Ratini. That would help ensure the footman's commitment to his task!

———

Six weeks earlier, while in St. Petersburg, Braxton had, through an intermediary, positioned his IO agents near the homes of his targets. Most of Mars' intended lived in various parts of Europe.

He had tasked the men with following their subjects and reporting on their activities. They were forbidden to contact the individuals and yet were expected do their best to infiltrate their lives on every level.

When their subjects later journeyed to Carnivale, the agents were to remain behind. They would resume their duties upon the subject's return home following Carnivale.

———

At last, Carnivale de Venizia arrived. Braxton emerged from his palazzo as the legendary Medici, Cosimo Pater Patria. A crowd of onlookers, assembled to witness Prince Braxton wearing what had become a fabled costume, cheered loudly and called out, "The prince! The prince!

Instead of heading directly to his first engagement via the gondola waiting to transport him, he walked amongst the crowd, occasionally drawing the veil to the side, and graciously accepting their approval.

There would be no doubt that he was dressed as the Medici patriarch.

Convinced his identity had been certified by many, he boarded the extravagantly decorated gondola festooned in streaming ribbons and covered by an ornate crimson canopy, launching an evening chock-full of festivities and intrigue. In other parts of the city, his plan had taken hold. There were no less than fifteen men and women attired in replicas of the costume.

The first event was held at the Doge's palace. Braxton mingled with the guests. He made a point of documenting his presence through conversation, and an occasional reveal, sliding the veil to the side. He made mental notes of where he had last seen his intended victims and details of their costumes. Braxton attended no less than four events hosted in the palaces and palazzos of the rich and powerful.

Just before making ready to depart the last event, he noticed a duplicate Medici-costumed guest arrive. How convenient, he thought. What could have been an awkward and unexplained departure was made easy. He exited the palazzo through a back entrance, confident none of the intoxicated guests would take note of his departure.

Braxton returned to his rented room and changed into his Mars costume. Retracing his steps, he again made appearances at the establishments he had previously visited. His golden costume created a sensation! Everyone wanted to know who this magnificent Mars could be. Men and women alike approached him with the intent of not only unmasking him but going beyond familiarity. This forward behavior suited his purposes. Mars focused his attention on his intended victims, brushing aside those with whom he had no quarrel. He exhibited an aggressive familiarity and behaved inappropriately with those whom later that morning would be given the Mars letter.

Mars placed men and women in what would appear to be compromising situations. The god would caress women, lifting their masks and passionately kissing them, always compromising them in ways to be remembered. Several men found themselves groped, kissed, and sometimes something more at the hands of the golden god. Be it excessive drink or whatever, few resisted. None directly challenged Mars, probably the only sober being in the entire city. He was efficient in his movements. Every target would at the least vaguely remember him and their moments with him. The god discreetly placed a touch of fragrance on the neck, wrist, or arm of all with whom he conspired to compromise, having never exposed his face in the light. The same perfume permeated the letters awaiting their delivery.

Later, Braxton headed toward the prearranged rendezvous with Carlo Ratini. Carlo stepped back spying the costumed Braxton and was about to flee when Mars hollered, "Ratini! Stop!" The footman came to an abrupt halt.

Mars handed him five cloth bags.

"You will find each sack contains unique liveried uniforms for you and your associates. Wear them when the letters are delivered. Make sure that no one engages in conversation with the addressees. You are charged with destroying the livery when the task is complete."

Braxton withdrew the packets of letters from his satchel. "Each of these are suited to the geographical delivery points. This will allow all deliveries to be made within the obligatory tight schedule. You and your men will deliver the letters to the addressees. The gravitas the livery provides will ensure easy access to the recipients. You will note that many of these deliveries will be done in public places. The deliveries must be witnessed by others. If for any reason a recipient is indisposed or not in public, ensure that there are witnesses, not just servants present to note the envelope's delivery."

Carlo listened intently to what Mars said. "One more thing. See those men standing over there? They are

my men."

Across the street and 50 yards away stood ten men, rough looking laborers, glaring in their direction.

Carlo looked toward the huddled mass. "Yes, sir. I see them," he said with a nervous tone.

"They will watch you and your men to see that you carry out your assignment. They are not forgiving men." Mars handed Carlo an envelope containing the payments he had promised. "Now go!"

Carlos gathered all that Braxton had given him and ran down a dark alley. Mars made sure Carlo was well away before walking toward his men.

As he reached the group he whispered, "Gentleman, thank you for your time. I have no further need of your services." He handed them payment for their brief and hopefully effective performance.

With the sun beginning to show light on the horizon, Braxton returned to his rooms, his task complete. Lighting the fire in the fireplace and removing the golden costume, he threw it and all he had brought into the roaring fire. He donned the Medici costume. Securing the door behind him, he took a circuitous route through the city, acknowledging anyone that might take notice. Certain that he and his costume had been seen many times, he hired a boat to transport him to the Venezia Mestre Railroad Station on the mainland.

———

Carlo and the men he had employed for Braxton's plan met with success. They entered what were, normally, inaccessible homes and establishments. Carnivale had intoxicated almost the entire city.

Palazzos, villas, and fine homes were left vulnerable as most of their servants had also celebrated to excess the previous evening. Livery worn by Carlo's men commanded respect. No one denied them entry.

The letters were, of course, opened immediately. The envelope's familiar fragrance alarmed some and excited others, the couriers departing before the contents were read.

Shock, horror, and disbelief took hold. Servants were dispatched to find who had sent the letter. Naturally, the recipients had a vague recollection of Mars. Some remembered a little more than others. Most felt indicted but were not sure what the indictment entailed. Had they done something that could have scandalous ramifications? Could there be consequences and how far-reaching might they be?

Word spread quickly through Venetian society and the entire city. Everyone wanted to know who had received the letters. All assumed that the recipients had compromised themselves. What power this Mars must have to shame such powerful men and women! The rumors grew in number and were widely distorted, extolling how Mars had used his power and the weaknesses and venality of his victims, men and women alike, most probably having had carnal knowledge with all of them.

Details, inuendo and fantasies were chronicled in newspapers and pamphlets from stories bribed out of servants in several households. Not even the most powerful families could put a stop to their publication. Word traveled beyond the city. Cables flew across Europe.

Mars Copulates with the Rich and Powerful at Carnivale!

With these headlines, Braxton had efficiently sidelined any short-term efforts his enemies had planned to thwart his interests. They had been sufficiently intimidated and humiliated. It would be a long while before they would risk conspiring against anyone.

The recipients and their families fled Venice returning to their homes.

Final payment was made to Carlo via general delivery. Braxton's note thanked him for his service and indicated he could expect to hear from 'Mars' again.

———

Smoke billowed from the engine's stack as the train departed Venice for St. Petersburg.

Braxton left instructions not to be disturbed. Casting off his Medici costume, he slept for fifteen hours. When he finally awoke, he took sustenance and met for an hour with his executive staff, issuing instructions regarding individual responsibilities. Dismissing the men, he returned to his personal car. Braxton stared up at the inlaid wood ceiling above his bed and thought to himself, Uncle Cosimo, Machiavelli would be impressed.

He then clasped his hands behind his head and said out loud, "Yes, the god Mars has his eyes upon you, all of you. Mars can rest easier now, for a little while."

Braxton began making plans for the upcoming tour of Russia and all it could promise to provide for his growing empire. And what of the other countries… Japan, China, Singapore, India… what treasures could he glean from these exotic lands?

Of one thing he was certain: His exploration of the lovely Valentina would continue. Where would this enchanting creature fit into his plans? He had no idea, but he intended to explore every inch of her being to find out.

ACKNOWLEDGMENTS

It would not have been possible for me to have finished this book, my first book, not my first published book without the support of some amazing people. Many of you know who you are. Please forgive me if I do not mention you by name.

As I did with my first published book, 'First Spouse Of The United State,' I am going to do something rather dangerous and randomly list many of those who have provided support along the way.

Thank you so much to my team. Their professionalism, mentorship, expertise, and patience have been invaluable: Trisha Gooch Stein, content editor. Teresa Espaniola: cover designer. Tamara Merrill: oracle, guiding light, and 'jack of all trades.'

Thank you to Travis Barrick for a very special contribution.

As in 'First Spouse Of The United States,' many of those same people and more continued to stand by me during this process transcending three years: Mike Norton, Elena Bazhenova, Jae Barrick, Dale Peronteau, Stephanie Burnham, Jan Toon, Anusha Venkatram, Ray Morgan, Linda Haymaker, Leona Norton, Pam Hill, Peggy Hinaekian, Helen Brahms, Everett Hale, Larry Tritten, Josh

Rutherford, Nick Darling, Johnny and Jackie Lazootin, Patty Saenz, Craig and Alex Shaw, Lucy Burni, Kris Brew, D Maria Trimble, Craig McLeod, Ashley Curtis, Jeanne Ferris, Michelle and David Lowenstein, Mike Vander Griend, Pamela Means, Lane O'Conner, and the unnamed family and friends that are always there for me.

ABOUT THE AUTHOR

J.R. Strayve, Jr. was born to a nomadic military family, attending nine schools before entering college. Following service in the United States Marine Corps, he raised a family. It is here that he discovered his talent for "spinning tales," regaling his young children with spontaneous bedtime stories. Soon his passion for history spoke to him.

He spoke back and wrote the epic alternative historical series, Braxton's Century. Book 1 was published in January 2021.

He is currently co-authoring a sure-to-be best-seller blockbuster nonfiction detailing a Whistleblower's Veterans Administration exposé.

His first novel was and remains controversial: First Spouse of the United States, published in March 2019. A sequel is soon to follow. A short story, The Lieutenant & The Vintner and the novella, Vainglorious are available now.

WORKS BY THE AUTHOR

Vainglorious Prequel to the Braxton Century Series

If you think Henry VIII was tyrannical… you haven't met the czar.

Growing up the grand duchess, Ekaterina's life was more gilded cage than glitz In this alternative history timeline. She had no choice but to follow her father, the czar's, every command or become "forever indisposed" like her mother was. This included marrying the womanizing and power-hungry Prince Gregor.

Determined to rule her own life, Ekaterina must go through great lengths to try and save herself. Can she find a way to thwart the powerful men attempting to control her, or will her dream lead to an even bigger nightmare?

A prequel to Braxton's Century Volume I, set in the fabulously glittering Russian court of the early 1880s, Vainglorious's look into Grand Duchess Ekaterina life enlightens readers as to why she'll later be so closely drawn to Prince Braxton.

———

BRAXTON'S CENTURY Vol 1

"A riveting escapist fantasy I couldn't put down."

When a fiery prank goes wrong, Prince Braxton, the third son of the fictional Prince and Princess of Wales, blazes onto the scene.

His fateful act sets in motion this alternate history of the nineteenth century that journeys across continents with the larger-than-life prince as a guide. Can the spare heir forge his own path to build an economic empire?

Start your journey into history's most dynamic century through the eyes of an undaunted, rakish, youth today!

This first volume of four scorches a trail spanning from 1860 to 1880. The entire saga features a century of world wars and engineering marvels that one might recognize with requited and unrequited love, romances that defy social morays, death, revolutions, and espionage that casts this tale into one that could have been had Prince Braxton been real.

———

Braxton's Century Vol 2

When Prince Braxton departs Vienna, following a night of debauchery dressed in gold as the ancient God of War, Mars. He leaves behind a tangle of threats, promises, and compromised nobles, his trading empire intact. Or is it?

Braxton's larger-than-life wheelings and dealings take him from Russia to Japan, Hong Kong, and India. But it's sucking every ounce of Braxton's being from within.

Continue your journey of history's most dynamic century as Prince Braxton tears through life on his own terms. When life forces him to decide his path, what—and who—will he choose?

This second volume of four scorches a trail spanning from 1860 to 1884. The entire saga features a century of world wars and engineering marvels that one might recognize with requited and unrequited love, romances that defy social morays, death, revolutions, and espionage that casts this tale into one that could have been had Prince Braxton been real.

———

First Spouse Of The United States

They thought he had it all. But what he had was secrets in his closet.

Lt. Ricardo "Rocky" Chambers has always been the epitome of what women want and who men want to be. Handsome. Star athlete. Fighter pilot.

Heroism and prowess do not clear a path for happily-ever-after, as a dark secret could derail all this family man, captain of industry, and gay civil rights advocate has worked for.

And secrets aren't meant to stay hidden.

With adversaries lying in wait, the secret is exposed in the national media. Can Rocky and his husband overcome the fallout on the quest for the White House?

In a coming-of-age story that parallels today's political and social unrest, there are no taboo subjects.

———

The Lieutenant & The Vintner (A Short Story)

When SS Lt. Georg von Reichenau is assigned to the French Burgundy after recovering from his battle wounds, he laments not the loss of his fighting days but the loss of a trip to the Olympics and his future as a ski instructor.

Under German occupation in WWII, Andre Beaulieu, a gold-medal-winning Olympian downhill racer works to maintain his family's vineyard, unable to forget the woman he met at Olympic Village. He's been trying to find her for the last five years.

There's something familiar about the man who came to the vineyard after recognizing the name. But memory can be fickle. Can there be more to this recollection than either realize?

www.ingramcontent.com/pod-product-compliance
Lightning Source LLC
Chambersburg PA
CBHW051542260626
47170CB00003B/1055